SONG FOR THE *Hunter*

A sequel to *Mist O'er the Voyageur*

BY

NAOMI MUSCH

Smitten Historical Romance is an imprint of LPCBooks
a division of Iron Stream Media
100 Missionary Ridge, Birmingham, AL 35242
ShopLPC.com

Cover design by Elaina Lee

Library of Congress Control Number: 2021942986

ISBN-13: 978-1-64526-338-8978
Ebook ISBN: 978-1-64526-339-5

Praise for *Song For The Hunter*

A few pages into *Song for the Hunter*, Naomi Musch earned a spot on my list of favorite Christian historical fiction authors. What a joy to find another writer who shares my heart for telling cross-cultural stories in a frontier/wilderness setting—and discovering that writer's gorgeous, evocative prose brought the setting to such vivid life that I found myself often lingering over the imagery conjured. Characters Camilla and Bemidii (and a large supporting cast) came leaping off the pages straight into my heart. I couldn't turn those pages fast enough to discover how they charted a course through desperately entangled paths to find a clear way forward. Hope triumphs in this latest offering from gifted wordsmith and lover of history, Naomi Musch.

~Lori Benton

Christy Award-winning author of *Burning Sky*
and the Kindred duology, *Mountain Laurel* and *Shiloh*

This beautifully written and immersive story will transport you back in time and keep you turning the pages! Naomi Musch's voice and style is the perfect balance of lyrical combined with cadence and word choice appropriate for the time and setting. Fans of Lori Benton and Laura Frantz will find this story a perfect addition to their libraries! Highly recommend.

~Carrie Fancett Pagels

Award-winning and bestselling author, *Behind Love's Wall*

In *Song of the Hunter*, the long-awaited sequel to *Mist O'er the Voyageur*, Naomi Musch transports us back to the waters of Lake Superior during the height of the fur trade. Cultures clash as an evil man sends ripples across the waters that will touch the hearts of many. It took strong people to survive the wild and unpredictable environment, and it would take strong people to find the truth and reconcile with it. The story is beautifully presented in a setting rich in the heritage of the people and the grandeur of nature. A must read for those who enjoy the rugged landscapes and rich cultures of America's northern shores.

~Pegg Thomas
Award-winning author of *Sarah's Choice*

Song for the Hunter is a sweet and satisfying love story across cultures and paints the Lake Superior shore so vividly I could hear the waves splash and smell the pines. What a beautiful tapestry Musch weaves of loss and longing, risk and reward!

~Shannon McNear
2014 RITA® nominee, 2021 SELAH winner, and author of *The Blue Cloak*, *The Wise Guy and the Star* in *Love's Pure Light,* and the upcoming *Daughters of the Lost Colony: Elinor*

Rife with tender romance and poetic prose, Musch leads readers through a cross-cultural love story that not only entertains but points to the hope that all of us seek—to be loved for ourselves and to give love in return. A finely tuned inspirational, historical romance, *Song for the Hunter* opens a window into the fur trade era of the 1700s and portrays a realistic and insightful glimpse into the life of Ojibwe and Métis at that time in history. Five stars for this captivating novel readers of Christian historical romance and Christian historical fiction will fall in love with.

~Jenny Knipfer
Bestselling author of *In a Grove of Maples*, first in the Sheltering Trees Series

A wholesome story with vivid descriptions and just the right amount of tension that will keep you turning the pages well into the night.

~Lori Hayes
Award-winning author of *Island Summer*, Crystal Coast Series

Acknowledgments

As I sit here listening to a Midnight String Quartet, thinking about how the rhythm reminds me of the gently lapping waves of Lake Superior, I am thankful I get to live in an area so rich with history. Every which way I turn, there is a story that happened in the past waiting to be told in a fresh way. I will never be able to write all the stories and histories that inspire me from this place.

For those who don't know, the Cadottes are a famous fur-trading family in the annals of Wisconsin and Minnesota history. The branch of the family which plays a role in these pages, Michel and his Ojibwe wife, Equawaysay (Madeleine), built a flourishing fur trade in Lake Superior's Chequamegon Bay region, at a post on the largest of the Apostle Islands, now named for her—Madeline Island. I'll include more about them in the historical note at the end of the book. Should any descendants of the family (of which there are many) happen upon this story, I hope you will indulge me the liberties I've taken with your ancestors in these pages and forgive me any details I've gotten wrong (which I hope are few). Their story, and the stories of many other fur traders, voyageurs, and explorers like them, have given me many hours of pleasurable reading as I researched.

I'm also grateful to everyone who has had a hand in helping bring this book to fruition—even those who may not realize their part. Foremost are the book lovers who read and reviewed *Mist O'er the Voyageur*, the novel that precedes this one. I am so happy that readers fell in love with Brigitte, René, and the rest of the cast. It is largely because of my *Mist* readers that the story continues here.

I want to express my appreciation to my agent, Linda S. Glaz, for her help and direction in getting this book ready for an editor's inspection. I'll never forget the day she made "the call" and had me bouncing around the house in joy for hours.

In that regard, I also owe a debt of thanks to my editor, Denise Weimer, for her faith in this story to begin with, and for catching all my repetitive words and helping me make this story stronger. We share a love of the more rugged aspects of North American history. Along with her and everyone else who brought this story from a messy Word document to a beautiful book at Iron Stream Media, I so appreciate you allowing me to continue this Lake Superior saga.

Finally, the saying, "It goes without saying" isn't true. It bears repeating: I am *blessed* with a huge and fabulous family—a husband of forty years, five adult kids and their spouses, and grandkids galore (seventeen at last count). I could never get through the editing schedule of a book's release—much less the writing of a novel itself—if it weren't for knowing I have their support. When things come down to the wire, they're all willing to make adjustments in their own lives so that I can finish on time. So yes, it bears repeating: I love you guys!

Dedication

To my Lord and Savior Jesus Christ, for His unquenchable love.

"He hath put a new song in my mouth, even praise unto our God:
many shall see it, and fear, and shall trust in the LORD." Psalm 40:3

CHAPTER 1

Did my mother take the decision of marriage too lightly, or were her choices simply as limited as mine? I have always wondered.

—Journal of Camilla Bonnet

Late June 1808

A stiff breeze snapped tendrils of Camilla Bonnet's hair about her wind-burned face as she clung to the gunwale of the long Montreal canoe. Its eight voyageurs leapt into the shallow lake surf, making the craft jerk and wobble, assuring Camilla she was indeed pregnant. Her stomach lurched with each opposing shift of their weight. No good would come of her losing her pease porridge in front of them all, for it was far too soon for her secret to be revealed. She had yet to grasp it herself.

Climbing to the wharf, factoring his own weight into the upset, Camilla's husband, Ambroise, turned and reached for her. "Steady now."

She offered him a weak smile as she slipped her hand in his and rose to unsteady feet. Swallowing down a sour knot, she lifted the edge of her skirts and stepped onto the long pier. She eased out a breath and smoothed the hair from her face to better study the gentle slope of Madeleine Island—christened after the trader's wife, said to be an Ojibwe princess. Dark-haired children ran chattering along the waterfront, evidence of a village nearby. Porters moved around her as they unloaded bundles of trade goods from the four thirty-foot canoes and carried them ashore. They marched in a line, past remnants of an old fort, toward the trading post.

Camilla turned about and shielded her eyes against the brilliance of the afternoon sun to peer toward the mainland across the bay. The natives and voyageurs called it *Ouisconsin*. Perhaps a league distant, its wooded headland rose gradually above the water.

"A beautiful country, is it not, and this island post so well situated?" Ambroise spoke beside her, then bent to fetch the trunk.

"*Oui*, it is." She inhaled a deep draught of air, hoping to ease the turbulence inside. Perhaps there would be something other than water to drink inside the trading post. Tea would suit best.

Hoisting the filthy hem of her gown again, she trudged behind Ambroise up the beach toward the giant, swaying firs, slowly gaining her land legs as she left the *Lac Supérieur* bay behind. Oh! To only get out of this dreadful sun and lay her pounding head on a soft mattress, should one be had. How very doubtful that was.

La Pointe was a primitive outpost, though she'd been led to believe that Michel Cadotte, the trader in charge, had been well-educated back in Montreal. Such remembrance gave her hope for some amenity. At least she would not have to travel any farther west, unlike her brother's brigade, which had left Montreal with them but paddled the lake's northern arch.

"Do you suppose Tristan will arrive at Fort William soon?" She spoke to Ambroise's back.

He chuckled. "His brigade has some distance farther to travel than ours, my dear. It shouldn't be many more days, however."

To Camilla, it really only mattered how long she would be able to rest here. "When shall we expect him?"

"Not until August. Precisely when is uncertain." He cast her a smile over his shoulder. "I am sure Madame Cadotte will make you comfortable until our season of venturing is at an end and Tristan's brigade arrives. And I will count on you to keep an adequate record of your own discoveries here in your journal." He winked before focusing again on his footpath.

She pressed against the deep pocket of her skirt, assuring herself her journal was still safely tucked within.

They would have at least a month's wait, and then they would journey back to Montreal, where she would settle into a long winter's preparation for motherhood. The thought of being pregnant shocked her anew, yet it would not be a dreaded thing.

How fine it would be to love someone with all her being who might return her love without condition.

She glanced at Ambroise shouldering her trunk and his satchel ahead of her, just as the porters. A young man from the post ran to meet him, and they shared some words.

Ambroise was a decent man, but to say she had fallen in love with him would be a lie. She bore him a mild affection, but marriage to him had been a means to escape. Had she waited much longer to choose a husband, the opportunism of her father might have seen her married to someone much worse—like that crotchety old Scot, Monsieur MacDaw. Ambroise Bonnet was neither handsome nor homely, and his personality was at times overly excitable. Still, he had been better than her other options with their fat wallets, wandering eyes, or aged disability her father had been considering for her. She might not love Ambroise wholeheartedly, but she could accept and endure him. She sensed in him the making of a better father than her own had been.

Then perhaps it was wishful thinking, and only time would tell, for with Ambroise's rise in her father's company, might not he yield to his father-in-law's influences in ways that stretched beyond business? *Please, God, he would not.*

They passed the place of the old fort, which must have been a pivotal situation along Lake Superior's southern shore during the wars. Madeleine Island was the largest of a collection of islands called the Apostles, though the voyageurs said there were twenty-two rather than twelve.

"Come, my darling." Ambroise paused to wait for her as the boy scampered off. "I will inquire as to whether Monsieur and Madame Cadotte have a room waiting for us."

Such an exhilarating thought. A room. Four square walls. No more nights on a bed of cedar boughs with only a tarp or *canot* over their heads—at least not until the return voyage home. No matter that the trader's house would likely be rustic and probably smell of seasoning hides. It was a room. Camilla quickened her pace behind him.

He directed her attention to a sprawling oak standing nearby like a sentinel. "Perhaps you wish to wait in the shade with your trunk while I greet *Gichi-miishen* at the storehouse." He smiled proudly at his use of the natives' name for Michel Cadotte. *Great Michel*, indeed.

A sigh escaped her. "Oui, that would be most pleasant." To avoid a smelly storehouse for the breeze beneath the shade would refresh her before she had to meet the Cadottes, as well as afford her a further study of her new surroundings.

"I will not be long. There is the house, see?"

She turned her attention in the direction he'd nodded, and her heart thumped in pleasant surprise. A modest, two-story home, built of sturdy, lathed logs nestled along the edge of the trees. Next to it, a rustic fence of upright cedar poles enclosed a garden. The tidy structure was a most welcoming sight and hinted at more civilization than she'd imagined in such a place.

"And there is the storehouse." He nodded toward another building constructed of squared logs joined in dovetail fashion at the corners.

Camilla sat on her trunk, and Ambroise went away whistling, as though he was one of the voyageurs and not the son-in-law of one the North West Company's most prominent merchants. Had he been more like Tristan, he would puff out his chest and take great advantage of his position as James Clarboux's agent and favored son-in-law. He would enlist servants to carry his bundles to and from the store, and he would esteem himself as a man to be catered to. Tristan would find means to please himself in every possible way during his venture. His self-centered nature would not be so easily appeased as Ambroise's boyish delight.

Camilla leaned her back against the bark of the broad oak, thankful her father had assigned Ambroise to a separate brigade and different route than Tristan, at least for now. Marriage to Ambroise had freed her from her father's scrutinizing oversight, though not as far as she would have liked. Yet for this season, and with Tristan elsewhere, there was distance enough.

She closed her eyes and inhaled the scent of pine on the fresh lake air. The crowded streets of Montreal, replete with the stink of its waste, was a distant memory. Here, freedom seemed possible, if only temporarily. If she could prevent Ambroise from knowing she was pregnant until the time came for their return, she might almost feel as if the constraints of her Montreal life didn't exist. On this island, she could hold her secret close while finding refuge from the July heat and humidity that hugged the inland country. It could be that the upcoming month might pass most pleasantly. She would write of her days and the hopes and dreams for her babe in her journal, her closest confidante besides God.

When she opened her eyes again, she took in the layout of commons and buildings more closely. Smoke ascended from what must be an outdoor summer kitchen and laundry. Chickens pecked in the dirt outside a small barn, and a woodshed was attached to another building. Tendrils of smoke carried on the breeze from cook fires somewhere beyond.

Camilla brushed the dry beach sand from her slippers. Ambroise should return any moment. She glanced expectantly to the door of the storehouse, but the next figure to emerge was that of a native or possibly Métis man. His face lifted toward her, almost as though he were aware someone watched from across the compound, for his eyes immediately found hers and widened. His steps slowed, and Camilla realized she was staring. For one heart-stuttering moment, she thought he might approach her.

She jerked her gaze away as discomfort wormed through her. She had avoided these wilderness men when her husband wasn't present—the voyageurs and especially the natives and Métis. Men of lower social rank were not like the bourgeoisie in Montreal who flirted and bantered, but whom she knew how to easily dismiss. In this country, they were unaccustomed to seeing a white woman, and her husband had warned her to be on her guard, for they would take their approaches to her more seriously and with greater curiosity. Who knew what dangerous thoughts lurked behind their dark countenances? She had enough experience of men to guess. In the moments she'd watched the stranger, however, she'd taken in his broad, bare shoulders and muscled torso. His hair was clubbed behind his head. He had a fine brow, and—she stole another quick look. *Penetrating eyes.* Watching her still, not turning away but settling on her as he halted his pace toward the shore and stared at her outright.

Camilla's breath caught high in her chest as she pulled her glance away again. *Take a care, Camilla, or he will think you are extending an invitation.*

Ambroise must hurry, and she must not let herself be separated from him again in this place without a chaperone.

Her husband stepped out of the warehouse the next moment, easing her unsettled nerves. She rose and edged away from the tree, anxious now to be at his side. A brief glance at the Indian showed him moving on, but again their glances caught, if only for a moment. In her weeks of travel amid these unfamiliar people, none had so provoked her with such blunt perusal.

"Shall we get settled in our lodgings?" Ambroise's voice reached her while he was still more than two rods distant.

She squared herself so she could no longer see the native and waited until her husband drew near. "Oui, darling. I fear I am quite in need of a nap. I hope our hosts will not mind." She lay the back of her hand across her brow where a sudden dampness had arisen.

Ambroise hoisted her trunk once again. "Monsieur Cadotte tells me that both he and his wife have expected as much. They have a room prepared for us. Come, let us go and introduce ourselves to Madame Cadotte."

Relieved, Camilla followed him toward the main house, but another turn of her head showed the same Indian, observing them from where he lingered with some others beneath the trees. She nearly bumped into Ambroise when he set the trunk on the stoop.

As he knocked on the door, she slipped her arm beneath his elbow.

A moment later, a girl no older than nine or ten opened the door. *"Bonjour."* The child was dressed in European style, wearing a short gown trimmed in lace. Nevertheless, her feet were clad in beaded moccasins, and her hair hung in two long braids beside a round, brown face. She called for her *maman* over her shoulder.

A woman stepped forward to greet them.

"Madame Cadotte? I am Monsieur Bonnet of Montreal, and this is my wife, Madame Bonnet."

"Ah, oui! Monsieur and Madame Bonnet." Though diminutive in size, the wife of Gichi-miishen bore about her a regal calm. She must indeed be the daughter of a chief. Her shining black hair was parted and braided in a long tail down her back, and her eyes snapped with kindness. Her lips curved slightly as she inclined her head toward them. "Come inside, please." She drew them within, and homey sights and smells surrounded them. "I am known to The People as *Equasayway*, but you may call me by my Christian name, Madeleine. It is my pleasure to make your acquaintance. Your journey was a safe one, I hope?"

Camilla schooled her features to hide her surprise. She had not expected the native wife of a trader to speak French so fluently, although she'd met other Ojibwe along the route who did so. This far west, she expected to only meet a few Métis able to hold such civilized discourse.

Ambroise gave a slight bow. "Quite safe and very productive as well. It is good for us to come to your country. We look forward to viewing its abundant resources."

"We are most happy you have come. Please, you must make yourselves comfortable." Madeleine led them into the main room of the house. A stone fireplace and hearth took up the center of one wall between a stairway and a doorway to another room. Two beds were fixed against an adjacent wall, and benches and shelves lined the others. A single window looked out the front of the house. Madeleine indicated chairs and a long table placed before the unlit hearth. She spoke to the girl who stood beside four younger siblings, the smallest only a toddler sitting on the floor. Then she looked at Camilla and Ambroise again. "Julie will bring refreshment."

"*Merci*." Camilla settled onto a chair.

"I hope you find your stay with us pleasant. You must not mind my children." One of the other little girls drew close to their hostess. "Two of our older sons work in the storehouse and fields with their father, but the girls and the two little boys remain with me." She pointed to each child from largest to smallest. "Julie, Mary, Antoine, Charlotte, Joseph." They grinned as she said their names, and Antoine, about five, swung his legs restlessly.

"They are very well behaved." Camilla smiled at them.

"My eldest daughter, Marguerite, has gone to the village." She excused the small ones to play while the girl named Julie served their tea. The children, except for the toddler, scurried out the door.

Ambroise cast Camilla a smile. "My wife will certainly enjoy the children's company. We have no children of our own as yet."

Camilla sipped from her cup, grateful for the distraction. Now was not the time to tell him that his wishes were soon to unfold. She would let her secret remain her own for as long as she dared.

Once they'd finished their tea, Madeleine showed them to their room. She led them up the narrow stairwell beside the chimney. "My husband and I delight in having guests here on *Mooningwanekaaning*."

A door stood on each side of the upstairs landing. Madame Cadotte raised a latch on the one to the right. "Here is your place."

The bedroom into which Camilla entered contained two rope beds holding cornhusk-stuffed mattresses covered with trade blankets. Ambroise set Camilla's trunk at the foot of one of them. The chamber must belong to the older girls, but she would not ask where they would sleep now. "Thank you for allowing us a place in your home."

"My father, the great chief White Crane, taught that it is good to show kindness to strangers, and it is the way of my husband in his business." She inclined her head.

Yet another relief coursed through Camilla. "Madeleine, I hope you will call me by my Christian name, Camilla."

Madeleine curtsied. "I will leave you to your rest. You will join us for dinner later?"

"So we shall." Ambroise had already removed his hat, and now he bowed graciously.

"Tell me," Camilla said, stopping her. "Are all the people here so gracious and welcoming as you and your husband?"

Madeleine smiled. "There are many who come and go, so I cannot speak for each one, but here on the island, our intention is to show hospitality to all."

"And your children play in safety?" she asked, despite having seen them excused to do so.

"Oui, Camilla. There is no one here to harm them. You must not worry."

Did she read concern into Camilla's veiled questions? Or perhaps they were not nearly so veiled?

Madeleine withdrew, and Camilla swept a glance over the spare room once more. Its only luxury was a writing desk that stood beneath a small window. She didn't want to offend her hostess, so she had not asked the real question on her mind—whether or not *she* could trust everyone on this island. For all she knew, the man with the watchful eyes could be some relation to Madame Cadotte. She dared not offend her hostess.

Ambroise turned to her. "What is this line of questioning? Are you feeling well, Camilla? You've not seemed yourself today. I expected you would be more pleased to have finally arrived."

"I am pleased. Only, I'm not yet used to this place. Ambroise …" She clutched her fingertips together. "I don't like to be left alone. There are strangers everywhere."

"You heard what Madeleine said. The people here welcome us." Another tiny frown tweaked his brow. "Has someone upset you? Is this room not to your liking?"

Upset her? No, not really. She'd been more upset by Old MacDaw in Montreal than by the man who stared at her as though he'd never seen a woman before. She shook her head. "It's quite comfortable. No, I …" She shook her head again. "Never mind. I'm merely tired, that's all. I shall be happy to close my eyes. I am unduly weary after this last leg of our journey."

Ambroise stroked her cheek, then abruptly turned away and began searching in his satchel. He seemed to dismiss any concerns. "I will leave you to rest and unpack, my darling. I am going to assist Monsieur Cadotte and will return to you later."

She strode to the little window and peered out of it. Although waving pine branches obscured the view toward the shore, she could still see several people mingling near the beach. Was the man with the scrutinizing gaze among them? She squinted for a longer look, but it was hard to tell. How his impertinence unnerved her. Yet there was something—she could not say what, some fascination—that made her want to return his study. She'd never experienced anything like it before. Simple curiosity perhaps, tempered by fear, for he was striking in a strange and foreign way, and there was danger about him.

"Should you have any need, you may send for me." Ambroise turned her by the shoulders and kissed her brow. "You have borne our travels well. I am proud of you. Your father would be proud also."

She nodded, but her smile felt wan. In truth, she cared not whether her father was proud at all.

He left her then, closing the door behind him. His heavy boots clomped down the stairs. She returned to the window. Ambroise walked with the gait of an anxious youth toward the trade goods store, but the people gathered by the shore had disappeared.

CHAPTER 2

Be watchful and wary of the traders. They are your brothers, eh? In trade? But they will steal you blind if they can.

—Etienne Marchal, to his son, Benjamin

Bemidii paddled in the bow of the canoe while his brother-in-law, the French fur trader René Dufour, steered from the stern. Bemidii's half sister, Brigitte, sat on a cushion of hides in the center of the canoe between them. With each rhythmic plunge and pull of his paddle deep into the choppy waters of the lake, Bemidii thought about the woman on Madeleine Island.

The flutter of her gown had caught his eye across the yard, and when she saw him watching, she'd momentarily met his gaze. Never had he seen such a one before, with bright yellow hair coming loose around her face and skin equally as golden. If only he could have been near enough to tell the shade of her eyes, for even from a distance, they appeared different than his own deep brown. Her chin had lifted, and she'd jerked her face away, yet he wished to see it again. He had waited beneath the trees, hoping for such a chance, but she did not come out of the house again after she'd gone inside with the Frenchman.

She must be the man's wife. The Frenchman had come with the porters into the warehouse just as Bemidii was completing his trade. A blustering man he was, entering like a windstorm. One who walked loudly, his boots striking the puncheon floor of the warehouse without cadence or grace, announcing himself to all. Bemidii smirked, then turned his thoughts away from the man and back to the woman. What brought her with her husband to this wild country? He would like to ask her, for he could plainly tell she was unaccustomed to the ways of the Upper Country. Such a shame that he would never meet her again. Already the islands had fallen into a line of shadow behind them.

He scanned the Ouisconsin mainland, where their canoe skirted along a shore covered with thick green forests, formations of sandstone cliffs, and wave-carved sea caves. He had come this far along Superior's southern shore only a handful of times in his life. The first was with his father, Etienne Marchal, when he was only a boy. This past spring was the first time he'd come with René and Brigitte, his sister by Etienne's second wife.

A pair of ducks lifted off the waves beyond them, quacking as they flew toward a tunneling of sea caves between tall colonnades of layered rock. The columns supported overhanging cliffs and trees above and disappeared beneath the green surface of the water below.

"You did not reach for your gun," René remarked, drawing him from his reverie. The ducks disappeared from sight.

"We have meat enough. Those will nest, and next year will provide food for some other family, perhaps."

"Perhaps." A smile enriched René's voice. The day waned, and the yellow sun melted into the watery horizon. The lake had grown calm. "Are you uncomfortable, Brigitte?"

Bemidii felt her slight shifting behind him.

"I am barely pregnant. I suspect my discomfort will come later. I could paddle if you'd allow it."

"Rest. We'll go on farther until darkness forbids it. Best we do our traveling in calm waters. If you grow too tired, tell me."

She let out an exaggerated sigh. "Have no worry for me, *monsieur*. You must remember, I have earned the title of *le petit voyageur*, and I can endure your paddling for many hours longer than this."

Both men chuckled and continued their even pace. Bemidii looked to the shoreline again, where the dipping sun bathed the cliffs in golden streaks. He began to sing in Ojibwe. In a moment, René joined him and then Brigitte.

"Will you play your flute tonight?" Brigitte asked when the song had ended.

He nodded. "If you wish it. I will play a lullaby for my niece or nephew."

"Oui. The babe will learn your voice and your flute and will always know when they hear it, you have come to play for them."

"Until he plays for his own woman," René teased.

Bemidii shrugged without answer, yet he smiled to himself. He looked forward to knowing this child his sister would bear. While no maiden had yet turned his head enough so that he might play his flute for her, he would play instead for this unborn one of Brigitte's, a girl, he hoped, like his lovely sister. This child would also be dark like her parents, for while he and Brigitte's mothers were both Ojibwe, Etienne Marchal had been swarthy as well, and so was René. There was no likelihood that any child of Brigitte's would be golden like the woman he'd seen at the post today. Of that sort of French blood, none flowed in any of their veins.

Twilight drifted down on them like a great, purple blanket, and stars smattered the sky. At last, René called for them to halt. They had paddled beyond the rocky shoreline and come abreast of clay hills and sandy beaches. They drew their canoe up gently onto the sand. Once the fire was lit and Brigitte had prepared *rubaboo* for cooking overnight, the couple settled down to sleep. Their voices soon drifted off to silence, but Bemidii unwrapped his flute and, as the fire's amber flames turned to embers, his notes whispered into the night.

Two Weeks Later

Bursting with the nations of people swarming in and out its gates, Fort William perched near the top of Lac Supérieur, just a short paddle up the *Kaministiquia*, the place of the Great Rendezvous held every year during the midsummer raspberry moon. During the month, the ranks of the fort swelled with thousands of traders, voyageurs, natives, Métis, bourgeois clerks and partners, and other more important agents representing NW Company commercial interests. Men and women of every ilk in their societies. There was business to be transacted and revelry to be made. René would take part in much of the business, while Brigitte would gather with her friends and acquaintances among the women to talk and sew and cook. They would make their own trades. Bemidii would be paid, and then he would take part in the games and other sorts of entertainment that pleased him.

They had raised their lodge among the hundreds of others springing up outside the gates and stretching in clan and family clusters along the river like a small city. Now he sat cross-legged on the ground at their outdoor cooking fire. He finished sharpening his knife and tucked it back into its sheath at his hip.

"Bemidii, you must eat before you go." Brigitte offered him a bowl of rabbit stew scooped from the big kettle over the fire.

"*Miigwech*, *oshiimeyan*." He nodded thanks to his sister as he accepted the bowl. "It will keep me from spending more of my earnings than I should at Boucher's store."

She eyed him. "You should stay away from that place, I think."

"What if I find another sister there?" He winked and scooped a bite of stew.

Brigitte made a face. He'd first seen her at Boucher's last year, suspecting she was the lost sister from his childhood, but the experience of their meeting had frightened her badly until he was finally able to explain who he was nearly a month later when he led her to their father's grave.

Bemidii chuckled, then lifted the savory bowl of stew to his mouth, shoveling down the rest. He wiped his mouth on the back of his hand when he finished.

"In truth, Bemidii, I do not worry about you at Boucher's. You have more wisdom than the many others I saw wasting their money there last year. As long as you and René hunt well, and I am able to dry and store our provisions carefully, there is no need for us to spend for more at Boucher's."

"René has gotten us the best trades inside the fort also. We will not lack." He handed back the bowl. "But I am off to see what I can learn of others' successes and failures this past season."

She dipped his empty bowl into a kettle of hot water. "Take care. I will be at Bluebird's fire until you or René return. He told me he would meet me there after he found Monsieur Jacques."

Bemidii gave her a farewell nod and moved off down the riverside through the encampment that stretched along its course outside the fort. He had gone inside the fort yesterday with René to trade their cache of furs. But for celebrations, only the upper class and the bourgeois middle who had business to attend to were permitted entrance. Such an arrangement was fine with Bemidii. He had no reason to dwell among the Montrealers inside. He was a hunter and content in his role. Tomorrow he would attend a ceremony among the visiting tribes, and there he would be respected as one of them.

Boucher's was crowded, as usual. Even before he stepped inside the door, sweet scents of tobacco and roasting meat assailed him, competing with the sharp smell of whiskey and the rancid sweat of men. Lights, heat, music, and laughter pervaded the space. Here and there, a voice raised over some disagreement would settle again into murmurs of assent. Men cast dice and played cards, ate and swore. Some told tales larger than they dared, standing taller than their audiences and stretching out their arms. An occasional native girl passed among them, plying her own sort of trade.

Bemidii was glad he'd eaten at Brigitte's campfire, or he might have been sorely tempted by many offerings. At the counter that ran the length of the long, low-ceilinged building, he tossed a coin for a cup of shrub. He accepted the drink with a nod and turned to study the gathering further. It was the same a year ago when Brigitte had come inside with the Métis named Rupert, her brown eyes bright and nervous, her face flushed. His sister looked beautiful that night, but it was recognition that had swelled Bemidii's heart more than her lovely countenance. He had believed in an instant she was Marchal's daughter, the one taken away from this place at only six summers old to be reared and educated in far-off Montreal, a place Bemidii had never been, nor likely ever would be. His stare had frightened her, but he could not resist studying her and seeking to discover if what he believed was true. In the end, they had forged a deep kinship that neither ever expected. Now she was wed to René Dufour, and a better match their father could not have sought for his daughter.

He could not resist watching her then any more than he could resist noticing the woman on the island, though for wholly different reasons.

He took another sip, forcing the thought of such untouchable beauty away. Perhaps someday such a match as Brigitte and René's would happen for Bemidii. He was nearing an age where his friends were beginning to wonder what kept him from taking a woman. There were plenty of men years younger who already had a household filled with children. Yet Bemidii waited. For what or whom, he had no answer. Perhaps here at the rendezvous, the Great Mystery would deign him a meeting with a maiden meant for him. He doubted he would find her here in Boucher's store, however. He would have better luck seeking out his interests tomorrow at the ceremonial celebration.

Near one of the two windows in the room, four men sat at a table in discussion. They caught Bemidii's attention, as at least one of them was dressed in finer attire than the others. A Frenchman or a Scot, he wore a striped linen shirt and cravat beneath an open waistcoat. On the table near his elbow stood a tall beaver hat. He must be no more than Bemidii's own age but clearly bourgeois, some company apprentice clerk or shareholder from the east. What was he doing here outside the fort? Bemidii stepped away from the counter and meandered closer so he could hear their talk. He leaned idly against a support post in the middle of the room.

The man spun a coin on the surface of the table in front of them. "My coin is yours if you can tell me." *Frenchman indeed.*

"Bah! You have scratched the wrong itch, monsieur. You are wasting your time." A hardy voyageur with a grizzled chin waved off whatever suggestion had been made and guzzled from his cup.

The others laughed, and the Frenchman tossed the coin in the air, capturing it in his fist. For a brief second, he glanced at Bemidii, but Bemidii turned his head, feigning disinterest. The Frenchman's queued blond hair put him in mind again of the woman at La Pointe. If she had come to this rendezvous, then Bemidii would have no trouble deciding how he would pass his time.

"I will spend my money elsewhere, then." Movement stirred at the table, and from the corner of his eye, he saw the Frenchman rise. "I need no one to do my wenching for me. I'm certain I can find what I am after. After all, aren't these *sauvage* females for the taking?" The Frenchman eyed a serving girl carrying a tray of empty cups to the counter and ran his tongue over his lips.

Coarse laughter followed as well as at least one gesture. Bemidii had heard enough. This man was only here to serve his appetites, the same as so many others. Being one of the bourgeois here in Boucher's meant nothing beyond that. He straightened away from the support pole, making to leave, but the Frenchman's voice reached him yet again.

"I am told that the women will wash themselves and dress in their finest for their ceremony tomorrow. Perhaps I will attend and see what selections can be reaped from such a crop." He laughed again.

Anger tightened Bemidii's insides as he headed for the door. The ceremony was a spiritual time and a time of refreshing for friends and families, a celebration of goodwill and provision. Perhaps it was good he'd come to Boucher's. He would watch for this man tomorrow, and perhaps he could spare some poor maid the Frenchman's unsavory attention.

Several hours later, after he'd found the camaraderie of some fellow hunters and taken part in a friendly game of chance that won him a small pouch of porcupine quills for Brigitte, he returned to their lodge. Darkness had fallen, and a soft glow came from within. He called a greeting before entering, and René bid him come inside. The wedded pair lounged side by side upon their bed, Brigitte's face flushed in the light of a tallow candle. Bemidii smiled inwardly, glad he'd stayed away as long as he had.

"Did you enjoy your evening?" she asked.

He nodded and withdrew the pouch of quills from his belt. "For you. Something to decorate René's moccasins."

She peeked inside the pouch. "Merci. You did not spend your money on them, I hope."

He shook his head. "I won them fairly." He grinned. "I would not play if I could not win."

She gave him a sideways glance. "So you say, but you may not always be so fortunate."

He took off his sash and sat on his own bed to remove his moccasins. "Tomorrow is the ceremony of the tribes. Will you attend?"

Brigitte looked over her shoulder at René reclining on an elbow behind her. She leaned against him. "I would like to go."

René kissed her temple. "Then you should. Go with Bemidii. I will come as soon as I can. I have a meeting with the partners, and I will be expected to dine with them as well."

"I will keep watch on her," Bemidii offered.

"I think that I am capable of keeping watch on myself. Besides, how do you expect to meet a wife if you always have your sister in tow?" She grinned at him and back at René.

Bemidii returned the look before stripping his shirt over his head. He settled down onto his pallet and stuffed his hands behind his head. "Trust me when I tell you, should a woman please me, I will leave you to your own wits faster than a fish slithering from my hands."

She threw a soft, small bundle at him and pushed back firmly against René. He and Bemidii chuckled. René leaned over his wife and blew out the tallow candle, but before they quieted to sleep, he spoke again. "I thank you for looking out for her while I am away, Bemidii. Any other woman would be blessed to know you."

CHAPTER 3

Ambroise has burst into the house this afternoon announcing that my father wishes both he and Tristan to make their adventure. They will represent him to the posts in the west. Ambroise has asked if I might accompany him.

—Journal of Camilla Bonnet

Camilla rose late on yet another morning with the violent need to retch. Thankfully, Ambroise was not with her to witness her discomfort. She had yet to tell him her news, though days had passed. No good would come of him hovering with worry over her. Not now, while she still might take pleasure in her temporary freedom. To her great surprise, she found the company of Madeleine Cadotte and her daughters much preferable to that of Montreal's upper class with its pecking order and licentiousness. In the afternoons, when she generally felt better, she sometimes sat with her journal in the shade near the shore and watched while Madeleine and her oldest girls sewed canoe gunwales with spruce root. Nearby, Monsieur Cadotte and his lads fashioned the frame of a new canoe. Sometimes she walked with the Cadotte's eldest daughter, Marguerite, along the shore in search of shells, which were useful both domestically and for decoration. Camilla had not seen the stranger again who'd goaded her so openly with his stare on that first day, and no one else ever bothered her. Other than her morning sickness, she'd grown entirely at ease here.

Such freedom might be lost to her once the others discovered her secret, Ambroise especially. Camilla hoped to keep her pregnancy undisclosed until they were well on their way from this island. Still, that journey was yet weeks away. If the sickness and weariness clung even after Ambroise returned from his hunting trip on the mainland, she might be forced to admit she carried a child.

She scrambled for the chamber pot beneath her bed and gave

up the contents of her stomach, which was little. She had not gone down for breakfast and had eaten only a small part of her meal the night before. The very smells of last night's deer steak cooking over the fire had turned her inside out.

Camilla leaned back against the flat, plastered logs behind her rope bed and draped an arm across her brow. Her throat and chest burned. Her stomach ached. *Merci, Dieu.* She breathed a silent plea for the sickness to pass. Little by little, her head cleared, and she reached for a cup of water on her bedside table. When a few small sips had settled, she rose shakily to her feet.

There was no way around it. She must reconcile herself to telling Ambriose when he returned, which could be as soon as today. Perhaps they might stroll down the shore away from the trading post and the comings and goings of the village of La Pointe to find a quiet place where she could speak. He would likely become excited and want to announce his coming patriarchy to the world. She would encourage him not to rush the news.

Ambroise had left her in Madeleine's care seven days ago while he embarked with a group of men serving Michel Cadotte at locations among the other islands and on the mainland. He had greatly anticipated fishing with the men and seeing the places where the wild rice grew, which the natives would harvest later in the season. Meanwhile, their party would fish for whitefish, a staple here on the island. Ambroise was no true hunter or fisherman, but Camilla credited him for his enthusiasm in learning everything he could about life in the Upper Country.

Hundreds of miles they'd traveled for her heart to believe it, but it did seem his zeal was genuine and not solely for the purpose of garnering further favor with her father. Hadn't her father already promised him a rising place in the Clarboux business establishment?

Once Camilla washed and dressed for the day and felt more like herself again, she left the house and found Madeleine mixing dough in the outdoor kitchen. The air was thicker today, even so close to the lake. The wind made the water dance in peaked, white curls and pushed puffy clouds across the sky.

"Bonjour. You have awoken." Not only was Madame Cadotte well-spoken in French, but Camilla was surprised to learn that her French husband spoke English fluently as well.

"Oui. Please believe me when I tell you I always rose much earlier to begin my days in Montreal, but I find that the changes I've encountered here in the wilderness have taken their toll—or perhaps it is simply the abundance of fresh air and sunlight. I am more apt to rest when I can."

Madeleine Cadotte pushed the sleeve of her homespun dress farther up her arm. "I found each time that I grew tired more quickly than normal."

"Each time?"

"Each time I carried a child. You are pregnant, *non*?" Madeleine's brown cheeks wreathed in a knowing smile.

Camilla flushed. "You knew?"

"I think you could not go on such a journey unless your husband thought you well enough and able, and so something else must tire you. Your face, it is pale, more so in the early part of the day."

"Oui, but that is just ..." She touched her cheek, then lowered her hand. What was the point in denying it? It would do her good, perhaps, to have the confidence of another woman. She allowed a smile to give way. "I suppose it is true that I am pale then, for I have been ill most mornings. If I am correct, the child will arrive in the full of winter." Thinking of the time and distance that separated her from her and Ambroise's warm home in Montreal, her smile faltered. Yet winter brought sickness and hunger at times, even to such a prosperous and growing city.

"You will give birth during the bear moon or perhaps sooner, during the spirit moon. It is a good time to give birth, a time to honor the silence and realize our place within all of Great Mystery's creatures."

Camilla tucked her chin in thought. *Great Mystery*. She knew Madeleine spoke of God, but she'd never heard Him called by that title. It seemed strangely apropos, for God's actions—or lack of them—had long been a mystery to her. Yet the fact that a tiny being rested in her womb was a satisfying mystery. She raised her head. "A time to prepare."

"Oui." Madeleine gave a nod as she brushed flour on her hands to shape a loaf of bread into a large round. "You will be far from here and back to your homeland by then."

"It seems a very long time from now."

"You've spoken little of your journey to us. I have been many places with Michel, but none so far as you have come."

Camilla inhaled and let out a deep breath as Madeleine set the loaves on a long paddle and slid them into the brick oven. "We left Lachine almost two months ago. I had no idea, of course, but I must have conceived before we embarked. The trip was, at times, frightening and exhausting by turns, but the voyageurs took great care to see us safely through the most difficult passages. Monsieur Bonnet took great pleasure in the adventure."

Madeleine dusted off her hands and poured Camilla a cup of raspberry tea, adding a lump of maple sugar. "Drink this often. It will help you during your time." Camilla thanked her, and Madeleine retrieved her own cup. "You have come across many waters. Your child will be stronger because you have endured much."

Camilla sipped. Oui, much indeed. Long nights of cold and rain, at night burrowed under damp blankets among the snores of men who reeked of tobacco and sweat, followed by more days of heat and bugs, yet tempered by the pleasantness of the voyageurs' singing. "I am glad we made it to our destination in one piece. I pray the return journey goes as well."

Would she be over her morning sickness by then? When her stomach had upset several times during their voyage, she attributed it to the waves. So did Ambroise. That she might be pregnant had not occurred to her then, mostly because they had already been married for nearly a year, and she had almost given up on becoming so. Was it knowing that she would, at last, be free from her father's heavy hand in her and Ambroise's lives that put her at ease enough for her body to conceive? Did the thought of leaving Montreal behind, if only for a season, grant her the peace she needed to bring about such possibility? She would never know, yet the thought of having a son or daughter grow up near her father's house galled her. If only she and Ambroise could move to another city. Quebec, perhaps.

Such wishing was futile. Ambroise had high hopes for his partnership to grow with the North West Company and in her father's business particularly. She would be forever tied to James Clarboux, even as her poor mother was.

She pushed away her dour reverie and brightened her demeanor. "Is there something I can do to help you today, Madeleine?"

"If you wish it. There is the garden. Marguerite will show you. There are herbs ready for harvesting, if you do not mind. After you have eaten."

"I would be happy to investigate."

Madeleine offered her a bit of rice, which sat well with Camilla. Then Camilla hooked a basket over her arm and headed out from beneath the shed roof of the outdoor kitchen toward the small garden enclosed within a tamarack fence. At home, she sometimes helped her mother and their servants in the garden. She felt comfortable doing the same here.

There had been one servant girl whose company she especially enjoyed, until that young woman, a girl who had not seemed to escape her brother Tristan's notice, grew round with child herself and jumped into the river. Had a nearby fisherman not pulled her out, both she and the baby would have certainly perished. Even now, Camilla knew not what had become of the girl after she was turned over to the authorities and brought to *hôpital*. There was little hope for the future of pregnant, unwed women or their illegitimate children in Montreal when the father would not accept responsibility. The poor servant girl had probably been sent to the workhouse.

A gust of wind pushed against Camilla's skirts as she let herself through the garden gate and took in the array of greenery cultivated in patches all about. Marguerite was bent over amongst the vegetation, busily filling her basket while she hummed a tune. "*Allô*?"

The young woman stood up and whirled. Her face brightened with a smile. "*Salute*."

"I have come to help."

"That is very good. There is much lettuce." She pointed. "We should pick it before the rain." As if in explanation, Marguerite gave a glance upward at the fat clouds scudding across the sky.

Many vegetables would not be ready for a month or more here on these northern shores. But as Camilla trod carefully between plants and bushes, she soon found the wild lettuce and dandelion that Marguerite pointed out, as well as several other bunches of herbs that she selected and plucked.

Another gust of wind carried a scent of blossoms. The Cadottes and their people had made room for cultivating small patches of other plants that normally grew wild. There were blueberry bushes full of green berries close to ripening and strawberry plants that neared the end of their season. Peppery bittercress, spinachy chickweed, fireweed, and wild mustard grew thick in one corner of the garden—all plants native to the land but corralled here inside the enclosure. In another corner, corn plants grew to her knees, and tender young squash vines trailed among them. Green bean plants bore blossoms, and root vegetables grew in hills where space allowed. Camilla soon had her basket full of greens.

The wind pushed harder against her gown and nearly took her straw hat away. She clamped it down on her head.

"We should hurry." Marguerite moved through the garden again, making her way to the exit. "The storm is coming."

Overhead, leaden thunderheads pushed away the bright white clouds and patches of sunshine. The wind rushed through the pine treetops, sounding much like the waves on Lac Supérieur, and once again, Camilla thanked providence that she was no longer camping along the wild lake, hurrying to help string up tarps or take cover in some meager shelter like an overturned canoe that the voyageurs were afforded during a squall. This lake was a tempestuous mistress at times. As much as the voyageurs respected and feared her, they loved her and willingly put up with her tantrums.

Camilla and Marguerite returned their baskets of herbs to the outdoor kitchen, where a Métis woman accepted Camilla's from her hand. "Where has Madame Cadotte gone?"

The woman pointed at the main house and spoke in Ojibwe.

"Merci." Camilla's skirts danced and billowed in the buffeting wind as she left Marguerite and the woman to handle the produce. She clamped down her bonnet in earnest. Perhaps the coming storm would serve as the best time to record the most recent days in her journal.

Heavy pelts of rain smacked the ground around her. The storm was clearly going to be a strong one. Hurrying to the house, she paused just outside the door to look toward the lake. The waves rolled, smashing into the beach and breaking over the wharf. A long burst of thunder made her jump, and Camilla rushed inside.

Madeleine was seated at the table with her children. Books lay open before them, and one of the little girls read aloud. The boys, Camilla had learned, had surpassed the age of their mother's teaching and now spent their days in the warehouse, learning the trade with their father. Camilla slipped past them, not wishing to disturb their education, and tiptoed up the stairs to her bedroom. Lifting the lid of her trunk, she withdrew her journal along with a quill and precious bottle of ink. She moved to a chair by the desk, where gray light filtered in through the rain-splattered windowpane, and wrote of her morning in the garden and the concern closest to her heart.

I will tell Ambroise soon, but today it storms, so I will not yet expect his return. Perhaps tomorrow ...

She laid a hand on her flat stomach where the child grew, too tiny yet to feel its presence. What did the future hold for this little one? A life like the one Camilla had known? Or if it was a boy, a life under her husband's and father's tutelage in business? Would they send him to a prestigious school as Monsieur Cadotte's parents had done? Almost certainly. And if the baby was a girl? Would she grow up in a happy home? Could Camilla and Ambroise give their daughter a life more fulfilling than the one Camilla had known? She jotted down a few of her feelings about the coming baby. A daughter she would certainly never allow alone with her uncle.

Light. She needed light. The air felt tight and heavy.

Camilla frowned and put the journal and pen away. She capped the ink and rose to peer out the window. She pushed the muslin curtains wider and stared beyond, though rivers of water smeared the pain of memory and blurred most of her view of the trees and lake. The sound of the storm's surging gusted through the thick walls. She wasn't sure how long she stood there listening to the storm as it passed, fighting against the current of her memories, but eventually, the darkness lightened just a bit, and the wind began to calm both outside and in her thoughts.

The rain turned to a patter, and now she could more clearly see the lake through the trees. The water still churned, but not like before. The voyageurs could manage such a small surf. She took a breath and was about to move away from the window when a belated display of lightning emblazoned the sky, splitting it in two like the finger of God dividing the heavens asunder. The crack of thunder that followed shook her bones, and Camilla jolted back as though pushed. Her heart jarred against her chest, and she gasped. Then silence returned, and she took a seat on the edge of her bed until her shaking passed.

A minute or two went by, and then came a pummeling below. Footsteps rushed to and fro. The front door opened and slammed closed. Shouting came from outside. The door opened again with a crash.

Camilla rose and went back to the window but could tell

nothing. Perhaps it was the children, then.

When the pounding of feet struck the steps and her name was shouted up the stairwell—"Madame Bonnet!"—she whirled.

She opened the door to one of the Cadottes' sons. Augustin was almost even with her height. "You must come." He spun on his bare feet and rushed back down.

Camilla's heart filled with warning. Had something happened during the storm? Some damage to their home? Was the household well?

Downstairs, the family stood in a line as Michel came through the front door. He closed it gently and removed his hat. Water dripped off him to the floor, and his dark eyes fell upon her. "Madame Bonnet."

What could be wrong? *"Qu'est-ce qui ne va pas?"*

He stepped close and took her hands in his warm damp ones. Her heart thrummed, telling her things she didn't want to hear him say.

"Your husband, madame. Monsieur Bonnet …"

"What is it?" she whispered.

"There has been an accident."

"An accident?"

"I'm afraid—"

"Ambroise?" She pulled free of Michel and rushed out the door.

The rain had nearly ceased as she halted just beyond the stoop to see a crowd gathered near the lakefront. She picked up her skirts and ran down the muddied path, her shoes soaking through and droplets of water shaking off the trees overhead to fall on her. Shouldering her way past natives and Métis, she stumbled to the front of the group where a boat had been drawn ashore. Four strong men carried two others and lay them on the sopping ground.

A cry caught in Camilla's throat. Ambroise's large frame lay there on a blanket. *He is hurt. Only hurt.* She pushed past one of the men and dropped beside her husband. She grasped his hand. "Ambroise." She squeezed. "Ambroise."

His face was like the belly of a whitefish, and an unwelcome scent came off him. A scent of … she knew not what. It was almost as if he'd been burned.

Non. It made no sense. "Ambroise. Darling." Tears choked her. He could not hear. "Ambroise!" Her body turned weak and shrunk in upon itself. Hands lifted her away, but she cried out, weeping. "Ambroise!" Over and over, she called his name as they pulled her away and covered his body with another blanket.

And far, far away to the east, thunder rolled.

CHAPTER 4

I have done things for which I am not proud. Decisions are sometimes made for us, and we must act. Decisions for which there is no going back.

—Etienne Marchal, to his son, Benjamin

Two long braids draped the shoulders of the shapely young Ojibwe woman facing Bemidii, and dimples poked in her cheeks when she smiled demurely back at him. Then the drumming and singing began, and the circles moved in opposing directions, men in the outer ring, women in the inner. A full rotation was completed. The next time he met her, each pair of facing couples turned side by side and moved together in one direction. Bemidii and the woman stepped forward, moving in cadence along with all the other newly formed dance partners.

He enjoyed the rhythm of the dance, and the woman beside him kept elegant time with her own shuffling steps. She was short, the top of her head coming only to his chin. When he looked down on her, she seemed smaller than his little sister, Shenia. The dance moved on, and he searched beyond the edges of the circle for Brigitte, but she was nowhere in sight. René must have come for her. That, or she had found others to keep her company. When the dance finally ended, he faced the young woman.

"I am Bemidii." He inclined his head.

"I am called Anang."

"It is pleasing to dance beside you, Anang."

She smiled, her delight at the compliment obvious.

He peered across the way to the outer edges of the campfire light. "Do you thirst?"

"*Eya'.*"

Bemidii invited her to join him for refreshment. Meanwhile, he peered about for Brigitte. Finally, as they were sipping from a cool herbal tea sweetened with honey, he saw her standing in the twilight. She waved and turned away. He refocused his attention on Anang, telling her he was from the *Makwa*, or Bear clan, and asking her about her own clan and where she'd come from.

"I am of the *Binenhshiinh*, the bird clan."

Bemidii raised his brow. Her people were known as those who foretold the future. "And what happy prediction do you make of the festival?"

She shook her head. "Nothing has been revealed to me yet." Her smile and the tone of her answer flirted.

A warm and welcome feeling coursed through Bemidii, and he considered her closely. Then another man stepped behind her. "Your mother asks you to come." He gave Bemidii a wary eye. "You can return to the dancing later."

She blushed and cast Bemidii another glance. "I predict we will see each other again." Dipping her lashes but revealing her dimples again, she departed.

The warmth that had briefly spiraled through him dissipated as she disappeared through the crowds.

He made his way to the place Brigitte had been standing, but she was not there. He approached the nearest group of women and asked if they'd seen her, and they pointed the way. He walked still farther. Laughter and song filled the evening. Savory smells of roasted meat, fish boiling with herbs, and sweetgrass permeated the air. He would find Brigitte and return to the dancing. Hopefully, Anang would soon return as well, and they might see what the evening held in store together.

To his right, he passed the gaggle of company men he'd noted earlier when he first arrived. The blond Frenchman was no longer with them. Hopefully, he'd abandoned the celebration and returned to the fort with his kinsmen. The man represented everything Bemidii's father had ever warned him of.

He turned his thoughts back to finding his sister. Perhaps René had returned and was with Brigitte now. Bemidii continued through the throng. At last, he found Bluebird. "Have you seen my sister?"

"*Gaa.* Not since she went toward the river."

"Was she with René?"

Bluebird shook her head. "She was alone but said she will lie down and wait for Dufour."

He should have known she would grow tired. It had been a long afternoon and evening. He'd forgotten for a moment that her pregnancy only manifested in the way weariness overtook her abruptly throughout the day. No wonder she wanted him to go and dance. It was as much so she could slip away and rest, no doubt. But she should have told him. She was a strong one, and she didn't like it when others hovered over her.

Bemidii nodded at those he met in passing as he trotted down the trail along the high riverbank. He passed lodges and campfires. Those who weren't at the festival sat around their fires, smoking, eating, and telling stories. Some called greetings and invitations to join them, but he waved and moved on.

Darkness had not fully descended but soon would. Already a three-quarter moon shone brightly off the river. Lovers stood behind a tree, embracing one another as he passed, and for a moment, he regretted his mission. He would make certain that Brigitte was resting, and then he would return to find Anang, the young woman with the teasing smile.

The ravine through which the river ran cut deeper into the hillsides. The pathway upon which he walked narrowed along the top, winding through tall pines. Bemidii's feet moved soundlessly on the carpet of shed needles as he drew closer to their lodge. When he reached it, no hint of firelight shone from within. He drew back the flap covering the door. "Brigitte?" He listened for her response, but not even a breath stirred.

For the first time, real worry struck him with a sharpened edge. "Brigitte?" he called a little louder into the darkness. Seeing no one else about the neighboring lodges, he made his way slowly back along the trail. Might she have gone to the fort in search of René? Such a likelihood was slim. He must have passed her in the crowd, or she was at another lodge fire.

Maybe she'd gone to relieve her needs privately and would be back among the celebrants at the dance by now, wondering where he'd gone. His shoulders dropped in slight relief. That was it. He'd lengthened his stride when a sound near the river below the path halted him—a *thunk* against wood and a rustling. Bemidii peered deep into the dimness where the bow of a canoe swung against the current next to the shore. He stiffened and listened again, but only a hushed voice and the stirring of movement came back. Did someone hope to spear fish this night, or had he stumbled upon another pair of lovers?

A gasp reached him, and his pulse pricked. "*Boozhoo*!" he called.

Stillness wracked the twilight, broken only by the gurgling of the water. Then there was a thud, and the canoe shifted again. Bemidii stooped and called out once more. "Boozhoo! Is all well?"

A low curse came from below, followed by another gasp. Bemidii slid sideways down the embankment, pine needles slithering away under his feet. To keep from going headlong into the river, he dragged his flight by grasping hold of passing tree trunks. He skidded to a halt, facing who knew what in the darkness of the riverbank. Two bodies pressed together in the shadows. Perhaps he'd been wrong to think something was amiss. Then moonlight glinted on a blade.

"Viens pas plus près!"

The sharp command set Bemidii's nerves tingling. What had he stumbled upon? Bemidii recognized the Frenchman's voice but pretended not to understand. He grunted and took a step forward.

"He said, do not come closer."

Bemidii froze at the sound of Brigitte's shattered voice speaking in his native tongue. Dread swept through him. He answered her in Ojibwe. "Are you hurt?"

"Gaa."

He held his relief in check.

"This man I know. He—"

"Speak French," the man growled to Brigitte.

"J'ai compris." She took a deep breath. "Do not come closer, or he will—"

"Or I will cut her. Now get out of here."

Bemidii ground his teeth and pulled his knife from its sheath.

"Bemidii, non!"

The Frenchman yanked her tighter. "You know this *sauvage*?" The stranger ground his words into Brigitte's ear. "Why am I not surprised, since you have become one yourself?" His quick appraisal of her accompanied a sneer.

Bemidii took another step, but the man raised his knife to Brigitte's throat.

"Try it, and I will make quick work of the woman. Who is he, Brigitte, your lover?"

She shook her head, and when she spoke, her words choked with tears. "My brother."

"Your brother?" Incredulity seemed to momentarily throw the man off his guard, and Bemidii took the instant to fix his stance for an attack. He must free Brigitte from this madman.

The Frenchman studied him. "Put away your knife, and we will bargain. I will pay you for her. She might be worth something for your inconvenience, non?"

"My sister is not for sale. She is wife to René Dufour, a company partner."

The madman's arm banded around Brigitte's middle, pulling her back against him so that she shielded him fully. "You lie. Now back away. Do not suppose I will not cut her." He slid the knife to her neck and held the point against her skin.

Bemidii narrowed his eyes. "If you harm her, you will be dead before you take your next breath."

"Bemidii." Brigitte's pleading sounded almost like a farewell.

The Frenchman backed her slowly toward the boat. "We will

step back into the canot, Brigitte, and if you make a mistake, it will cost you dearly." His gaze hardened on Bemidii while he moved, the knife nicking the skin beneath Brigitte's ear.

Bemidii flinched but held his ground. He spoke in Ojibwe again, assuring her with gentle tones. "Be brave. He cannot keep you in his grasp for long." A sound on the hill above them caught his ear. He could call out, but what if it were a woman or a child, or even another Frenchman like this one coming down the dark path?

Brigitte stared at him while she allowed Tristan to move her into the wobbling craft. "*S'il vous plaît*, Tristan. You cannot think to get away with this."

He settled in the stern, keeping her in front of him as he pushed the canoe into the current with a shove off an overhanging branch.

The boat swept gently into the stream farther from shore as Brigitte's captor tucked his knife away and drew out a pistol instead. Aiming it at Bemidii, he released his hold on Brigitte and reached for a paddle. Distance between Bemidii and the canoe widened, then the small boat rotated in the current.

Bemidii plunged into the river and dove. A bullet plugged the water beside him. He surfaced and stroked hard, keeping an eye on the drifting canoe and this Frenchman she'd called Tristan, who was reloading his gun.

"René!" Brigitte cried out, and her captor struck her across the face so that she fell back into the canoe. Then he raised his gun a second time.

Bemidii ducked beneath the surface again. This time, the bullet sliced through the water near his head, but he was nearer the boat when he resurfaced. The Frenchman clamored for his paddle, but with another solid stroke, Bemidii reached for the hull of the craft and grasped the gunwale. He hoisted himself up and pushed down again with all his might, unsteadying the Frenchman before he could strike at Bemidii with the paddle. As the man stretched his arms to find balance, Bemidii slid his grip farther along the gunwale and repeated the action, this time upsetting the canoe so that both occupants tumbled into the water. Brigitte flailed, and the Frenchman reached for her, but Bemidii shoved the canoe away and pushed through the water toward them, forcing the Frenchman to release her. Brigitte swam for shore, and then Tristan turned toward Bemidii. A flash in the rising moonlight showed he'd drawn his knife again.

The current swept at them, and Tristan took a breath and slunk beneath the surface. They met, and a sharp, burning pain ripped through Bemidii's side. He gripped the man's arms, and the Frenchman grasped him in return. They grappled, half in the water, half out. Then they slipped apart from each other, and Bemidii reached for his own knife. Tristan swam toward shore, where Brigitte was just gaining her feet, and Bemidii followed, ignoring the searing pain in his side.

They met again in waist-deep water. Locked hand to hand, Tristan's grip on his knife extended above their heads, while Bemidii grasped his weapon at their sides. Close now, in the moonlight, Tristan's eyes bore into him with icy hatred. Bemidii broke the stare and let his legs collapse into a bend, flipping Tristan over his head. But as the man rose, he leapt back at Bemidii, bringing down his knife.

Bemidii brandished his weapon as a shield, and as the weight of Tristan's lunge brought him forward, Bemidii's blade slid between Tristan's ribs.

Like statues frozen in time, they held until Tristan's eyes bulged and his mouth gaped. Then Bemidii pulled the blade free. He stepped back. They stood there in the stream, staring at one another in the moonlight, as Bemidii huffed for breath and sounds returned. The river gurgled around them. Brigitte sobbed. Then Tristan staggered back, stumbled, and slipped into the water.

"Bemidii!" René called.

Bemidii turned, a spasm of fresh pain coming over him. He blinked at the smattering of people gathered on the bank above, but mostly he saw René holding Brigitte close, their eyes upon him.

He took a wobbling step, then another. René let go of Brigitte and rushed down to pull him from the water.

CHAPTER 5

I hate Tristan! I hate him! And Papa too. He never listens. When I grow up, I will marry a fine man, and I will never do what they tell me again.

—Journal of Camilla Bonnet, ten years of age

Two weeks had passed since Camilla buried her husband. Her shock had dulled, but her uncertainty for the future had only grown, day by day adding to her sense of weakness and dependency. She would be forced to return to her father's house, though he would surely waste no time in procuring a new husband for her. Likely, some widower who needed a mother for his children or perhaps a much older man who would strike a bargain with her father, bearing in mind she was coming to him with a child. Someone who would expect her to take care of him in his dotage. Someone like old MacDaw who made her skin crawl.

Meanwhile, the gentler shock of finding herself pregnant had worn off. The smallest roundness now hid beneath her stays, and a flutter came from within, like the wings of a butterfly, reminding her that all too soon, she would be responsible for an infant while at the same time, she would be dependent upon her father's provision.

She recorded her fears in her journal as she sat in the shade of an oak above the sandy shore. She raised her eyes to the calm, blue waters of Lac Supérieur and peered across the bay toward the mainland. How hard it was to fathom the violence those waters could churn. Ambroise should not have agreed to venture across that day. He had complained to his native guides of being wet and tired, and some said he had insisted against their advice that they go back to St. Michel as soon as the storm seemed to have passed. They told her he had been anxious to return to a warm hearth with his wife.

It was her fault, then. Another burden she must shoulder alone.

Today was hot. This morning, she had gone with Madeleine Cadotte and her daughters to pick the blueberries, which had been ripening at almost a daily rate. After they returned, she had helped prepare a rack of whitefish for drying. She was thankful for these tasks that both filled her time and made her feel as though she had something to contribute in payment for her hosts' kindness and generosity. After all, she was dependent upon them until such time as Tristan returned for her.

Perspiration clung inside her dress, soaking her stays and sticking to her waist beneath her petticoats. The gentle lapping of the water made her wish she knew how to swim. Even not knowing, she longed to take off her shoes and walk in it. To keep going and never turn back. She closed her eyes and dreamed of the cool water caressing her, covering her. Was this how the serving girl in Montreal had felt before the fisherman dragged her from her death?

Perhaps Camilla could at least touch her toes into the edge. No one was about to see her. She laid aside her journal, ink bottle, and pen and unlaced the ribbon of her leather shoes. She looked from side to side and behind her again, making sure no one was present, and stood up. The prickly grass tickled her toes, and, in a moment, she was pushing them into the hot sand, hotter than she anticipated. With a lift of her hem, she scooted to the water's edge. As she stepped in, the cool water closed around her ankles, and Camilla shuttered her eyes in a rush of relief.

A man's voice startled her. "Bonjour."

"Oh!" Camilla dropped her hem and jumped back. Too late. Water had already soaked the edge of her gown, and now it collected particles of sand.

"My pardon, mademoiselle."

She straightened, curling her fingers into a clasp in front of her. "No pardon is needed, and it is *madame*. Madame Bonnet."

"Madame Bonnet, oui." He was not a tall man, and he must

be of middling age or thereabout. He fisted a cap in his hands and dipped his dark head, then took a step toward her. "I meant no intrusion on your reverie, but I had hoped to speak to you privately."

Now Camilla recognized him as being among the Métis porters in Monsieur Cadotte's employ whom she often saw carrying goods to and from the warehouse.

"My name is Victor Pilon."

She inclined her head, acknowledging him.

"I knew your husband only in passing, madame. I met him just before he left with the others for the mainland. I am very sorry for your loss." A line appeared between his brows, and his lower lip pushed out.

"Merci, Monsieur Pilon. Your kindness is appreciated."

"But …"

But.

Her heart skipped a beat, and she stiffened. Did he have some knowledge of the accident she had not known about? "What is it? *Qu'est-ce qui ne va pas?*"

"I am also sorry you are left alone. I have come to offer for you."

She frowned. "Offer for me what? I do not understand."

He squeezed the cap in his hands. "For your hand, of course. In marriage. You cannot remain alone, a French woman in this wild country. Who will care for you now? Who will provide?" He took one step, and then another. "Who will shelter you? You cannot rely on the grace of the Great Michel forever. You will need a protector, someone vowed to—"

"Monsieur Pilon! I insist—"—she put a hand to her chest to calm the breathless racing of her heart—"I insist you speak no further." She lowered her trembling hand to her side.

"I assure you that I am a good man, madame. I have no other wife—"

"No other wife?" She gasped.

"No native woman bearing my children in the wilderness." He shrugged. "As is the custom of some."

Her toes curled in the sand. She wished for her shoes, wished she could flee this man's presence.

"You must marry again. It is right. It is safe."

"Monsieur, you misjudge my predicament. Oui, I have lost my husband, but I am not alone without aid. My father, James Clarboux, is a very important merchant in Montreal. Surely, you have heard of him. Even now, his agent, my brother, is on his way from Fort William to collect me and return me to our father's house." She pushed back her shoulders and lifted her chin. "I have no intentions of marrying anyone here on this island or anywhere in this country. I must go home."

His gaze drifted down the length of her to her bare feet poking out from beneath her soggy hem. "Should you change your mind …"

"I will not."

He squeezed his cap and nodded. "I will leave you, then."

"Bonjour."

"Bonjour, madame." Much more slowly than she would have liked, and not before another sweeping glance, he finally turned his back, thick with bunched shoulders beneath his shirt, and strode away from the beach.

Camilla sagged with relief and rubbed her hands down over her face. As soon as he was gone, she took shaking steps back to her shoes and sat to put them on. A total stranger asking for her hand! A Métis! Begging to marry her and live here in this godforsaken country! It took long moments for her trembling to cease.

At last, her pulsed calmed. She exhaled a deep breath as a movement almost unnoticeable far out on the water caught her eye. She shaded her eyes and squinted. It was not a bird, but something larger. Soon she recognized it as a lone canoe, gliding toward the island. A fisherman, perhaps, or maybe a message-bearer from one of the villages or other posts on the mainland.

The pages of her journal fluttered open beside her. She picked it up and smoothed it closed. She would write of Victor Pilon's strange proposal later. Perhaps, with time, she might even laugh at it.

Camilla rose, pocketing her quill and ink bottle. She hugged the book to her chest as she raised her eyes to the bay again. The approaching craft was indeed one of the typical birch bark canoes she'd seen so often cutting along the shores and rivers. This one was manned by a native. He sat nearer the back than the center but far enough forward to keep the bow from riding high and catching the lake wind. The craft rode light upon the water. It must not be heavily laden with goods. He raised his paddle and twisted it to the other side, sending droplets of water sparkling in the sun as he dipped it in again. She stared, mesmerized by his symmetry of motion.

Paddle, paddle, paddle, paddle.

Swing, spray, dip.

Paddle, paddle, paddle, paddle.

Again …

His body was bare and bronze to the waist. Tattoos, too far away to discern their design, marked his neck and biceps. His hair draped his chest in two black braids. Soon he was close enough for her to see the sinew of his muscles move with each graceful stroke. Even his neck strained until he laid the paddle down and allowed his canoe to slide toward shore. Then, before it could catch the rough lake bottom and be damaged, he rose and leapt into the thigh-deep water, guiding the craft to the beach. He wore only a breechclout like most of the native men did in the summer heat. Many natives had come from the nearby village of La Pointe, right here on the island, and from other places to trade with the one they affectionately called Great Michel, but this man was one she had not seen before. Unless …

He raised his face, and Camilla stepped back against the tree, drawing a hand to her throat. Oui, she had seen him before. Weeks ago. On the day of her arrival, this man had left the fort, searing her with a long, curious look and imprinting the memory of a face that was at once probing, strong, and purposeful.

She dared not move lest he notice her standing there, but even in that intention, she failed, for his gaze searched the shore as if seeking someone, and then found her. His eyes glinted like obsidian and, she was certain, with recognition.

CHAPTER 6

"Some will try and cheat you. When you make your mark, use the letters I taught you. Your name will win the trader's respect."

—Etienne Marchal, to his son, Benjamin

Bemidii had never expected to return to this island post so soon, yet during his long voyage back, he could not deny having thought often of the golden-haired woman he'd seen here only weeks ago. When he settled his canoe on the sandy beach, scanned the rise, and saw her, it was almost as if he had conjured her there with his thoughts.

His breath halted for fear she might disappear. She stepped back farther beneath the shade of the tree. Her mouth opened slightly as though startled—as though recognizing him too. Air returned with a swelling in his chest. She would not disappear.

He straightened to give her a longer study while ignoring the pulling at his side where the wound had closed but remained tender, especially after crouching long hours in the canoe.

On the night of his fight, Bluebird had packed Bemidii's wound with steamed yarrow, then wrapped his torso in a bandage while his sister explained who Tristan Clarboux was—or, more importantly—who Tristan's father was. Bemidii heard the worry in her voice as she spoke of this powerful man, and he sensed, even then, he would not be given a reprieve to rest and heal.

René had gone alone to speak to the authorities, giving them his word as company partner that Bemidii had only acted in defense of Brigitte. Still, the clerks and lesser-ranking officials at the fort feared speaking against the son of James Clarboux. They repeatedly pointed out that the elder Clarboux was one of the company's most important members of the Beaver Society. Surely, they insisted, the Métis man had provoked Tristan. Perhaps the man's sister had done so as well.

Despite stirring René's ire at such innuendo, they pressed on. Why had she gone alone with him? Why had the three of them ended up on the river? No gun had been recovered. Had Clarboux been unarmed but for his knife? Did the Métis intend to rob him? Implications tumbled out against Bemidii in defense of Clarboux's son. Despite René's insistence that Tristan had accosted his wife, his word was received reluctantly, and the other company men determined Bemidii should be arrested and sent to Montreal for trial. James Clarboux would insist upon it.

Undoubtedly, he would expect recompense for his son's life.

When Bemidii heard that, he and René made arrangements to meet at the end of summer, and Bemidii left them, joining some Indians traveling southwest. What hope could there be of receiving a fair trial with this *James Clarboux* at the top of the bourgeois chain of authority? René would continue to use his persuasion, but Bemidii would not wait for a different outcome.

At the Pigeon River, several of his party turned inland, while he and two others traveled on toward *le fond du lac*. Bemidii took shelter for two days with his mother's household outside the St. Louis River post before paddling on with another pair of hunters heading toward the rivers spilling into *Gitche Gumme*—the Great Sea—or as the French and his sister called it, Lac Supérieur, at the southern shore. Perhaps he should have continued with them deep into the inland Ouisconsin posts, but he did not. At the mouth of the Bois Brule, they parted ways.

Now, after another two days' paddling, accompanied by fair weather, he at last arrived at the islands they had visited more than a month ago. He had not expected to see this bay again so soon, if ever, but as René and Brigitte had discussed the plan for joining him again, Bemidii had thought of the sweetness of the islands and the country surrounding Chequamegon Bay, not to mention the great distance which they lay between here and his troubles at Fort William.

And of the brief glimpse he'd taken of a particular woman.

In no hurry to take his pack from the canoe, he basked in the sight of her again.

She pulled her lips closed and shifted, her fingers tightening on some book she held. Then she lowered her eyes and hurried toward the fort before he could speak.

His heart lightened, for she was like a bright blossom in the sun, *wabigwaan*, a wildflower. He would think of her so until he learned what she was called. He followed at a distance, but when she turned to the house of Michel Cadotte, he continued on to the post.

The place was quiet now, with so many gone to rendezvous and others out fishing or up at the La Pointe village. Only the one called Great Michel was present, along with one old Indian purchasing tobacco. As he finished his trade, Bemidii came forward.

"Boozhoo," he said with a nod.

"Boozhoo. How can I help you?" Michel Cadotte was of average height, a farmer-tradesman from the sun-and-windburned looks of him. He wore a homespun shirt tucked into his brown cotton breeches, the sleeves rolled up to his forearms, but he donned no waistcoat or other overshirt. His hair, dark with little gray, was drawn back in a short queue, and he must have shaved only recently. The man raised a strong chin and eyed him over a fairly prominent nose that pointed to native blood in his lineage. "We have met before."

Bemidii gave a nod. "Only a month past. I came for the fishing with one of the North West partners. He is gone now."

"Ah, yes. You brought good pelts. You came back."

"I am thinking of staying here until the falling leaves moon. Perhaps, before the ice comes, I will go to hunt on the mainland. If you have need of porters or meat, I am willing to help."

"I have no need at present, but that will change with the season. What is your name?"

"I am called Benjamin." Brigitte had suggested he go by the

name their father called him so as to keep anyone who knew of Clarboux's death from bringing trouble on the head of Bemidii.

"Benjamin, eh? All right. Where will I find you? At the village?"

"I will set my camp along the southern shore"—he thumbed in the general direction where wilderness forest stretched above jutting layers of rocky sandstone lapped by crystal clear waters, a good place and away from the village—"but I will not be hard to find." One corner of his mouth moved in a slight smile as Cadotte turned a ledger to face him.

"Make your mark so you will be counted among my employees when I have need. In the meantime, I will take any fish you can spare."

He nodded and signed the mark for Benjamin as he had been taught by his father.

Cadotte pulled the ledger back and looked. "Very good, then." He closed the cover. "Can I get you anything else?"

Bemidii shook his head. He wanted to ask about the woman and her husband, but he would know of them soon enough. He would find out from one of the other workers if a brigade would leave soon, now that all the summer rendezvous had passed. Perhaps she would be here a few more days, at least. Though she was married, he might still enjoy her presence, for no harm could come of admiration. Who knew if ever again he would see a woman whose hair shone like the very sun?

He went back to the beach and retrieved his canoe. With a last glance toward the home of the Cadotte family, he set the craft in the water and pushed from shore, this time paddling around the southern tip of the island to the east—just far enough for privacy and quiet. Many days had already passed, but perhaps more would be required for René to make Bemidii's case before the authorities. Surely, time would give them reason. They would see that he had only defended Brigitte and himself. Still, he must be patient, for men of the Beaver Society and the North West Company were not easily put off. They considered themselves wisest of all men and the betters of The People and the Métis.

Along with such a wait, he would have to be patient while René made stops with his traders along the way. He could be of great service to Cadotte during that time, and perhaps, speak to the woman as well. He would like to hear her voice.

Bemidii soon came to the place where rugged sandstone outcroppings made almost a stairway to the shelf of land above. Tall pines with long needles danced in the breeze overhead. Beyond, the forest made a floor bedded with soft fern and pine needles. A good place to set his dwelling. He and his Dufour family had done so in this very place for a week during the raspberry moon, the days Brigitte called July. They had built a small hut of long poles covered in bark and pine boughs, similar to a *wiigiwaam*, but not quite as large as the home belonging to his mother, Keeheezkoni. They had tucked the poles in the woods, and Bemidii knew where to find them. By evening, his structure was complete. Tomorrow he would find fresh boughs and bark to cover it. For tonight, he would sleep beneath the stars.

The next day, Bemidii finished the shelter and tasked himself with finding bait for fishing. After turning over logs and rocks until he'd captured enough worms, he took his canoe out again, paddling it close along the shore and dropping his line. His catch was small but sufficient for his supper. By midday, the wind picked up, and working the canoe became both troublesome and a bit dangerous. He paddled back to camp and cooked his meal over a fire. After he had eaten, he took out his flute and relaxed on a woven mat with his back pressed against a birch tree. In the shadows of the massive trees, he gazed out over the wide, blue waters. He could see no distant land from this spot, only the sparkling dance of the water. His flute picked out a melody both sweet and somber, for he was filled with something of each the pleasant and the sorrowful.

What if René's good word did not prevail among his fellow partners, or what if they did not forget this incident with time? What if Bemidii would never again be safe to go to rendezvous, to hunt and trap and trade? What if he was even found out here in this faraway place?

Yet was returning to a solitary life a bad thing? He was in the company of the Great Mystery, who René claimed was no longer a mystery but a loving Father. If that were so, then he must not dread this isolation. Would he not be welcome again in his mother and stepfather's village? Certainly. Yet he would endanger those he loved if this older Clarboux, Tristan's father, was determined to punish him as Brigitte feared.

Bemidii put the flute away. Only a fortnight ago, he had wondered if he might soon find a maiden for whom to play his song. Now, he thought of survival.

Twilight gathered, and with it, his thoughts turned to the French woman on the beach. Even now, she might be brushing out her hair and preparing to lie beside the boisterous Frenchman Bemidii had seen in the trading post last month. As sour as the thought of her going to such a one might be, he could not stop imagining her eyelids lowering and her lips bending in a silky smile.

He turned to his side with a grunt and pulled a robe over his shoulders. He should not allow his thoughts to wander in such a way.

A blush of dawn crept over the horizon when Bemidii awoke. He rose and gathered fishing line and hooks, along with innards from last night's catch he'd kept from drying in a bowl of water. They would make a fine bait. He soon pushed off in his canoe, the gentle dip and drip from his oar the only sound breaking the day as he skimmed the surface of the calm lake. In the distance, a loon dove beneath the surface, barely ruffling the water. As the sunlight stretched toward him, he dropped his line into the water, lowering it until he guessed it to be only several inches from the bottom. After several tries, he hooked his first fish.

By the time his stomach began growling for food, he had two walleye and two perch in his woven basket. Too bad he didn't have a gill net for scooping the whitefish in these waters. If Cadotte wanted fish, Bemidii should consider trading for a net with one of the women in the village who made them. Nevertheless, even without the net, he headed back to camp later in the morning with enough fish to dry and pound for pemmican as well as plenty for his dinner. This evening, he would try again, and he would take any extras to the post to trade for some flour or cornmeal.

After he'd eaten a meal and then prepared the remaining fish for the next step in making pemmican, he strode toward the swamps deeper in the island in search of sapling brush to make a fish trap. Until he owned a net, he could catch any number of fish or shellfish with such a trap or two.

The afternoon had waned even as the day had grown sultry. Evening was not far off by the time he returned to camp with a bundle of twigs. Already the lake had begun to calm, and soon he could put his canoe back into the water to fish again. Right now, even in high summer, the lake was cold but not too cold. After his long trek through the woods, being pestered by mosquitoes and black flies, the notion of a bath pleased him. He set aside the twigs and climbed the sandstone back down to the water's edge.

Wearing only his breechcloth, he leapt in up to his waist. The icy water sucked away his breath, but he let out a gust of breath and dove in. His body shuddered from the shock, and the stitch in his side made him cringe, but it felt good to clean himself of fish scent, sweat, and bug bites. Stroking his way nearer the shore, he dug his fingers into the sand beneath the water and scrubbed himself. Then he dove again, sluicing off the sand and scouring his scalp.

After a prolonged swim, he finally pulled himself out of the water. Gooseflesh ran its course up and down his body, and his hair dripped a river down his back. He shook himself off and climbed the rocks back toward camp.

A movement on the trail to his left jarred him to a halt. The island was full of bears, and at the moment, Bemidii was defenseless. But it was not a bear, nor was it a deer or even some inhabitant of the village. From a sun-kissed face, the Frenchwoman's eyes widened like green lake stones as she stood there staring at him.

Water ran down his temple, and he raised a damp forearm to wipe it away, but his movement made her startle. She reached into the deep pocket of her dress, and Bemidii stood motionless as she pulled out a pistol and pointed it at him. The long bore shook, and she steadied her hold with her other hand.

He held up his hands, though it must be clear he carried no weapon on his nearly naked body. *"Wabigwaan ashwiyaa."* He spoke softly, more to himself as he considered the way she stood there, arming herself against him.

"*Arrêt*. Do not come closer."

He held his pleasure in check. The sound of her voice was musical though breathy.

He turned a palm up at his side, and she took a step back. He did not want to frighten her further. In fact, he did not want her to leave. He would remain still as long as she did not flee.

Her eyes flitted over him, and she blinked as a rosy flush crept up her neck and cheeks. Did his nakedness embarrass her? Bemidii fought a smile. If she was afraid, why did she not leave?

CHAPTER 7

If I could learn the task without flinching, I might nearly find my mark. Ambroise insists it is not so difficult as I make it seem. But I have never had cause to fire a pistol.

—Journal of Camilla Bonnet

The weight of the pistol dragged at Camilla's arm. Did he wait for her to weaken? She shrugged her shoulder as she tightened her grip. "I am going to leave now."

He did not move, but those eyes … *those eyes*! The dark obsidian glinted with something between humor and evil intent. Camilla couldn't tell which. She didn't dare wait to find out—after all, how could she shoot a man? She might threaten with her pistol, but if it came to shedding his blood …

Her husband had come to the west with a brace of pistols. One went to the bottom of the lake when he was killed. The other he'd left behind in her chest at the Cadottes', and she wielded it now. It was loaded. He'd taught her to use it, with minor success, before they left Montreal. Bear roamed the island. She'd seen a sow and two cubs near a berry patch last week when she'd gone out with Madeleine and the girls. The women had left the bears alone, going home with empty baskets. Since then, she made sure to take the pistol with her whenever she wandered away from the Cadottes' alone. Madeleine assured her that it was wise, especially if she were going to pick berries. Madeleine also urged Camilla to stay on the main trails or within sight of the lake to avoid getting lost.

Camilla had done both. She had walked the Indian trail just along the sandstone crest of the shore, this time without her journal. She only wanted to see more of the island and to get away from pitying eyes. Everyone there pitied the useless French woman whose husband had died. It frustrated her so badly. She only wanted to get away to a place where she could think and pray without the concerned perusal.

When would Tristan come, and what would he have to say of Ambroise's foolish decision to paddle across rough seas? She could only imagine how Tristan would sneer at her husband's foolhardiness, and then he would grouse at the need to take care of her all the way back to Montreal. Would he offer any comfort? What's more, did she want him to?

Would she survive her encounter with this savage long enough to find out?

The man still hadn't moved, and Camilla was afraid to turn her back on him. She couldn't run without him catching her. There was no one to whom she could cry for help. Even the gun in her hand offered little consolation, for the more she wavered, the more she doubted she could ever pull the trigger.

"I do not know who you are or why you look at me that way, but my husband is only back there." She jerked her head to indicate some unrevealed distance behind her. "He will come if I scream. Or … or someone will," she added lamely.

The Indian's lips twitched. Did he mock her?

She scowled and motioned the gun again. "You had best go about your business and leave me be."

He looked toward the bushes, and she couldn't help but follow his glance. Was that a camp? Did he live so close by, and she had not known?

He said something in his language. It was the second time he'd said those words. The first time he'd merely whispered them. What did that mean, anyway—*wabigwaan ashwiyaa*? She should have paid more attention to the natives' speech on her journey. Perhaps she would have picked up more understanding beyond *boozhoo*—hello—and *eya'* or *gaawiin*—yes and no. There were a few other words, but none she could draw upon to help her now.

He slowly raised his hand and rubbed his chest. The tattoo on his arm resembled a bear.

She licked her lips and took a backward step. "Go on now.

About your business. I am going back." Dare she lower the gun? He still hadn't moved.

Then he raised and dropped one shoulder, and his lips definitely lifted in a smile.

She backed farther and lowered the gun as she turned and, without pause, hurried back up the path. Would he follow? Her breath hitched in her chest. What if he leapt from the bushes and grabbed her? Wasn't that what these wild Indians did? They weren't like the tame ones, the men who paddled the bourgeois and upper class across the lakes and up and down the rivers to the trading posts. Her stomach fluttered—or was it the baby? Camilla laid her hand over the protected place. She did not see the root in her path. Her slipper caught, and she pitched forward, landing hard on her knees and losing the gun in the brush beside the path.

Pain shot through her right knee and up to her hip. Too late, she clamped her mouth on a cry. And too late, she heard the sound of feet behind her. She hissed with pain and twisted, stretching for the gun, but it lay too far away. The Indian loomed over her. Then he dropped down on one knee and looked the length of her and back again. She flinched as he reached for her skirt, then she slapped his hand.

He let out a loud sigh and rubbed his brow with a thumb. Then he held out both hands, palms outward. He pointed with one finger at her feet and, moving slowly, reached for her ankle. She instinctively drew back, but his movements were non-threatening. She gritted her teeth, waiting to see what he would do. He gently touched her foot, then slowly stretched his fingers toward her ankle. She flinched again.

"It is turned." She bit her lower lip, and he nodded. Did he understand?

Leaning back on his haunches, he held out a hand and searched her eyes.

Camilla hesitated, but what else could she do? Perhaps it was only his bearing that frightened her, and he hadn't meant her any harm. She gave a tiny nod and took his hand.

He stretched his other arm around her shoulders and, girding her arm, helped her to her feet.

"Aie!" She could put no weight on her right foot. He kept her from falling, his strength bolstering her. As she slowly sought her balance, she became once again aware of him in other ways. His hand was warm to the touch, but the arm that brushed against her felt cool, even in the day's heat. He must have been swimming, for his hair was still wet. The water that had slicked his brown body earlier had dried. Sinewy arms braced her, and she dared a glimpse of his face outlined by a strong jaw and high cheekbones. He was taller than some of the other aborigines and Métis she'd met. Too tall for a typical voyageur, but not for striding these wild woods.

"Merci. Now, if you will help me to Monsieur Cadotte's trading post, *si'l vous plait*." She wobbled. The gun. She'd nearly forgotten it. "Oh." Dare she point it out and ask him to retrieve it? What if he used it to hold her hostage? What if he stole it from her? But there was nothing for it but to ask. "My—my pistol." He would not understand. She waved a hand at the brush. "There."

He followed her direction. As she supported herself against a tree trunk, he gently let her go and stooped to pick up the gun. He turned it over in his hands, seeming to admire it. Again, their eyes met, and this time, she did hold her breath. Turning the gun around once more so that the grip was turned her way, he offered her the weapon. She took it from his hand and wobbled again as she released the tree trunk to put the gun inside her pocket.

"Merci," she whispered, unsure what else to say. Her ankle throbbed, and now her neck heated with embarrassment that she had threatened to shoot him. She had brought the injury upon herself. Her eyes stung, and she despised her tears, yet it was all just too much. She swayed, and his hands shot out to steady her, his grip sure. "I don't think I can walk." She let out a hollow laugh as she floundered and gripped his forearm. "And you don't understand a word I speak." She sniffed and raised helpless eyes.

"Je le comprends."

She blanched and pulled her gaze away. What a little fool she was. He'd understood her all along and hidden the fact. "Oui. I see now that you can," she said between thin lips.

"If you will allow me, I will carry you home." He spoke fluently, and she cringed again. Carry her! Why ...

"*S'il vous plait.* I will cause you no harm. I will return you safely to your husband."

Her husband, who she'd claimed was waiting just up the path. She looked at him again to see if he realized the truth. His expression gave no indication that he did. Finally, there was nothing more she could do. The painful pressure in her ankle grew to a throb. It must be swelling furiously. She gave a jerky nod. "If you would be so kind."

With little effort, he scooped her up, and she had no choice but to put her arms around his neck. He set off down the long path back to the trading post, the heavy gun in her pocket wedged between them.

He did not stop once to rest. His chest expanding for breath between his long strides, he moved with silence and grace at a steady pace over the terrain. Camilla tucked her chin to avoid looking at him, only now and then peering farther down the trail. When at last the clearing near the trading post was in sight, she shifted against him. "You may release me. I think I can stand."

He stopped and lowered her gently, steadying her as she gingerly set her foot to the ground. Her breath hissed between her teeth at the horrible jolt shooting up her ankle.

The Indian was quick to grasp hold of her. "I will help." Lifting her wrist, he wrapped her arm around his neck and swept his other arm around her waist, nearly raising her off the ground but not quite. Forward she limped, with him taking almost the entirety of her weight on the right side. As they came into the yard, John-Baptiste Cadotte, the son who most often worked in the store with his father, lifted his head from where he was pedaling a sharpening stone beside a shed.

"Madame Bonnet!" He laid aside a tool and hurried toward them. "You are hurt?"

"I only turned my ankle."

"Let us take you inside." He moved to her other side so that she was nearly suspended between him and the Indian.

At the door, she stopped them and looked at the man, whom she now suspected might be Métis. "This is fine. Young Monsieur Cadotte can help me from here." She offered him a stiff smile of thanks as he released her, but his gaze still held. "Merci."

"I am called Benjamin."

"Benjamin." She nodded and would have departed, but he touched her arm, stopping her.

"What is it you are called?"

She felt his perusal and raised a hand to her hair self-consciously. "I am Madame Bonnet."

"Bonnet."

He had heard the lad call her so but must have expected her to tell him more. She let out an exasperated breath.

"*Mino dibikad.*" He smiled.

"Oui, well …" She turned her back to let the Cadotte lad help her inside.

"He says it's a good night," the young man said, granting her a smile akin to suspecting an interest between them.

Flustered, she reached for the door handle. Then, at the last second, she looked back over her shoulder, but the man who called himself Benjamin was finally going away.

CHAPTER 8

Diplomacy is hard-earned wisdom, a mutual respect among peoples whose opinions and desires do not always agree or are not clearly understood. You must develop this skill if you are to live in two worlds, that of red and white.

—Etienne Marchal, to his son, Benjamin

The waters were calm for paddling, and the load easier to carry in a canoe. Nevertheless, Bemidii walked the shaded path to the trading post carrying two stringers of fish. Cornstalks stood tall and tasseled inside the garden fence near the Cadottes' house, but no one was outdoors as he passed by. He set his face toward the storehouse, passing a man about his own age who was pulling a chaw off a new hunk of tobacco.

Entering the building, the breezy scents of summer were replaced by the earthy combination of tanned hides, tobacco, dried herbs, and even the metallic smell of gunpowder. He approached Michel Cadotte, who stood behind the counter.

"I have fish to trade." Bemidii handed him one of the stringers.

Cadotte noted the weight and number of the fish and credited them in his ledger. He tipped the feathery end of his pen at the second stringer. "Those as well, or are you taking them to the village?"

"Non. I bring them as a gift to the Great Michel and his guests. No trade." He laid the four, fat whitefish in an empty basket beside the scale.

Michel's brow rose along with his glance. "Guests, you say? You must mean Madame Bonnet. Did you travel with her and her husband here from Montreal?"

Bemidii shook his head. "I am a hunter only, not a voyageur."

"And a fisherman," Michel said with a one-sided smile. "I accept your gift with pleasure. Madame Bonnet has not said she is tired of fish for her supper yet."

Bemidii tipped his head. "I will also purchase two dozen hooks." While he was well supplied in shot and traps, he hadn't gotten enough hooks at the rendezvous. At that time, he did not anticipate quite so much fishing.

As the man packaged the hooks for him, Bemidii looked over some of the other offerings in store the trader had to offer. "You have many goods now that the season's furs have gone east."

"All but those over there." Cadotte thumbed toward a table in the corner. "They'll ship soon. When Bonnet's brigade arrives from rendezvous."

"Bonnet's? Monsieur has traveled on to rendezvous?"

Cadotte slid the small package across the counter, his glance finding Bemidii's. "Non."

Bemidii palmed the package.

"I forget you did not arrive until recently. Monsieur Bonnet is no more. He was killed only weeks ago here in the bay. Struck by lightning along with one other."

A jolt passed through Bemidii at the revelation, but he schooled his features with a small frown. "I had not heard. I am very sorry." His thoughts swam toward Madame Bonnet. *Ashwiyaa*. How bravely she had defended herself, while in her heart, she must quake at being so alone. Her husband was—dead. He rubbed a hand over his chest as though it might help to settle the quickening of his heartbeat. "Then my gift to Madame … you must also tell her I send it with my condolences at her loss."

Cadotte eyed him momentarily, then turned his attention back to the open ledger, where he recorded the trade of the hooks. "I will give her your message. Your name again, it was Benjamin?"

"Oui."

Cadotte nodded. "The brigade that comes will take her to her home again in Montreal. Her brother will be among them."

Bemidii kept silent. He did not trust the tone of the words that might come from his mouth. If he should only say *I understand*, he might sound too concerned. If he should ask a question, he might sound too curious. It was best he said nothing, so he tucked his small package into the leather bag strung from the belt at this waist and departed. He must learn more about Bonnet's death and the brigade to come, but he had no wish to arouse undue curiosity from Cadotte.

The same man who'd been pulling at his tobacco leaned against the outside wall when Bemidii exited the store. He raised a chin and spoke over the tobacco in his lip. "You are new here. I saw you only once before."

Bemidii gave a nod. "I am Benjamin."

The man turned his head and spat. Then, with a stained smile, he stretched out his hand. "I am *Wiisagi-ma'iingan* among The People, or Coyote, if you prefer."

"It is good to meet you, Coyote."

He was of a stringy build and a few inches shorter than Bemidii. "My mother named me Red-Haired Coyote, though you can no longer tell." He grinned and ran a hand over his head, smoothing the dark hair, clipped at the shoulders, behind one ear. "You are staying long on the island?"

Bemidii shrugged. "For a time, until the season for hunting comes. Then I will move in from the lake and find a place to set my traps. And you? You are a hunter or voyageur? Or do you live here?" He didn't wish to answer too many of this Coyote's questions. It was better to turn the questions to him.

"La Pointe is my home. Where is your camp?"

Bemidii poked his thumb over his shoulder in a generalized direction. "Down the south trail."

"Would you like to come to my lodge? I have a bottle of rum, and the day is getting on."

His offer did not appeal to Bemidii, but neither did he wish to be thought unfriendly. Such a demeanor would draw notice. "Perhaps another time. I have fish traps to mend."

"I saw you had a good catch when you went inside."

"Eya'. Good fishing this morning. You did not go out?" He turned as though to move along, and Coyote fell in stride beside him.

"I should have, true. My wife is making a new net. When she is finished, I will take it out. Better to take a catch all at once than over many hours of dipping a line."

If you are so fortunate. Bemidii bit his tongue against the thought. He strode toward the beach, not wishing to have Coyote trail him all the way back to camp. "You had good trading this year?"

He glanced at Coyote's noncommittal expression. "It was not bad. Not as good as could be either. I will find a new place to hunt this year. Perhaps I will join you," he said with a wink.

One of the Cadotte daughters had come outside and was playing a game of pretend in front of the house. Coyote followed Bemidii's quick glance. Bemidii continued making his way down the path to the water's edge. He squatted to wash his hands, scrubbing sand between his palms. "I have heard there was a tragedy during a storm here not many weeks ago." He raised his head to peer across the wide bay.

Coyote dropped beside him, resting his forearms on his pointed knees. He gave a long, slow nod. "My wife's cousin was killed along with the Frenchman."

"Why were they on the water?"

Coyote's sniff sounded like a huff coming out his nostrils. "*Le Bourgeois*. He wished it. Some said he was tired of the wet and sleeping on the ground, and he was too much in a hurry to be in his wife's bed again."

Bemidii shook the water from his hands and rose. "So his foolishness has left her alone."

Coyote stood beside him and nodded. "Not for long, I expect. She has been offered for, but she is determined to return to Montreal."

"She will go with one of the brigades heading to the Sault?"

"They say a brigade comes for her as it was supposed to come for both of them. They will be surprised to learn her husband is dead. She will travel under the safety of her brother's oversight."

"When are they expected to arrive?"

"They should have come already. The season is passing, and soon the leaves will turn. The trip will not be pleasant for a woman unable to keep warm beside her husband, especially one who is grieving his loss."

Bemidii patted Coyote on the shoulder with a friendly smile. "It is good you have no such worries, eh?"

Coyote chuckled and held out his tobacco pouch for Bemidii.

Bemidii shook his head. "I go back to my camp now." He paused for a moment. "Perhaps you will fetch me if this brigade arrives. I am drying fish and could sell some to the voyageurs before they move on. You will easily find my camp along the trail."

Coyote agreed. "It is a good thing to make your acquaintance, Benjamin."

The next day, Bemidii lowered his traps into the water beneath skies that looked like trade wool. The waters weren't too rough, but a bit choppy, nonetheless. He would have to move swiftly in case a storm blew in. Instead of heading back to camp when he was through, however, he paddled along the shore until he came around the tip of the island where he'd first arrived. He couldn't say why—for the woman would not be there now. She surely hadn't healed. Her sore ankle would keep her indoors for a time yet, perhaps even until the brigade came for her. Yet if he could catch even a glimpse of her golden hair, he would be satisfied.

He made slow strokes in the water, allowing the paddle to trail as he observed a loon diving for fish in the distance and reappearing fifty yards farther away. Bemidii smiled. Cadotte's wife, Equasayway—or Madeleine—was the daughter of White Crane, the principal chief of the Ojibwe, although some were saying that honor would soon belong to White Buffalo, a member of the Loon clan. Perhaps the bird diving in the water ahead was making its presence and opinion known.

Bemidii took several more strokes, rounding the bend, and looked toward the beach. His breath caught in his chest as a glance up from the distance caught his—her face framed in loops of sunny yellow. She sat beneath the same tree she had the day of his arrival. She did not rise, but he noted the way her body straightened as he allowed the canoe to drift to shore.

He laid the paddle down and raised his hand in greeting. "Boozhoo, Ashwiyaa."

Was that a tentative smile on her lips? "I do not know what that is you call me. I heard you say it before."

"It is my name for Madame Bonnet. Ashwiyaa is 'defends oneself.'" He climbed from the boat and gently tugged it onto the sand.

A single one of her brows tilted slightly. "That hardly seems comely."

"I do not know *comely*. Is it a beautiful woman?" He took several steps up the shore, enjoying the flush that spread over her cheeks. "Your foot is getting better?"

She reached down and tugged the hem of her dress over her ankle. "It is still painful but not as swollen as before. The color is awful."

He hardly heard her, for he could not stop staring at her face. Freckles dotted her nose an even deeper shade of honey. From what he'd heard of white women, they were not pleased by such effects of the sun. Again, she had the same book tucked on her lap. "What is it you read?"

She picked up the leather-bound volume and turned it in her hands. "It is not for reading, but for writing inside."

"You keep records like Cadotte?"

"In a manner of speaking. I keep a record of my days."

That seemed like a useless pursuit, but Bemidii nodded. "I do not write much in the French letters, only my name and numbers and those few marks my father taught to record my trade of furs."

"It's pleasant to know how to pen one's thoughts and feelings."

He studied her for a quiet moment, then nodded. He had no wish to interject sorrowful thoughts into their conversation, as surely, such would overwhelm her feelings these days.

"Did you receive my gift?"

"Oui. Food is always welcome, though, in truth, I am hungry for some red meat these days." She lowered her head and swept her eyes up again. "I apologize. That sounded very ungrateful. All food is a gift from God." She sighed. "'Every creature of God is good, and nothing to be refused if it be received with thanksgiving,' as the Good Book says. So for your gift, Benjamin, I thank you." She rubbed her lips together and looked away with another blush. Was it because she had spoken his name?

He came nearer. "You are most welcome, Ashwiyaa." He spoke the name with near reverence, causing her eyes to fly open wider.

"I am not so accustomed to using a man's Christian name when we are so barely acquainted."

He glanced pointedly up the hillside toward the trail to his camp. "Is it not enough that I carried you close to my breast for such a distance to say that we are acquainted well enough to speak our names? I am happy to be called by Benjamin and no other name."

She shifted as she seemed to consider his remark. Finally, she raised her chin again. "Oui, well, that might be so. You may call me Camilla if you would like."

"What means Camilla?" He made a face. He was teasing her now.

She shrugged. "I really have no idea. Some eastern flower, I suppose."

He chuckled and was rewarded with another flush of her cheeks. "A name most fitting. Wabigwaan Ashwiyaa." Another step, until he stood at a comfortable distance to speak without seeming over-imposing. "She is a flower who defends herself."

"That seems most contradictory." She blushed again, but a smile tugged at the corners of her lips. "What brings you to the post today?"

"I do not go to the post. I decide only to paddle along the shore."

"Oui, I see." She laid a hand over her stomach and seemed to caress the material of her dress. "I want to thank you again for helping me get back to the house when I fell."

"No thanks are necessary. I am sorry for frightening you." He had taken a bit of pleasure that day in her response, but knowing now how her husband had been so recently killed, guilt gnawed. "I should have taken more care of your impression, as you are new to this country."

She gave the tiniest nod. "Oui, I am new, but I do find it a pleasant country. I have never known anything beyond Montreal until this year. Montreal, with its fine homes and shops. Wares beyond what you can imagine. Silks and jewelry, sauces, and sweets. You have not the like of such delights anywhere here in the Upper Country. Yet …" She pulled in a long, deep breath and exhaled it slowly. "There is much to be commended for this beautiful land and even this treacherous sea." She peered beyond him, and a fleeting cloud passed over her features.

"I regret your loss," he said, his tone turning solemn. "Had I known you suffered, I would have shown greater kindness to you that day."

Her eyes flashed to him. "You were not unkind."

"Not unkind, but not thoughtful either."

She shrugged and shook her head as if to rid herself of such gloomy thoughts. "Tell me, Benjamin, where are you from? Did you grow up here on this island?"

"I come from the west and only visit this place on occasion. My family is from the place you call *le fond du lac*, near where a wide river empties into these waters. There is a village there where my mother lives with my younger brother and sister and my stepfather. I hunt and travel with others now."

"Others?"

"From the company as well as family members." He didn't elaborate on that. Let her suppose he meant brothers or uncles, not a sister or her husband, a Frenchman from Montreal such as she. Perhaps she knew him. The reality that she might be acquainted with his Dufour relation sent a tingling of uncertainty through him. It might be better if he did not familiarize himself further with Ashwiyaa, yet how could he resist? He must turn the conversation from himself. "Will you stay here now, to be near the place your husband is lain?" He knew her answer but wanted the thought to lodge long enough inside her head and heart to consider.

"Non. I will return with my brother, though what awaits me in Montreal, I ..." Her expression turned shadowed once again.

"Perhaps, before it is time for you to go, I will see you again. Your injury is unfortunate. I have found a newly ripened blackberry patch that has not yet been raided by other pickers. I could show you." He softened his expression with a smile. "I would make sure you are safe from bears."

Her lashes fluttered, and her gaze lingered across the water for a long moment. Finally, she brought it back, and her hand moved over her dress front again. "Such an offer almost makes me wish I could stay longer." She lowered her eyes to the book in her lap, and she smoothed the cover. "Dried berries for the journey would be welcome."

Though he wished to linger and speak with her further, he could think of no other excuse. "I wish you well, Camilla," he said, trying her name on his tongue.

Her forehead smoothed, and with it, the corners of her eyes. "And I, you, Benjamin."

CHAPTER 9

Without my pen and ink, the hours in the canoe would be unbearable. The men that surround me reek of unwashed bodies and tobacco. Their stories are raucous as well, but I fill my pages, pretending not to hear. Yet I would not trade my journey for all the fine parlors of Montreal.

—Journal of Camilla Bonnet

Camilla was sorry for the rain. Marguerite and Julie had moved with her back into the room they'd so graciously vacated for Camilla and Ambroise. Though the Cadottes had allowed Camilla a period of mourning and adjustment, it was clear she was crowding their family by keeping the eldest girls from their own beds. She went to them, insisting they return to the room upstairs she now shared with them, which meant her privacy was at a premium. She had grown to enjoy Marguerite's company, for the young woman was near Camilla's age, and Julie was young but unintrusive. Nevertheless, Camilla had no place indoors to be alone.

At last able to walk again without the assistance of a cane, and with only the slightest discomfort, Camilla had looked forward to strolling farther away from the house. She didn't intend to go far. Just a short walk down the shore. Not as far as Benjamin's camp—or so she told herself. But with the steady drumming of the rain on the roof and no sight of a break in the slate-gray clouds, she would not leave the house today. Even if the rain were to stop, the forest would be soggy, every leaf and blade of grass drenched.

Perhaps the storm would delay Tristan a while longer. And if it did?

She shouldn't have admitted to Benjamin that leaving raised uncertainties. After she'd wished aloud for more time here on the island, she'd had to include a desire for berries for the journey, or he might have mistaken her longing. The thought of returning to Montreal set her on edge. What would her future hold? What would be worse, being forced to quickly marry some man of her father's choosing or being forced by circumstances to remain in her father's house?

She could not bear being under his thumb again, especially not with a child to raise. Yet, surely, he would waste no time in marrying her off again or in allowing her to be choosy. Not with a baby on the way. She could almost hear her father now, berating Ambroise for his idiotic decision to try the lake during a storm. The poor man was dead, but that would not save him from her father's tongue lashing, a tongue lashing she would bear on Ambroise's behalf. Her *père* would look at her with narrowed, twitching eyes, sorry to have to take on the responsibility of her provision once again. He would resent the burden she'd become. Then he would present some man willing to take her and the child together, and if Camilla refused …

If Camilla refused, her father would likely force her to give the child up. He'd send the babe to the nuns and maybe her, too, or worse. There were institutions for women deemed unreasonable. Deemed insane. It only took a word from a respected man like her father to make it so. He had once threatened to send her own mother away when she had the courage to speak up to him.

Camilla sat on the cornhusk mattress of her bed and caressed her womb. As if aware of her thoughts and feelings, the child stirred. Love and protection poured through her, filling up every space. She would not let the baby go, no matter what her father said or did. If she had to, she would even marry someone as old and pawing as Monsieur MacDaw, who lived alone with his eccentricities in a tall, narrow, and cold house near the cliffs. She'd seen the way his eyes roamed over her and spittle would gather on the corner of his mouth. He'd pinched her once …

Camilla shuddered. She would prefer to stay on this backcountry island rather than face such a distinct possibility. A while longer, anyway, even if it meant the brigade must travel home in the cold of autumn, and she must do without the comforts of her other life. Just long enough until she could determine some course or idea to present to her father.

Gentle thunder rolled. Had it really been only weeks since Ambroise died? Was he cold, there in the wet ground where they'd buried him? She stretched her hand across his pillow. Then she laid down on the bed and pressed her face against it, willing some scent of him to linger still, to help her remember. But non. The bedding had been washed more than once. Ambroise was lost to her forever. Even the finer points of his features seemed already dim. How could this be?

While a man she barely knew—had only spoken to twice—appeared in her thoughts with vivid clarity?

Careful not to disturb the two girls who remained asleep in the other bed, Camilla pushed herself up from the bed and went to the little writing desk beneath the window, where she opened her journal and dipped her quill into a nearly empty bottle of ink.

It seems Ambroise has been gone much longer than he really has. He is like a passing ghost in my mind. What kind of wife am I to miss him so little? He deserved better. Yet I cannot help but wonder, did he love me more than I loved him?

The final lettering of her question appeared faint. Camilla scratched the bottom of the bottle to reload her pen, but alas, there was not enough ink. She pulled open the tiny drawer in the secretary, but no spare ink could be found there. Perhaps Monsieur Cadotte had some in his store. Then again, he probably only kept enough on hand for his own needs. Hunters and trappers had no need for ink. Ambroise had ink, but it had disappeared on the day he was killed. Sunk to the bottom of the lake with his pistol and pack.

Camilla nibbled on a fingernail, considering her dilemma. She could hardly get by without being able to write in her journal. What did one use when they had nothing to write with? There must be something. She glanced up at the tiny windowpane, streaked with rain.

Berries. Berries could be made to substitute for ink. She lifted her shoulders, feeling lighter to have thought of an answer. Of course, the blueberries were almost finished, and the patch where she'd picked them with Madame Cadotte and her girls was well scavenged. But Benjamin said he knew of some berries. Blackberries. They would make a fine ink for her quill. She could mash them and bottle some of the dark juice for the long paddle back to Montreal.

Resolved to find blackberries once the rain stopped, she closed the journal and rose from her desk. Surely, Madeleine would have tasks for her to fill her day.

The rain continued all day long, lashing against the house at times, and thunder rumbled well into the night. Then at some point, the storm passed, and the raindrops on the rooftop lessened until they ceased altogether. When morning broke over La Pointe, sunshine rushed to brighten the sky. The air felt lighter, released from the canopy of rain. Instead, a warm breeze dried the island, a perfect day for carrying out her plans.

Camilla wrapped her ankle well for extra support and wedged her slipper on. Testing her steps, the modicum of support felt much better. She hobbled downstairs, where Madeleine had already cooked their breakfast and was serving her family.

Camilla took her seat at the table. "I will be out today." She ladled hot porridge into a wooden bowl. "I am restless, and I am out of ink. I thought perhaps I might find some berries and make some."

Michel raised a spoon, heaped with steaming porridge, to his chin. "Excellent idea. I have heard the blackberries are ripening."

"Can we go, too, Maman?" The littlest Cadotte girl, Charlotte, turned pleading eyes to her mother.

"Perhaps later. Not this morning. We have lessons, and then we must gather beans."

A collective groan came from the children, but Madame Cadotte was not moved. She gave a small smile to Camilla. "You must wear boots. Blackberry vines are unforgiving and will ruin your slippers."

She had not considered that. She had a tall pair of moccasins among her things. Ambroise had purchased them for her at the Sault, partly with the thought that she might need them and partly as a souvenir of sorts, but she had yet to try them on. The very notion of shedding her slippers for such primitive footwear seemed almost savage in itself. Now, for the first time, the idea carried some practicality. She returned to her room after breakfast and found them. Soft and sturdy at once, she was surprised at how comfortable they felt. Since they laced, she was able to snug them over her ankle wrapping without too much difficulty, and they added extra support. Minutes later, she hooked a basket over her arm and slipped away from the house.

She left for the high sandstone path along the shore where she'd walked that fateful day a week ago and was carried back by Benjamin. What would he think of her turning up at his camp today? How was it that she felt as though he might be a friend here where she had none? Madeleine was kind and giving, and she even seemed to understand Camilla's French ways. Yet they hadn't grown particularly close. And Camilla was lonely.

She took her time walking slowly along the trail that was covered in a thick layer of spent pine needles, careful not to stumble over any tree roots knobbing out of the ground like veins in a sleeping giant's hands. A breeze blew off the lake, sending a sparkling sheen across the water. Ambroise had loved his adventure so. Perhaps he could not have wished for a better way to meet his Maker than during the very epoch of his journey.

She glanced down at her moccasins as she traveled. Her husband's gift had been more thoughtful than she knew at the time. Portaging with the voyageurs over much rough terrain, she had worn through one pair of shoes. Ofttimes, she had needed Ambroise's assistance when he might have served more purpose in helping the voyageurs carry the heavy packs.

With these moccasins, she would have little need of Tristan's assistance on their journey home. She could walk quite easily in them—especially once her ankle healed completely.

Her breath came more quickly as she hiked through the forest, and once, she startled at the screeching of a red squirrel, who scolded her from a branch high above. She had forgotten the pistol. She halted. Maybe she would be wise to return for it. After all, she was still alone here, despite Benjamin's assurance that he would protect her from bears. And did she really trust the man himself?

Oui. She did. Was she a fool to do so?

Several panted breaths later, she continued on. If she was a fool, she would soon find out.

She emerged at a crest on the pathway where the trees opened up to a wider view of the lake and sky, framing vivid blues in tree and rock that descended to the water's edge. Off the path to the left, amid pine and fern, stood Benjamin's shelter in his small camp. Her heartbeat still hadn't slowed, and now it ticked with as much nervousness as exertion. What would he say upon seeing her here? More yet, what would he think? Would he think her bold or wanton? Did the Métis think in such terms, or was that reserved for the fine homes of Montreal? She huffed a breath of air, purposing not to worry. It didn't matter. She'd come here to find berries so she could write.

Then she saw him. He was in his canoe some distance out from shore, but she knew it was him. In so short an acquaintance, she'd learned the shape of his shoulders, the leanness of his torso, the tilt of his face to the water or sky. Warmth swam through her limbs.

Foolishness.

She had not felt so silly since she'd been the naïve girl who'd asked her family's *au pair* whether or not the woman would marry Tristan. The question seemed reasonable at the moment, what with the things Camilla thought she saw pass between her older brother and her nanny. The woman was not such a great many years older than he, surely. Yet the au pair had reddened and scolded Camilla, seeming altogether more shocked and embarrassed than angry. No, Camilla had not been so silly since long before she learned the true ways of the world and the men who ruled it.

She pressed a hand again to the babe nestled inside, her eyes on the man in the canoe.

Benjamin pulled a long rope from the water on the end of which a cage of sorts dangled. He settled it in the bottom of his canoe. Then he picked up his paddle and stroked at an angle toward the shore.

Camilla stepped closer to the edge of the rock face. Her ankle was somewhat sore but still felt strong. She had never been much of a girl to climb and run outdoors, but only because she hadn't been allowed. She lowered herself and placed her feet with care as she descended the rocks. Soon she stood on a wide slab that jutted out into the cove.

As though she'd called him, his face turned toward her, and she lifted an arm. With hesitation at first, and then with more courage, she waved at Benjamin.

"Ashwiyaa!" His voice reached out to her across the water.

She waved again. "Benjamin!" She laughed at his shout that followed, a hoot, really—some native form of exuberance that lit a joy inside her.

His paddle stroked the water with the rhythm it had that first day she saw him. She felt each pulse run through her as though she herself were in the boat. In only moments, he drew near shore. He leapt from the craft and stopped the boat before it touched the rocks, steadying it as it bobbed in two feet of water. After he unloaded his fish trap, a small net, bait, and paddle onto the rock beside her, Benjamin leaned across the canoe, and with a flip, hoisted it over his head.

She'd seen plenty of voyageurs do the same, but not with their body's every muscle gleaming in the sun. He settled the boat securely on the ledge before saying anything to her.

Then he smiled. "You have come for the berries."

She still held the basket on her arm. "Oui. No fish today?"

He shook his head. "The wind is wrong. It is a good day to pick berries. They are very plump and fine for eating. I will dry some for pemmican as well."

"I intend to turn some of them into ink."

He shook his head. "Ink. I think they will tempt your tongue before you can do so." His quick glance at her mouth made her lick her lips, and he smiled again. "Come." He climbed to the first rock and held out his hand.

His fingers curled around hers, making her step easy.

"Your ankle is better?"

"Much better, and the moccasins help support it."

"Well-made," he said, with another glance, this time to her feet. No man had ever looked so casually at her feet before except Ambroise. Yet she was not uncomfortable that Benjamin did so.

"I suppose they are. My slippers would have been ruined." Even the leather moccasins had gotten damp on the walk in. Now, though, the leaves and grass were drying. "Is it far to the blackberries?"

He pulled her up the final bit of the climb, this time taking both hands. "Not far." Then he released her, and with grace and agility, leapt back down, rock to rock, and retrieved his equipment.

She clutched her hands together with the basket dangling on her arm, the feel of his touch still vivid. His hands were stronger than Ambroise's. Her husband's hands felt like putty until their voyage hardened them a bit. Nothing about this man looked soft or weak. Noticing so only made her cringe inwardly at the thought of the sort of individual her father would next marry her to—unless she chose a husband for herself. Was there a man in Montreal, a good, kind man, pleasing in both countenance and temperament, who would care for her and a child not his own as well? A man who wasn't her father's age?

Bitterness boiled inside as she waited while Benjamin stored his belongings and hung the trap from a tree. He went inside his shelter and returned a minute later wearing a trade shirt, leggings, and tall moccasins much like her own. He picked up a small copper pot and appeared ready.

"You are sure you do not mind my intrusion? You must have many things to take your time."

He shook his head. "This is a good thing and important. Man cannot live on fish alone."

She smirked. "Do you not mean bread?"

He raised a brow as he came to her, and they turned to the path again. "Should I?"

"I—I thought you were referring to the Scripture that tells us man shall not live by bread alone, but by every word that proceeds from the mouth of God."

"Bread. Fish. Does it matter? Is not the point that nothing satisfies without God's teachings?"

She hadn't thought of it quite that way, but it was true. "Are you a Christian Indian?"

He cast her a quizzical glance, one laced with humor. "I am familiar with the teachings. Members of my own family follow the teachings of Jesus."

"But not you?"

Benjamin shrugged as they strolled. He moved aside a branch in their path for her to pass. "I consider it, but I am undecided. I trust in the Great Spirit, but I am still weighing the matter of this man who claimed to be his Son."

Camilla had never weighed her faith. She had known only the faith her mother insisted upon, such as it was, weak and unfed. She considered it her responsibility to maintain a modicum of religious observance. Yet, without the tiny seed it was, what else was there to cling to? She nodded. "I understand. I suppose I, too, have much to be uncertain about." Especially since Ambroise died. She had never entertained the notion in her journal of God having let her down or abandoning her, but perhaps He had. Maybe He had never been with her at all.

"Perhaps we will talk about this further and come to understand together." There was warmth in his voice that pulled her step closer.

"Perhaps we will."

Their walk took them another quarter mile down the shore, then Benjamin guided her inland through a maze of brush. "You must tell me if your ankle grieves you. We can rest, and I will help you."

"All right. It is fine at present. Merci, Benjamin."

They soon came to the berry patch, a tangle of briers creating bowers taller than Camilla. She had worn her most serviceable dress. It had seen rough wear, and she had needed to stitch up the hem more than once. She'd even patched a tear acquired during a portage. Thankfully, she could easily conceal the mended rip beneath an apron like she wore now. After today, she might need to do more patching. The thorny bushes tore mercilessly on her clothes, and she found she was safest staying along the edges of the patch. In places, there appeared to be tunnels through the middle of the thick vines. Tufts of hair caught on a thorn here or there and bear droppings beneath told her she and Benjamin had not been the first to find the berries, after all. Still, there were plenty, and they were as plump and black as Benjamin described.

He was right in another thing. It was hard to add the berries to her basket. Her hands were soon stained purple, and she suspected her tongue and lips were too. She collected enough of the ripe fruit to crush later and turn the juice into ink for her quill, as well as enough to share with Madeleine to do with as she liked.

Benjamin periodically added his own handfuls to her basket, though she also saw him tilt his head back and pour generous portions into his mouth. He caught her looking once, his mouth full to bursting even while he smiled, and Camilla laughed.

When had she last laughed? She couldn't even remember. It seemed as though it had been years since her laugh had been real. Genuine. Filled with contentment.

Before long, her basket was full along with her stomach. Benjamin came from the brush, scratches on his hands bearing witness to his determination to reach the fattest berries. His copper pot brimmed with black treasure. She turned beside him with a limp.

"Take my arm." He held up his free arm and carried the pot in the other. "It will make it easier. You've been long on your feet."

She did not argue. The sustained walk and steady picking through the brush had increased the ache above her foot.

He assisted her slowly through the woods. "I can carry you again if you wish it."

She heard no teasing in his voice and swallowed against a sense of self-consciousness that told her her feelings were not to be trusted. "This is fine."

"When we are at my camp, you will rest before returning to La Pointe."

She only managed a tiny nod and tightened her hold on his forearm, the tendons of which could be easily felt beneath his thin linen shirt.

They reached his camp, and he rolled a log from the brush for her to seat herself upon. He took the berry basket from her and set it aside. "I wish to see this ink you make when you are through. And to see you write. I have watched my sister write."

"Your sister reads?"

"Oui, and I, though not as well as she. I read only the words I must know for trading."

She frowned over the puzzle he'd become to her. "Did you grow up near a trading post?"

He nodded. "At the Fort St. Louis post at *le fond du lac*. But there is talk there now of it moving. There is talk everywhere of the Americans taking over these posts east of the *Messippi*. I have heard it said that even Gichi-miishen will soon serve the American company."

Ambroise had explained this to her during their journey. "I was told he is working now for the new company at Michilimackinac to help the North West Company smuggle goods into America to avoid the taxes."

Benjamin took a seat on the log beside her and rested his arms on his knees. "Fewer packs are sent to the Kaministiquia each year from these posts, and last year, many hunters and traders were persuaded by a Shawnee prophet to take up arms against the Americans instead of hunting and trading."

"I have heard of the Prophet also. Michel told my husband that his trade suffered a great loss last year when this prophet and some of his Ojibwe followers plundered Michel's warehouse in another place."

"*Lac Courte Oreilles*," Benjamin supplied. "It is several days' journey south." He pointed toward the lake in the general direction of the Ouisconsin forests.

"So perhaps it is true that Michel will soon be working for the Americans. What of you, Benjamin? If the Americans soon push all the British out, for whom will you hunt?"

He turned his face to her, his eyes so close she thought she could sink into them. "I will hunt for myself, my family, and those I love. I will take my furs to the one who can pay the most, for my first thought is for those I call my own."

She swallowed. "You have mentioned a family—a brother and sisters."

He gave a slow nod. "I have no wife."

Her pulse throbbed in her neck as his gaze passed over her face.

And then a volley of musket shots fired in the distance. Far across the woods, the echo carried from the post.

CHAPTER 10

"If you do not understand, you must always ask. Only a foolish hunter would keep silent when he does not understand while he is still learning. His very life in the wilderness depends upon it. So, you must ask, for there is survival in knowing."

—Etienne Marchal, to his son, Benjamin

Ashwiyaa's back straightened, and she raised her head. "Gunfire—do you think it means they have arrived?"

Bemidii studied the curve of her jaw. He reached up and pulled a blackberry leaf from her hair, catching her attention once again. "It is possible."

"I remember they fired guns at the other posts when the canoes came. Do you think it is the brigade from Fort William?"

Bemidii shrugged. It could be anyone. The fishermen from the village. Someone's family returning to La Pointe. Yet he did not really believe it was for such a common arrival a volley was fired. The brigade from Fort William was late and most likely had finally come. She would depart from this island soon. "When you are fully rested, I will take you there to see. First, I will look at your injury again." She seemed about to protest. "You have strained it much today."

She nodded. "You are right."

"It would be best if you could set your foot in the cool water to bring down swelling and ease any bruising that remains. I will help you down. Afterward, I will paddle you to the post instead of walking."

Rather than protest his suggestion, she followed his guidance as he assisted her down to the water's edge. Her hand felt small and light in his, and the only time he released it was to encircle her narrow waist and lower her to the next rock. He had never held a woman so, and he let go reluctantly. "I will help you remove your moccasins."

Her glance flew to his, and a moment's hesitation sparked her green eyes, but she nodded and sat. Then she let him unlace and gently pull her moccasins free. She still wore the bandage and stockings. Without her permission, Bemidii gathered her foot in his palm and unwrapped the ankle. He looked askance at her concerning the stockings.

"My stockings can use a good soaking," she said and lowered her feet, stockings and all, into the water.

Bemidii stood and moved behind her to remove his own moccasins and leggings before dropping down beside her and putting his legs into the water. The coolness was enlivening, the view tranquil, and being beside such a woman, as intoxicating as the sun's brilliant sheen on the water. They relaxed in silence for a long moment before she spoke.

"I don't know what has kept the brigade so long. I would have thought them to arrive days ago. Now that they might have finally come, I fear I do not feel ready to leave." Her voice was wistful as she looked out across the blue. A flush infused her cheeks. "I should not say so, perhaps, but I do not know what awaits me when I return to Montreal without Ambroise. Or rather … I do." She swished her feet and stared into the glassy water below.

"You have family."

She nodded. "My mother, father, and brother. Ambroise had a brother also. Their mother passed away several years ago."

Bemidii mulled over the distance that would soon separate them forever. "They will have missed you."

She gave a dry laugh. "I hardly think so. My mother, perhaps."

"And your friends?"

She shrugged. "What about you, Benjamin? Tell me more about your family."

How much to say? Even here, safe on this island from the reach of those who would see him hung for Clarboux's death, he must speak carefully. The world of the fur traders and voyageurs was both large and small at once. "My father died when I was a boy. He was French, like your father. My mother is Ojibwe. She was given other children by another husband." He paused as he thought of what more to tell. "My French father had another wife who died also, but she, too, bore a girl. That is the sister I have come to know well. She and her husband."

"What is her name?"

He glanced at her. Brigitte had come from Montreal. Though it was unlikely that the two had ever met, he must not take the risk. "Aamoo. Is means 'Bee.'" It was his name for her and the pet name their father had sometimes called her.

"Bee."

Bemidii nodded. "She is married and will have a child soon." They shared a smile, and Ashwiyaa cupped a hand over her abdomen. A fleeting thing, like the shadow of a bird's wing, flitted through his thoughts. He turned his face outward again.

"That is very wonderful for her and for both of them. Do they …"

He glanced at her.

"Never mind."

"You have a question. You must speak it."

"It is a foolish question."

"No question is foolish. Speak."

"Does this husband of hers love her very much?"

He grinned. René was a fool for his sister. His love was as wide as this water. Bemidii pressed his hands to his thighs, then leaned back and stretched his arms behind him, bracing himself on the rock. This way, he could see her. "He has loved my sister for much longer than she knew. He was afraid she would not have him, but my sister loved him too. They were ridiculous."

She chuckled, and the sound warmed him … emboldened him.

He would not speak of the dead or presume upon what lay in the man's heart, but he could ask her of her own. "Did you love your husband so?"

Her shoulders stiffened slightly, and her legs stopped their small movement of circling her feet in the water. She stared ahead for a long time. So long, he regretted his question. Then she gave a small, slow shake of her head. "Not as I should." She turned to see him, and he sat up straight again.

"I apologize for asking such a thing. Your pain is fresh. I was thoughtless."

She laid a hand on his wrist, touching him freely for the first time, and the sensation nearly drowned him. "You must not apologize. There is no reason to say that our marriage was perfect. He was a generous man, and I had no fault with him. It is just … we only …" She shook her head. "Perhaps we loved each other enough."

Her hand still lay on his arm, and he moved only enough to capture her hand and hold it gently.

She let it rest in his for almost a minute. "I should return."

She should—only, he wished to keep her here a while longer. If the brigade had come, they would stay a night. Two at most. She would be reunited with her brother and prepare for her journey. He would not see her again.

He pulled his legs up and stood, then drew her to her feet. "I will get your basket and see you safely back."

She nodded, and he leapt up the rocks to the top of the ridge. Picking up her basket of berries, he paused. Perhaps there was a gift he could give her so she would not forget this day. Nor him. He slipped into his shelter and unfolded a leather wrap. Inside lay two eagle feathers. Both were sacred to him. One had been given to him at birth along with his name. The other he'd earned as a young man for strength and bravery. A long and severe winter had threatened his village with hunger. Bemidii was only a boy of fifteen summers that year. Yet he had strapped on his snowshoes and gone into the woods during the deepest cold. There, he'd eventually found a bear's den. He'd killed the bear with a thrust of his knife when it emerged groggy and disturbed. The people of his village had prepared a feast, and Bemidii was given the feather.

He picked up one of the long, black-and-white plumes of his namesake feather and stroked the stiff vanes. The feathers were meant to be displayed, for they were given only as a great honor. Here, in this camp, they could not be displayed unless he wore them in his hair, which he only did upon special occasions. But this hard, white quill would make a fine writing instrument. He refolded the leather over the remaining feather and slipped out of the lodge. A moment later, he returned to Ashwiyaa's side. He set the basket of sun-warmed berries on the rock and stood before her.

"I bring you a gift. When you make your ink, now you will have a new quill to write with also." He raised the feather over her head and held it there. "I do this to give you a blessing. I wish you bravery and happiness." He smiled and laid the feather across his palms, handing it to her.

As she accepted his gift, a soft sheen in her eyes showed she understood this might be a sacrifice. "Thank you, Benjamin. I will treasure it always. May I use it to write of my adventure here on St. Michel's?"

"It is yours to do with as you wish."

She nodded and held it close.

His heart pushed at his chest, and to manage the strength of its beating, he turned away and took care of the business of setting the canoe in the water. She held the feather and her moccasins. Then Bemidii helped her into the canoe, his every touch as able and gentle as could be, savoring. In another minute, they were moving along the shore. The sound of his paddle touching the water spoke the only words between them.

It took less than ten minutes to round the tip of the island where the shore was busy with people moving to and from a brigade of five long Montreal canoes. Each thirty-foot craft was laden high with bales, furs that would be carried east and then sent on merchant ships to Europe to be made into hats and cloaks. Men from La Pointe brought two empty canoes to join them. These,

Bemidii knew, would be filled with bales from Michel's own stores. As they approached, Coyote's familiar face lifted, and he waved.

Bemidii gave a nod and let his paddle drag, coasting them easily to shore out of the way of the other craft. Coyote came to meet them. He stood aside as Bemidii exited the canoe and tugged it gently close to the sand so Ashiwayaa could exit. She glanced at the other man briefly as she stepped into the water's edge in her wet stockings while letting the hem of her dress dip into the water. Bemidii steadied her by the hand and helped her to the shore. She let go as he lifted the canoe with care onto the sand.

"Benjamin." Coyote eyed them with curiosity. "You are full of secrets."

"She is the guest of Gichi-miishen."

"I know who she is."

Bemidii retrieved the basket of berries and handed them to Ashwiyaa. "She required assistance, and I offered. What is this commotion?" He jerked a nod at the brigade and the people scattered about, pretending not to know but effectively redirecting Coyote's interest.

"A brigade from Fort William."

"The northern lake route is shorter."

"They have business." Coyote glanced at Ashwiyaa again. "Madame Bonnet must know."

Bemidii ignored the remark and held out his arm. "I will assist you through the sand."

She took his arm and limped alongside him up the beach toward the gathered people. As they gained level ground, she released him and turned to face him. "I must thank you again, Benjamin, for all your help. For your friendship as well. My time here under such … circumstances"—she lowered her eyes—"would have been much more difficult to endure without your friendship." She turned the feather in her hands and raised her eyes again. "I will face my family soon with the news about Ambroise. With your gift, I will write my thoughts before I go and see them—except for my brother, of course."

"He will comfort you."

She gave a small nod. "Perhaps." Her chest lifted and fell. "Goodbye, Benjamin."

"Goodbye, Ashwiyaa." He whispered her name, and a smile drew up the corners of her mouth before she blinked quickly and moved away toward the crowded trading post.

Coyote waited. "This brigade has come a long way for her."

"It is because of her brother. He is here to join her and her husband—the man who died in the storm." Bemidii strode back toward his canoe with Coyote following.

"Yes, so I hear. She will be surprised to learn that the Montreal agent who was to lead this brigade died at Fort William."

Bemidii halted. "What is this?"

"I am told there was a company man in charge who was killed shortly before they intended to depart."

It could not be the man in Bemidii's thoughts, who sat in a canoe shooting at him. "That is unfortunate. He was overcome by the journey or injured somehow? Not drowned," he said, his voice reflecting that they both must be thinking of Monsieur Bonnet.

"Non." Coyote folded his arms. "Murdered, they say."

Bemidii frowned. "Too much brawling, I suppose. It has happened before, with some regularity." He brushed off the deepening discomfort worming through him. He gentled the canoe back into the water.

"You should come to the village. Join us for festivity. Some of my friends have signed on to Gichi-miishen's brigade. It is the last night to celebrate before they leave their families. They may not return until the ice is ready to form."

Coyote's story held danger, yet Bemidii must not seem aloof. To run to his camp and hide in obscurity during a fête would only mark him with suspicion. "I will join you. It has been a long time since I enjoyed a good feast. Fish, is it?" He grinned, for what else would there be?

Coyote laughed. "I will ride with you." Without an invitation, he settled into the bow of Bemidii's canoe and let Bemidii paddle him along the island's western shore until they came to the main village of La Pointe. The scent of fish and boiling corn made Bemidii's stomach rumble, despite his remark. All he'd eaten this day was the berries.

After beaching the canoe, Bemidii followed Coyote to the home the man shared with a worn-looking wife and three dirty children. Coyote clapped his hands at the eldest girl and told her to bring tobacco for him and his new friend. Bemidii took a seat on a mat outside their lodge and accepted the pipe Coyote offered after lighting it. He pulled the smoke in, and as it released, he cupped his hand as if to capture it, then guided it with strokes up to the sky, down to the earth, and over each shoulder, then he passed the pipe back.

"You like some rum?" Coyote asked him, with a light in his eyes.

Bemidii shook his head. "I am not interested in rum."

Coyote grunted. "I thought as much after the last time I asked you. You have other ways to lighten your heart. The French woman at the post, she lightens it, perhaps."

"She is someone who needed a friend."

"A friend." Coyote handed him the pipe, then reached into a shirt pocket and pulled out a small flask. He uncorked it and took a swig, then rubbed an arm across his mouth when he was done. He plugged the flask and returned it to his pocket before accepting the pipe from Bemidii again.

"Her husband has died. Her heart is sore."

"Sore or not, it will not remain empty for long. Nor will her bed, I am certain."

Bemidii's anger glowed like coals deep in his chest. "You should not disrespect the dead by speaking so."

Coyote let out a raucous laugh. "I can tell I strike deep."

Bemidii cooled his temper by gazing about them and smiling at Coyote's youngest child. She showed dimples before hiding behind her mother's skirts. The mother pushed her loose, scooped up a bowl of food, and brought it to Bemidii.

He dipped his head at the woman as he accepted her generosity. "*Miigwech.*"

Coyote emptied the ash from the pipe with two taps on the ground beside him. Then he accepted his own bowl of fish stew. Bemidii ate his meal in silence while Coyote devoted himself to his own food. Finally, having finished, Bemidii was ready to ask the question burning inside. "This man who was killed up north—have you heard his name? No one from *le fond du lac*, I hope."

Coyote pulled the rum flask from his pocket again. He shook his head as he uncorked it. "Non. Not one of the wintering partners. It was the son of a merchant. A man named Clarboux, they say. A young man. His father is"—he waved his hand in a circle—"something, so they say. There is talk he will offer a reward once he hears."

Bemidii schooled his expression. "This merchant, you mean? What is the reward to accomplish?"

"To find the murderer. They say he's run off. Some Ojibwe or Métis. I think it more likely one of the Sioux were involved." Coyote took another long swig, emptying the flask. He let out a sigh. "I would not mind finding him. Such a reward would keep me by my fire this winter and spare me freezing my feet off in the woods trapping beaver."

Bemidii nodded complacently while he fought unsteady nerves. "You are right about that. Especially if the killer is Sioux." To speak the word *killer* set his teeth on edge.

"Oui, Madame Bonnet will be surprised."

"Will she? She is thinking only of her brother now."

"Of course, her brother."

Slowly, the frayed edges of his nerves bound together into a ball. "What do you mean?"

"The dead man, Clarboux, he is her brother. Did you not know her father is the merchant I spoke of?"

Bemidii stared at the hard-packed earth, his lungs seemingly turning to stone, then shook his head. "I did not. I had only heard of Bonnet, her husband. She never—I never heard anyone speak of her father or give the name of her brother."

Coyote fell silent. It was a moment before Bemidii noticed how the man regarded him. At last, the man's gaze fell away. "Yes, so she has lost both a husband and her brother on her journey. Your woman *friend* has proven to be more enduring than both." He unfolded his legs and pushed himself to stand.

Bemidii followed. He held out his hand. "I thank you again for the fine meal. You must tell your wife. I have been too many days cooking my own food."

Coyote shook his hand. "I am glad you decided to join me. Come again tomorrow to see off the brigade. My friend Victor is going with them. He also expressed an interest in the Widow Bonnet. He will be more than happy to be traveling with her, I am sure, especially now that her brother will not be along to chaperon." Coyote grinned and slapped Bemidii on the back.

Bemidii laughed as was expected.

"I will walk you back to your canoe." He turned and barked an order to his wife. She scowled and scolded in reply. "She is never satisfied, that one."

Bemidii acknowledged the remark with a glance at her over his shoulder, though he suspected the woman had much to complain about. "You need not come. I will see you again tomorrow."

Coyote let him go. Bemidii strode casually to the beach where he'd left his canoe, though his footsteps felt as if he carried the weight of a bear trap clamped tight. He would have to put in an appearance tomorrow among the crowd, at least. It would do no good for anyone keeping an eye open for a suspicious native to wonder over Bemidii's aloofness. Perhaps, if nothing else, he could catch one last glimpse of Ashwiyaa before she left. His heart ached to do it, but he would remember how she looked at him with friendship because if she were to ever find out he murdered her brother, she would despise him.

CHAPTER 11

People ask me if I am afraid to go on this journey with Ambroise. Afraid? How can I be afraid? There will be hardships, certainly, for I am unaccustomed to living in the outdoors. Is that what I am to fear? I am more afraid to live my life here in this never-changing existence like my mother's. Living dangerously is better than dying hopelessly.

—Journal of Camilla Bonnet

Camilla hurried as quickly as she could on her injured ankle to the Cadottes' house. Voyageurs' glances fell her way en route, grazing her with looks she had come to know well on her journey west. For that very reason, she had always remained close to Ambroise. She would remain almost equally close to Tristan on the way back to Montreal. These men all carried themselves like beasts, hungry for a kill, or in her case, hungry for a woman. Hadn't their appetites been sated at Fort William? Ambroise had delicately explained some of the sorts of behavior that took place at rendezvous. Goodness, hadn't she seen lasciviousness enough even at these small trading posts when drinking and revelry got out of control? How thankful she was again for the safe harbor she'd found in the Cadottes' home. Civility, even. And then there was Benjamin. Never a kinder man had she thought to meet in the Upper Country. He was as civilized as any she'd known in Montreal, more so than many.

She let herself inside the house, where only the girls were gathered.

"Where is your maman and Marguerite, and your brothers?"

The second eldest girl, Julie, raised her pretty head, her two long braids draping to her waist. "They are helping our père at the store. Maman said we were to stay here until you returned."

"Oui, I understand. I will stay here with you now. I had only wondered … did, by chance, any of the men from the boats come here looking for me?"

All the children shook their heads. "Non, madame. No one."

"All right." Tristan had probably gone straight to the store with the others. He would be seeking Ambroise. Likely, he'd probably already been given the news of Ambroise's demise from Monsieur Cadotte. How would he receive such a shock? "Look what I have brought." She showed the children the berries. "Have you eaten?"

"Non, madame."

"I am hungry," Antoine, who was five, said.

"Follow me. I will give you some of the berries with cream." She led them to gather around the table, her hands needing to busy themselves.

"You have a feather," the middle girl said. "Where did you find it?"

Camilla glanced down at the eagle feather poking out the top of her apron pocket. "I was given it as a gift."

"You are very honored."

Camilla paused. "Oui. Very honored."

She dished up some of the berries into bowls for the children and poured cream over the top. Then she mashed the rest in small amounts with a pestle. She poured the liquid into a separate dish. "I am making ink," she explained, as the children ate their berries. "For my trip back to Montreal."

She'd barely finished when the front door opened. Camilla rinsed her purple fingers in a bowl of water and met Madeleine's and Marguerite's glances.

"You are back." Madeleine loosened the strings of her bonnet and removed it.

"Oui. The girls are eating berries. I saved some for you and Michel as well." Camilla smiled, but it felt weak and nervous. "I saw that the brigade has arrived. Has Monsieur Cadotte told Tristan about … about my husband?"

"Please. Sit." Madeleine folded her hands together and nodded toward an open bench seat near the hearth. Marguerite lowered herself in an opposite chair, her features drawn. Camilla tucked her skirt beneath her legs and curled her toes under her hem, remembering her stained stockings. Madeleine did not sit, however. She paced in front of the cold hearth, now wringing her clasped hands. "The brigade did arrive. They plan to depart again on the morrow, as early as can be."

Camilla shifted. "I must hurry and begin my packing, then."

Madeleine paused and touched a hand to her brow. "You must consider. There has been unfortunate news."

"Unfortunate?" What news could be more unfortunate than the death of her husband? Had something happened to their father or mother, and Tristan left it to Madeleine Cadotte to break the news? "What is it?"

"There will be no partner or merchant returning to Montreal with this brigade. Your brother—"

"He is wintering in the Upper Country?" Such a sudden decision by Tristan would not surprise her in the least. Yet it instantly angered her that he had not sent word before now. He could have written. Perhaps he had. "Is there a letter?"

Madeleine shook her head. "Please, madame. This is most difficult."

Camilla's gut tightened, and a cold fear trickled down her spine. "Is Tristan in trouble, Madeleine? You must come out with it if he is."

"Tristan—that is—Monsieur Clarboux is … is dead, *mon amie*."

Camilla pushed to her feet, wavering. The baby fluttered inside her. She blinked.

Marguerite jumped to her feet. "*S'il vous plait,* Camilla. You must not—"

Camilla waved away the hands urging her to sit again. "I cannot. I must …" What must she do? Something. Anything. "How? Why?"

Madeleine's mouth turned down, and her brow curled. "I

am so sorry, my dear. He was, unfortunately, killed in an attack. Someone—they say it was a man attempting to rob him—stabbed him with a knife."

"Tristan …" His name ushered out between lips nearly too stunned to speak. "Oh, Tristan." She did sit again and lowered her face into her hands. Madeleine laid her warm touch on Camilla's shoulder. "It is all right to weep."

Tears fell, but they were silent tears. Tears of sorrow, yes, for he was her brother. Tears of uncertainty, absolutely. Tears of fear for the days ahead. She hated the tears, but they came, anyway. *Benjamin*. How she wished it were his hands on her shoulders now, comforting her, assuring her that the future would not be as dark as she believed. What would her father do now, without his son and heir, without even a son-in-law to take the reins of his business someday?

Again, the baby moved. The child was growing. The movements felt stronger now than they had only days ago. She held the infant cradled in her palm. If the baby was a boy …

My father will not send the babe away. But now, more than ever, she knew what lay before her. Marriage to someone like old Monsieur MacDaw with the drooling lips and grasping hands. Without her father having a son and heir, this child must be raised by a man of wealth and means, so that someday he could step into the Clarboux business shoes. And Camilla would be powerless to have a say, either in her own life or the child's. Even if the child was born a girl, it would be too late for Camilla.

Her hand brushed the feather protruding from her pocket. *Courage and happiness.* How were such things to be hers now? Especially happiness? She withdrew the quill and smoothed the vanes. "If you will excuse me, I should like to lie down."

"Oui. You must rest. It has been a shock. Tonight you will speak to Michel, and he will help you. There is a man in charge, a Scot who has agreed to carry you to your home or to Michilimackinac if you prefer."

She shook inwardly as she stood and made her way to the steep, narrow stairs. A Scot. Another stranger. A burly voyageur of whom she must be wary. If only Benjamin would sign on to the brigade. She didn't know him well enough to be sure, but she believed she could trust him enough to see her back to Montreal.

She set the eagle feather beside her journal on the desk and lay down on the bed. Surprisingly, she fell asleep but woke again hours later. Darkness had fallen upon the house, but she could not tell the hour. *Tristan, dead.*

The thought brought a new wash of horror and dread. Had he been simply minding his business when he was attacked? Had he been alone in his encampment? Had he been deceived by a woman? Such a thought was dreadful yet would not surprise her. Women of ill repute often picked the pockets of the men they drew into their lairs, and it was not unlikely that some man who owned them would kill for more. Had Tristan met his end over such a fiasco?

Her brother was a sinner, to be sure. Perhaps one of the worst. Hadn't she tried to warn that young woman he brought home some two years past? Whatever was her name? Brigitte? Yes, that was it. Brigitte Marchal. Camilla had tried to warn the young woman of her brother's tendencies and of the crudeness she had known at his hands as a younger girl. Shortly afterward, the girl had simply disappeared.

And yet … for Tristan to die brutally.

Camilla rose from her bed and moved to the window where a full moon outlined the world in stark and contrasting shadows. She was not cold, but a shudder passed through her, and she clasped her arms about herself. "I am alone." She spoke aloud but softly into the night, her voice and movement waking the infant in her womb who stirred. *Not alone.* Rather than bringing comfort, the awareness heightened her growing uncertainties about the future. In the morning, she was to leave this island, but she had fallen asleep rather than pack her belongings. How could she travel on with this brigade of voyageurs who had not so much as one of her father's company men among them?

Anxiety spiraled tighter in her chest. She remembered the way some had looked at her as they journeyed here in springtime. They had been courteous as long as she had Ambroise close at hand. Once or twice, one of them had brushed too close or stared openly when Ambroise's back was turned. How would she be kept safe among them without him? Who was this Scot that Madeleine spoke of? The voyageurs might not lay a hand to her for fear of her father's and the company's repercussions, but to what lengths might they be willing to go? Enough to cause discomfort, surely. Enough to make her wary and nervous.

Would it help if they knew she carried a child? Perhaps, and perhaps not. Her pregnancy beneath her full skirts might not be obvious to many until near the end of their journey. For some, it would not matter. There were many like old Monsieur MacDaw from all ranks of society, hungry for a woman.

Camilla returned to her bed. Now she did not sleep, however. She wearied her mind with possibilities until daylight pushed back the moon and the first stirrings of wakefulness came from before the hearth below. Then she pushed back her covers and rose again. She had not undressed since yesterday, so she washed her face and coiled her hair on her head. Then she swept a hand over her berry-stained and wrinkled dress and limped downstairs.

She walked into the main room where Michel stood with his back to her, his hand on his wife's shoulder. She held little Joseph on her hip. The other young children still slept in their beds along the wall. Michel whispered something into his wife's ear and kissed her head. Camilla cleared her throat gently. The couple turned.

"Ah, Madame Bonnet. I hope you have rested well." Michel's cheerful expression was kind, even though she knew his animation was for her own benefit rather than out of any genuine feeling. He pulled a chair from the table, urging her to sit. "My wife will soon have your breakfast. You must be sure and fill yourself today."

"I have prepared extra food in a satchel for your journey,"

Madeleine said, as she stirred a pot at the hearth. "The growing babe will make you hungry, and you must not have to wait for the men to stop."

"Merci."

Michel took the seat opposite her. "You must allow me to express my deepest sympathies over Monsieur Clarboux, your brother." His voice sobered. "I am sure he was a good man, and such a loss is deeply felt by all in the North West Company, but especially for you and your family. It is unfortunate that you must return to your home with such heaviness on your heart. Indeed, to have lost both a husband and a brother on one summer's adventure …" He shook his head and sighed. "Madeleine and I are very sorry."

"Merci." Her tongue cleaved to her mouth. Could she think of nothing else to say? She licked her lips. "Tell me about the Scot who leads the brigade." She glanced up only to see Michel briefly knit and smooth his brow.

"He has led many brigades and is a master of these waters. You have nothing to fear for your safe return."

"What kind of man is he?"

"Kind of man?" He leaned back as Madeleine set bowls of porridge before them.

"Is he a–a family man?"

Michel shrugged. "I suppose that I do not know. We've never spoken of such. We only deal with business matters."

Madeleine came forward and sat down with her own food. "Michel, you must see that Madame Bonnet is uncertain about traveling with strangers."

"Oui, I understand. Yet, what else is she to do? Perhaps you will only need go as far as Michilimackinac this season. We have friends there and can send a letter so that you will find a place with them until someone else can take you up the rivers to Montreal—someone sent by your père, perhaps."

More strangers. She thought of the feather upstairs in her room. She must call on courage now. She nodded. "I will consider it. If you will be so kind as to write a letter. Should it turn out that it is best for me to go all the way to Montreal with Monsieur …" She fumbled for his name. "The Scotsman, then I will do so."

Madeleine tilted her head, her eyes soft with sympathy. "I would not hesitate to ask you to stay with us until spring, but it will only be harder to travel once your child is born."

"Merci, Madeleine. I understand." Camilla looked at the steaming bowl before her but could not muster the desire to eat. "I have not packed."

"Marguerite and I will help you." Madeleine laid a hand over Camilla's. "But you must eat." Her words carried the weight of a command, such as when she spoke to one of her children.

"It will be another hour before the brigade is ready to depart. There is time," Michel said, and he scooped a bite of porridge into his mouth.

"I hear the children waking." Madeleine abandoned her breakfast and rose to fetch more bowls.

Michel wolfed down the remainder of his breakfast and stood as the two older girls and then the boys wandered into the room, rubbing sleep from their eyes. "I will see to the store and the voyageurs now." He turned to his two eldest boys. "Come to me after you've eaten." Then he left them.

While the children clamored for their breakfast and their mother and oldest sister tended to them, Camilla took small bites, forcing down as many as she could. This would be her last meal here. In an hour, she would be squeezing into a position in a crowded Montreal canoe laden with bales. How many weeks would it take, rocking on the waves amid the smells of stinking hides and sweat-soaked men? The very thought turned her insides. After stomaching as much for the day as she could, she pushed the remnants of her breakfast aside.

"I will help you pack when I am through feeding the children," Madeleine said over her shoulder.

Camilla left the kitchen. She set her foot upon the stair and halted. First, before she gathered her things, there was something she must do. She would never lay eyes on Ambroise again, but perhaps she could find a moment's peace in her heart there at his graveside. She slipped out of the house. She would only be gone a few minutes. Madeleine need not worry for a single one of them.

Her ankle felt stronger today, almost whole. Only a few others crossed her path as she walked across the dew-laden grass toward the tiny cemetery where they'd buried Ambroise. A strong brogue voice let out a string of curses down at the beach, and she glimpsed a thick-shouldered man with flaming red hair who must be the Scot. Her breath quickened as she hurried on.

A few sprouts had begun to push through Ambroise's freshly mounded grave. Michel had seen to it that a cross marked the resting place with Ambroise's name along with the dates of his birth and death engraved upon it.

She touched fingertips to the rough wood and stepped beyond it to face the sun lifting into the morning sky. A sob crept up her throat and burst out. "What—will—I—do?" She pressed her hand to the babe and dropped to her knees. "*Cher Dieu, que vais-je faire*? I am to have a child, and I have no one to care for us. Must I submit to someone of my father's choosing? You are my Father, *n'est tu pas*? Am I to be despised by You that You would abandon me so? You have taken both my husband and my brother—my only protectors. Would you now have me commit my life and this babe's to strangers, and then have me give my flesh to a man like Monsieur MacDaw? What am I to do?" Her stomach clenched around her sobs, and she had to bite back the bile in her throat. "*What am I to do?*"

The wind rose. She heard it brush through the pine tops before she felt it. The scent of earth stirred beneath her as the breeze washed over her shoulders. Camilla gulped and sniffed. She sat back on her legs and wiped her tears with the back of her hand. She imagined she could hear the dip of the paddle—not the paddles of the voyageurs' canoe, but Benjamin's paddle. *If only.*

If only it was him and not the Scot taking her away, she might be able to bear it. He would see to her comforts. Wouldn't he? Did she really trust him to such lengths?

She did.

She bowed her head again. "*Père Dieu,* I will go home if You will it. I will get into the Montreal canoe awaiting me this moment if, indeed, You wish it so. Yet my heart is not there, not in Montreal, not in my earthly father's house. I have been chattel far too long. Perhaps I am thinking the worst when it is not so, but ... my heart tells me I am not wrong. Perhaps I am disobedient to You and to my father to even speak the things of my heart. Nevertheless, I will speak them. I wish them. *Seigneur*, I pray for some other choice. Some way to escape this fate. Will you not show me a way?"

She raised her eyes, and the wind blew again. She closed her eyelids and breathed the scent of the pine and blue sky. In the distance, she heard voices—Madeleine's girls, no doubt. Oui, they called to her.

"Madame Bonnet!"

Camilla rose from the dirt. She didn't bother to brush it from her skirt, nor did she look at Ambroise's grave again. She walked toward their voices, knowing what she must do.

CHAPTER 12

"I know you want me to be sorry I left your mother. Oui, there is always room for guilt. Guilt eats and is never satisfied. Yet we do what we do and endeavor to put aside regrets."

—Etienne Marchal, to his son, Benjamin

Bemidii remained at his camp, sharpening his knife on a stone. Today was not the day to venture to the trading post, not with the North West brigade preparing to leave. Not with Ashwiyaa about to depart with them. For a few brief days, he had allowed himself to imagine playing his flute for her. He had envisioned taking her into his arms and making her his own. Then the revelation came crashing through his daydreams, driving through him like a knife in his chest—the man he'd killed was her own brother.

His fantasies were foolish, for they could never be. Especially now.

She would hate me. Her fear would return ten-fold, and she would despise me if she found out. The thought of anger and hate filling those beautiful green eyes and turned on him was enough to wound him. He must forget her entirely. He had no choice, anyway, for soon she would be gone.

Meanwhile, he must continue to bide his time here until René and Brigitte arrived. Then they would depart St. Michel's for the winter's hunting and trapping. By next year, the memory of Tristan Clarboux would be forgotten—hopefully, at least, Bemidii's role in it. Ashwiyaa would find another man to love. A Frenchman. She would mourn her brother with her family and some new husband. There was yet a chance Bemidii could dance with some other maid. Perhaps Anang would not have married before next year.

Yet it was hard to recall the young maiden's face when Ashwiyaa's filled his thoughts. He tucked the gleaming knife blade into its sheath at his hip and stood. When would his sister and her man arrive? With Ashwiyaa present, time had not mattered. Now the days seemed suspended instead. Never before had he known such a feeling of impatience and hopelessness.

He sorted through his fishing tackle as time dragged by and the sun inched upward through the trees. Finally, he walked toward the ledge above the lake and searched the blue expanse. He'd heard nothing, yet perhaps the brigade had gone by now. They would follow the Ouisconsin shore toward Bahweting and then cross over to another lake he'd been told was like unto this. From there, the long canoes would proceed to Michilimackinac. Before long, Ashwiyaa would be among her people.

A shout followed by a chorus of voices drew his attention. There was no mistaking the sound of a *chaunteur* and the song of the voyageurs. They were leaving only now. Wishing he could see her in the colorful cluster, Bemidii strained his eyes at the canoes in the distance, moving southeast across what seemed an endless body of water. Did she, too, glance his way across the waves? He raised a hand in farewell, though no one could see from such a distance, and in his heart, he told her, *I am sorry, Ashwiyaa. I did not know he was blood of your blood.*

Now all would return to normal, and Bemidii would be safe again, but his heart would not forget. As the men in the canoes shrunk smaller, his heart did as well. The beating diminished along with their song, and soon the sound of the breeze stirring the treetops and the gentle wash of the surf against the rocks was the only sound. For long moments, he stood in the silence.

"I did not go."

Bemidii jerked about, his breath catching at Ashwiyaa's voice behind him. At her approach, his heart revived and pounded against his ribs—for love or guilt or both, he could not say.

"Ashwiyaa, your escort leaves." He raised a hand to the brigade melting into faint dots on the horizon.

"I have no escort."

"But the brigade—"

"I was afraid."

He frowned. Had a spirit told her the truth, and now she came to accuse him? Yet she did not look like one coming to condemn. "What caused your fear?"

A sheepish smile touched her lips. "The unknown. Your feather, I'm sorry to say, did not provide the courage I needed."

"Yet you have courage to remain in a strange country among people not your own." He gestured toward the trading post and the village, including himself.

"I am not so sure. I have a letter for a reputable family in Michilimackinac with whom I might stay until I can return to Montreal with a suitable chaperone."

He took a step toward her, his puzzlement growing. To his relief, she did not step back. "And how will you go to Michilimackinac, now that this brigade has gone?"

"I thought perhaps … that is …" A rose bloomed over cheeks that had been kissed gold from the summer sun. "You might see me there." Her eyes steadied on him as she pulled in a breath. "Might you take me there, Benjamin?"

Words failed him. How could he do such a thing? He'd never been so far. The fort and post she spoke of lay many days east, across treacherous waters. He would need a brigade in itself. *She would not ask if she knew what I have done. She would run from me.*

She seemed to hear his first thoughts. "Michel was not pleased with my decision. He did not say so, but I could tell he worried over my delay. Yet he assured me that he would be sending one or two canoes himself as far as Michilimackinac this fall. He promised I could go then, if I am ready. I will only be ready if you will be my guide, Benjamin. I trust myself to no one else unless it were to be Michel himself leading the way."

He ran a hand over his jaw. She trusted him, but what was he to do with such responsibility? His heart had soared the moment her voice reached him, and to see her standing there before him released a tightness in his chest. Yet to take her to Michilimackinac himself, especially with such a dark secret between them? It was not possible.

"You are unhappy that I've asked for your assistance."

"Gaawiin. Non." He held out a supplicating hand and lowered it. "That is not so. I am pleased to have gained your confidence. You are right to believe I would see you safe and unharmed in any circumstance."

Her shoulders fell in a soft sigh. "Merci, Benjamin."

"But …" On his word, her breath hitched almost imperceptibly, and he wished he could tell her he would do just as she wished, but he couldn't. "I am unable to leave this place. My sister will come here to find me, and I must not waylay her husband from his own wintering adventure."

"Surely, your brother-in-law would understand if you could not wait for him."

He shook his head. "We have made an agreement. They will travel a far distance themselves to reach me. It is too late to change our plans."

"I see." She lowered her eyes, and her hand fell to her middle with a caress in that manner she had, a manner that now grabbed hold of his awareness. She gave a self-deprecating shake of her head. "I was being very foolish. I only supposed—"

He took a long stride forward and spoke with only a step between them. "You were not foolish. You were frightened of that which you could not see. You have been left without your man to care for you, and the journey is long. What if, during your journey, you had need of something and no one to ask? What if you were cold or hungry or …" He let his gaze linger on her hand where it rested as though cradling a treasure. Eya'. A great treasure. "What if you grew uncomfortable with the child you carry, and there was no one there to offer you ease?"

Her chin jerked up, and her eyes looked like those of a frightened deer, only wide and green like the very leaves of the trees around them. "How did you know?"

"I am sorry for speaking of something that is private to you. I did not know. I only guessed."

"You could tell?"

"You"—he laid a hand against his own abdomen in the way she sometimes did—"often hold the child as if he or she is already in your arms. You protect it with all that is in you."

"Do I? You do not think it is merely an unconscious habit?"

"Does not the Great Spirit give us the instinct to protect? Is it not part of our very natures when our children are in danger?"

"You said you have no wife or child."

"And so I do not. What I say is true, nonetheless. Do you agree?"

She nodded.

"When will your child be born?"

"In the winter, I'm afraid. That is why I must make certain I am well situated by then. My father …" She paused and cleared her throat. She pinched her lips for a moment longer before she went on. "My father, you see, will make very certain that I have someone to look after me while I look after Ambroise's child."

He frowned, determining not to understand that which she hinted at. "He will provide you with a servant, perhaps."

"Non, not a servant. A husband. I believe that the moment he hears of Ambroise's fate, he will have someone in mind. Someone he had earlier intended for me before Ambroise sought my hand."

Bemidii stiffened. She had nothing to worry about, then. She would eventually return to Montreal, either before or after her child was born, and settle again as wife to some other man, much like Bemidii's own mother had done—yet it was not the same at all. For his mother was never forced to marry. She chose a man who loved her.

"Are you not able to choose yourself whom you will marry?"

She half turned away. "It has never been up to me. Not really. Only this time …" She slowly squared herself to him. "This time, I am deciding not to face it yet, at least not to return without the aid of someone I trust. In the meantime, I have prayed and asked God to provide another way. I would not marry if I did not feel forced."

"Here, you are not forced." He did not let go of her gaze. "Here, you are safe. What is wrong with this place?"

"This place? Why, nothing is wrong with it. It's a beautiful place, but …"

"Will Great Michel give you shelter until—as you say—you have another way?"

"Madeleine has said as much." Her voice fell softer, sounding regretful. "I fear I have burdened them greatly. They are crowded in their house as it is, and winter will come in only a few short months."

"You can ease Madame Cadotte's burden by helping her in her tasks. There is no need for you to feel a burden yourself."

She stroked her hand down over her abdomen, and as she did so, the slight mound was visible against her tightened skirt. Bemidii's heart swelled, conflicted.

"Then you do not think I should go to Michilimackinac?"

"You will know what to do when the time comes, even as you knew this day. And if the time does not come at all, you will know that too."

She lowered her arm beside her, and the bump disappeared. "Merci, Benjamin. I knew that if I spoke with you, I would be sure."

He cringed inside. How differently she would have chosen if she knew her brother's blood colored the ground between them. "Did you not already speak to God, and He made it sure? After all, the brigade has now gone its way."

She nodded. "I did speak to God, and I thought I heard His voice."

"Then you will know if He speaks to you again." He smiled, urging her to do the same, and was rewarded with a lift of her lips.

"Until such time as I find my way to Michilimackinac, I will search for ways to assist Madame Cadotte. Perhaps I can begin by picking her more berries."

Her smile widened, and her own relief passed into him. As foolish as it might be, Bemidii could continue his friendship with her. He would push aside the past, as he had before finding out Tristan Clarboux was her brother. He would think only of how he might please her. "Then you will need a guide," he answered with another grin.

"Again, I say, merci, Benjamin. I know not what I would do had I not met you. I am very sorry I was frightened at the start. I know now that my fear was unfounded. You are a kind man. A good friend."

He laughed, though his insides curled. He must be more careful than ever, for if she were to discover the truth, the price upon his head would be hers to claim.

CHAPTER 13

My mother urges me not to delay should Ambroise seek my hand. I suspect that if I do not choose soon, my parents will insist upon someone who displeases me more. Ambroise complements my father's vanity with his interest in trade and company matters, which is sure to win him favor, despite the fact that his family's wealth is very limited. I must consider carefully.

—Journal of Camilla Bonnet

September 1808

Camilla sat on a chair in the shade, a mountain of cornhusks in a basket at her feet. The brittle husks had been soaked overnight to regain their pliability. With a lengthening cornhusk braid in her lap, she carefully held the braid in her right hand, then folded a husk in her left with a twist of her fingers and wove it into the piece. Madeleine smiled encouragement at her. Soon she would have a rope of cornhusk long enough to stitch into a sleeping mat. When she returned to the east, she could take the mat with her as a comfort against the hard ground.

Ten-year-old Julie worked across from her, twisting husks into the shape of a doll and teaching eight-year-old Marie how to do so. Julie handed a doll she had already made to little Charlotte, who ran around them, waving it at their mother and crying, "Look, Maman! Look!"

Camilla warmed at their delight. What if she carried a baby girl? Would her child one day delight in a simple cornhusk doll, or would only a doll of French porcelain with painted eyes do? Or perhaps she carried a boy like little Joseph toddling at Madeleine's knees.

Madeleine spoke in a flurry of Ojibwe, and Camilla need not know the language to understand the shared joy between mother and child.

Madeleine raised her head as the little girl scurried around them with her doll. She laid aside her own braid of husks that was easily twice as long as Camilla's and rose. "Come. The children will be hungry soon, and your fingers will be tired from braiding. We will have our tea." She hoisted Joseph into her arms as she waited for Camilla to tie off the piece of braid and join her. "After your tea, you will rest. It has been a long morning."

"I am not sleepy. I find the work quite restful in itself," Camilla said.

Not only was the work restful, but interesting. It reminded her of when her mother taught her to do needlework as a little girl. Her mother had always been very patient with her many mistakes and the knots she created. Now Camilla had a fine hand for needlework.

"Nevertheless, it will help you to rest when you can. Soon enough, the time will come when restfulness will be a memory. Your infant will not allow it."

Camilla chuckled. "I do not mind the thought." She brushed a hand down her skirt front again. The mound was still so small, she could hardly believe that Benjamin had noticed it at all, though now it was beginning to be visible even with her heavier skirts. Yet he had said his sister also expected a child. Perhaps he was familiar with the signs, despite being an unmarried man. She took Charlotte's hand and urged her along. Five-year-old Antoine gathered up the sticks he'd collected and fell into step alongside them.

At the house, Camilla poured their tea while Madeleine and Marguerite prepared food for the children. When the task was finished, Marguerite left the house carrying food in a basket for her father and younger brothers at the store. For not the first time, Camilla wondered why the Cadottes' eldest daughter had not yet married, for she must be nearing twenty. Then, perhaps no suitor had proved worthy of her affections. If someone such as Monsieur Pilon were the type of suitor to be expected, then Camilla could understand.

She dabbed a cloth at food smeared on Charlotte's face. Had Marguerite noticed the handsome hunter Benjamin on their island? Why had he not noticed her? A more eligible pair Camilla could not imagine. Perhaps Marguerite was content to be home with her family, like a second mother to her smaller siblings. At least, her father did not seem in any hurry to send the girl away or see her married for whatever sum she could bring. Michel was not like Camilla's father.

"Merci, Camilla. Joseph, non." Madeleine thanked her and scolded the little boy in the same breath.

"I do not know how you manage so well. My family was not large. I could not imagine my mother handling so many. She tired easily." Camilla nibbled her bread thoughtfully and took a sip of tea.

"It is what is to be done, so one does it. And now you are here to help as well, like my Marguerite."

Camilla nodded. "She is a great help to you."

"Oui." Madeleine cleared their dishes. "A great help, indeed. And now, I must put this one in his bed." She scooped an increasingly cantankerous Joseph into her arms. He pushed at her and rubbed his eyes. "Come now. No more fussing, Joseph. You and Antoine come, too, Charlotte."

"Maman …" Charlotte whined.

"Bring your doll."

Charlotte slid from her bench and followed a bit less reluctantly. Antoine went without complaint.

Camilla cleaned up their lunch. Julie and Marie helped her without being asked. It took very little, and soon they were finished. The girls wandered off to play, and Camilla took the stairs to her room.

The baby stirred inside her. The movements were getting stronger now. She was nearly five months along, more than halfway, and it was hard to imagine that before long, she would be tending her own little Joseph or Charlotte. Her pregnancy would no longer be hidden. Anyone who looked closely could tell she was to bear a child. She had already let out her skirt and underpinnings. In a hastily written letter sent to her parents with the brigade, Camilla explained her reasons for staying behind, adding to her confession of being pregnant that she suffered frequent bouts of illness and could not bear the thought of riding in the canoes. A lie. She hadn't felt ill in many days. In fact, she had never felt more robust. However, the remainder of her reason for staying she did not reveal to them, and now she took a seat and penned the explanation in her journal with honesty.

I could not go without someone I trust, at least a little. Not without a man like Benjamin there to protect me…

She twirled her goose feather quill in her fingertips. She could not bring herself to use the gift of Benjamin's eagle feather in such a way, even though he had urged her to. It seemed sacrilegious somehow. Or maybe it was only that she wanted to keep it as a treasure. For it was a part of him somehow and represented his name. Didn't he say so?

The special feather lay at the top of her desk, and now she looked at it, then picked the goose quill up again and dipped it in her ink made of berries and charcoal.

He took me berry picking again, though the berries are nearly finished. And I spoke to him yesterday outside the store. Nearly every time we meet, why, my heart almost stops. I fear I have developed an attachment to him that I have been afraid to admit. How can it be? We are so very different. Our worlds are so vastly opposed. Yet I would know more of his.

Yes, so much more.

He was not indelicate concerning her condition, yet there had been several times since she'd admitted she was pregnant that she had seen him looking at her in a tender way. When he became aware that she noticed, he would ask if she was well, if the child was well, if she was resting enough. He was like a worried father, the very thought of which made her neck warm.

He is so kind. Maybe it is because of his family, whom he speaks well about. I would like to meet this sister and brother he tells me of. I suppose I shall do so when they arrive. Yet I do not wish it. For when they come, Benjamin will go away with them.

She paused and frowned. She hadn't thought much of his going before. Now it felt imminent. Was it really that she could not bear it? Were her feelings running so deep as that?

How I wish he would not leave, even though I know he must, for he says so. I have come to feel welcome here. More welcome than anywhere I have been. This island, this wilderness, this family, and the beautiful man who shows me natural things—they touch me in a place I did not know existed. How could I not feel welcome?

She put the quill aside and sprinkled sand over the letters, absorbing the excess ink. She shook the granules into her palm and blew off the page as a soft knock fell on the door.

"*Entrez.*"

Marguerite slipped inside. "I am sorry for disturbing you."

"It is all right. I am neither busy nor resting. In fact, I am thinking of taking a walk. Would you care to join me?"

The young woman's eyes brightened. "Oui. I will come. Shall we look for berries?"

"Last time I went, they were nearly finished. To tell you the truth, I would like to put my toes into the water before the weather changes."

Marguerite chuckled. "I am happy to join in that."

The weather had already begun to change. Sometime in the

past week, Camilla had felt the need to add a blanket to her bed at night. Though the days were warm and bright except for an occasional chilly rain, the evenings drew close earlier, and she suspected a frost could come any time. Tomorrow they planned to harvest the winter squash, and the early apples had already been gathered from the trees.

She and Marguerite left the quiet house and walked down to the shore, where now only two empty canoes were turned upside down on the beach. These were the Cadottes' boats. Now and then, another was found there, but not today. Today no one came or went. They had the lakefront to themselves, and they wasted no time in removing their shoes and stockings. The sand was not hot like it had been a month ago, and when the surf washed over her feet, the water felt crisper after the longer nights.

"May I ask you, Marguerite, why you have not married?"

The other girl shrugged as she swished the toes of one foot across the surface of the water. "The right man has not called nor played his flute."

"Is it true that your mother is a princess?"

"A princess? Hm … My grandfather is White Crane, a great chief of The People, so oui, she might be so."

"Then you are a princess, too, by heredity."

Marguerite gave a warm smile.

"I would suppose your parents would not be happy for you to marry just anyone."

"Non. My father is an important man."

Camilla nodded. "I have not seen many men here who might meet his expectations for his eldest daughter. While I am not as esteemed among the French as you and your mother are among your people, I understand the need for a wise choice. My father, too, is an important man in Montreal. Have you never considered the hunter named Benjamin?"

Marguerite cast her a glance rife with curiosity. "The man whom you have befriended?" One brow lifted. "I know nothing about him. This Benjamin only arrived this summer, just as you did. He came alone, though my father said he had been here once before with two others, a company man and his wife."

"A company man?"

"Oui. A Frenchman from the east. A partner."

Confusion swam through her, mingling her thoughts like the water mingled the sand around her feet. Benjamin had never said anything about his brother-in-law being French or, of greater import still, being a partner in the company. Surely, Marguerite was confused about that too. "Then you have never met him? Benjamin, I mean?"

She shook her head. "Non. I have only seen him with you and once when he was trading here before." She smiled again. "Perhaps he will court you, and you will not have to go away."

Camilla looked across the water again to hide the feelings she feared showed on her face. "That would be impossible." But she spoke without certainty, and her cheeks warmed when she glanced back at Marguerite, who smiled knowingly. Camilla raised her chin. "In Montreal, you would keep such thoughts and suggestions to yourself."

"We are not in Montreal, madame."

She squinted into the glinting water. "Non. We are not."

"He is a handsome man, and I have seen the way he looks at you."

"Have you?" She bent and swirled her fingertips in the water, her movements matching the whirling of possibilities stirred by Marguerite's words. Why should she not marry Benjamin? Why go back home—ever?

"Oui. I have also seen the way you look at him."

Enough. The conversation had gotten out of control. She straightened and wiped her fingers on her skirt. Benjamin had made it very clear that he would leave with his own family soon to hunt and trap. She could not go with him into the wilderness like that. Never could she, and especially not with a child coming.

Ambroise's child. What would a man like Benjamin want with a child not his own? Camilla exhaled a long breath and stepped out of the water. "I will continue with my plan to go to Michilimackinac, just as soon as your father sends the canots."

"I will be sorry to see you go." Marguerite's tone turned sure. "But then you will find a man able to take good care of you."

Camilla shook the sand from her stockings as though she meant to shed her foolish notions with the grains. She could not marry someone like Benjamin. She was a lady born and bred, and she was intended for marriage into society. She knew nothing of life in this country outside the four walls of the Cadottes' home. During the few weeks spent camping along the way here, she had been cared for and coddled by her husband and those he commanded around them. But to live in the forest and off the land? She could never …

Yet the idea of belonging to Benjamin allured her in ways she should not let into her thoughts.

CHAPTER 14

"Much can be gained when you bring your goods to the traders, but trade wisely. Save some of what you will need later, for you cannot eat trade beads or be warmed by gun powder."

—Etienne Marchal, to his son, Benjamin

Bemidii paddled along the shore toward the post. Hills tinted with hints of red maple outlined the distant mainland. Before many weeks, the entire lake region would wear a shawl of red and orange. The deer had put on coats of titian, too, their bodies glistening in the sun when they came to the water to drink.

As soon as René and Brigitte came for him, Bemidii would head back to the mainland to hunt and trap. They must be visiting the villages and posts along the way, but any day they would arrive. Perhaps even this day.

Until then, how wrong could it be that he sought out Ashwiyaa? Nothing could come of his feelings for her, and yet he could not go away without seeing her as often as he dared before his departure and hers. He had not courted her, and it was improper for her to spend time alone with him, and yet, she was no inexperienced maiden, nor he a besotted youngster.

Well, a bit besotted, perhaps.

He rounded the point and coasted his canoe alongside the wharf, climbing onto it rather than stepping into the cold water. The air was breezy and cool today, so he was dressed in a shirt, buckskins, and knee-high moccasins. His hair, parted in the middle, lay freely down his back. From the dock, he dragged the canoe close to shore, where he would pull it gently onto the sand. From the bottom of the boat, he took up a stringer of fish. Soon he would have red meat to trade and eat. He was ready for a change in his diet. But many needed to eat in La Pointe, and his fish would be welcome there.

He looked long toward the Cadottes' home as he passed by to the store. In the backyard, a trio of women worked over something. Ashwiyaa raised her head and waved. He nodded as he passed by.

Inside the dim trading post, Gichi-miishen and his two sons bent over their tasks of counting and weighing bales of fur. Bemidii had learned that yet another son, the eldest, also named Michel, had gone to a mainland post some miles south of the big lake.

"I have come in need of settling our trade," he said, laying the fish in a basket provided. "I will depart for the winter hunt soon and would gather an awl and a new trap. The rest I will take in gun powder."

Gichi-miishen opened his ledger on the counter before him. "It is good you come now. Supplies will not last long once the season begins. You may have heard my stores were robbed at Lac Courte Oreilles last year. It has been a slow recovery."

"Eya'. I have heard. A hard loss for all who depend upon the generosity of Gichi-miishen." He dipped his head in acknowledgment of Michel's good standing with the people of the land.

The man thanked him and gathered the items he requested.

After Bemidii signed his name for the transaction, he picked up his bundle and left, passing by way of the trader's home again. The women had gone inside the house now—all except Ashwiyaa. Did she wait for his return? She raised her head again, and her smile beckoned. She sat on a chair, lacing a snowshoe.

He strolled up to see her work. "You have gained a new skill?"

She nodded, her hair shining on her head. How he wished he could touch it.

"Madeleine and Marguerite have been very patient in their instruction. I think I am finally learning."

"The lacing looks tight. When the leather strips dry, they will serve well, I am certain."

She seemed to glow beneath his praise, shifting so that she tucked her feet beneath her skirts with only the toes of her moccasins poking out.

"Soon you will need to make other preparations for the cold—preparations for yourself and your journey."

"Oh? What preparations? I have blankets and a warm capote."

He pointed at her feet. "You have broken your moccasins in well, but when the cold comes, you will want them lined with fur."

"Ah, oui, I see your point."

"I have soft rabbit hides, a suitable fur for such a lining, if you would like to have them."

"You would give your hides to me?"

He smiled and let the offer rest.

"Merci. I would like to have them."

Bemidii cut his gaze away, considering. "Does your work have all your attention, or might you like to come with me to my camp to collect the hides? There may not be many more opportunities." He looked at her again.

"The snowshoes can wait. I think we have much of the year left before they will be needed." A shy smile touched her lips, and she laid her work aside. "We will take your canot?"

"Eya'."

Ashwiyaa stood, collecting her shawl around her shoulders just as a young girl came out of the house and paused to look at them.

"Julie, please tell your maman that I am going to visit a friend. I will be back later."

The girl nodded and spun to go back inside.

Ashwiyaa took a deep breath. "Shall we go?"

Bemidii led the way back to the beach. He set his purchases in the middle of the canoe, then pushed it back into the water alongside the wharf. He stepped down into the craft, and it wobbled slightly beneath him, but he smiled confidently at Ashwiyaa as he reached for her hands. "I will not let you fall."

Her fingers clasped his, and she stepped down, leaning near him to keep her balance. Tightening his hold so she would not slip, he inhaled the scent of her skin. She moved carefully to her place and sat.

"You are comfortable?"

She nodded and drew her shawl closer about her as a gust of wind rippled the water.

Bemidii made his way deftly to the rear of the canoe and picked up his paddle.

"You have spent many hours of your life on these waters," she said over her shoulder, her voice filled with reverie, as though she could imagine his upbringing.

"From a young age, I was taught—first by my father, and then by my mother's second husband—to paddle, to hunt, and to fish these waters and the rivers that feed them. To make my own canoe."

"I watched the voyageurs patch their craft, and I have seen places where they are built. It is a great skill."

Bemidii tried to push back against the pride her words caused, but he could not. She glanced back as if to measure the success of her compliment, and he returned her smile. This thing that was happening between them—he could not deny it. Nor did he wish to. Yet …

The dark reality came crashing over him as a cloud put out the sun overhead, turning the water beneath his paddle gray and depthless. In front of him sat the woman whose brother's life Bemidii had taken with his own knife. The blood he'd spilled had been her own. How she would despise him if she knew. His joy evaporated.

She was quiet the rest of the way as Bemidii paddled them to his camp. Did she sense the fruitlessness of their friendship as well? Tomorrow they might wake to never cross paths again. Would these moments together only make that inevitability more difficult to face? He knew the answer. He should stop now, turn around, and return her to the post. He could bring the rabbit skins and leave them at Michel's store for her. There was really no reason to bring her here except to be alone with her.

His mother, Keeheezkoni, would scold him for behaving so with a woman. He smiled at the thought. His mother wished him to take a wife and give her grandchildren.

He paddled next to the flat rock and steadied the boat as he climbed out. Ashwiyaa placed her soft, white hand in his brown one. His mother would not wish him to attach himself to this French woman. Only hurt and separation could come of it. Nevertheless, he did not get back inside the canoe and return her to the Cadottes' home. He assisted her to her feet, then hauled the canoe from the water and settled it safely upside down on the wide shelf of stone.

"Take care not to slip." He let her go in front of him this time, steadying her as she made her way over the uneven, rocky ascent. A glance toward the lake showed more clouds gathering, with bright spots of sun bursting through intermittently. "The sky changes quickly. Perhaps another storm will come. We will gather the rabbit furs, and I will return you to your lodging."

She faced him at the top of the rise. "I would rather not leave just yet. We've only just come. Please."

A storm brewed inside him. "You may stay if you wish. Are you hungry?"

"You must not use your supplies on me. I ate a generous meal earlier."

He smiled. "You did not answer my question."

He squatted by a firepit and stirred the ash with a stick. A few coals glowed. From a small pile of twigs beside him, he crisscrossed several atop the coals and bent to blow on them gently. As tiny flames licked the fuel, he added more. Soon he was able to add larger pieces of wood. "I cooked a pot of rice, corn, and fish for my meal last evening. It needs to be eaten."

"All right. If you insist."

He went into his lodge and came out with his copper pot containing the remnants of the meal. He hung it on a green, crotched stick angled into the ground above the small blaze. As the food began to warm and bubble, he stirred it with another green branch cut for such a purpose.

She sat on the log he'd placed beside the fire. "It is too bad I did not know you meant to feed me my dinner. I would have brought bread to contribute."

"I would be pleased to eat bread at your hand," he said, and her eyes sparkled with his words as she took in their intimate meaning.

He should not speak so, for he played with a fire hotter than that which cooked the wild rice in the pot. If she knew what he had done, she would throw the food into his face.

His spirit darkened, and he turned his face away as he stirred and ladled some of the food onto the inside of a smooth piece of bark. He rummaged in a rolled-up leather satchel and produced his only spoon. "You will want this." Handing it to her, their fingers touched, and their gazes intersected. He quickly let go. "I will get the rabbit furs."

Inside his lodge, Bemidii took deep breaths and clenched his fists at his sides, as though he could control his desires by doing so. For it wasn't only his desire to touch her and be with her that tormented him, but his desire to put the past away into a dark place, the way he could easily put away his cooking utensils and fishing gear. If he could tamp the truth away so tightly, it might never come between them.

Yet such a thing was impossible. Having her here with him was impossible. If René and Bridgitte would come, he might seek their wisdom. René would tell him to seek God's will. They would speak sense to him, remind him of the risks, and take him away. If Bemidii were to ever tell Ashiwayaa what he had done, not only would she despise his affection, but she would undoubtedly see him brought to justice.

But what justice? Her father did not seek justice, yet he would want revenge, or so it seemed if the rumors Bemidii heard before leaving rendezvous were true.

He quickly dug through his bundle of spare hides, the things he saved for his own winter's use, and pulled out two of the softest, thickest rabbit skins he could find. He had taken them in the coldest of winter last year when their hides might be the warmest.

He could not face Ashiwyaa with the truth, and he could not hold her love, but it would please him to know she wore his rabbit hides inside her moccasins on her journey back to Montreal when the waters beneath the canoe bottoms turned icy.

He ducked back outside to see her finishing her meal.

"I have learned to love the pleasures of simple food. Somehow it tastes even better here today than it would in the finest dining room in Montreal." Her lips curved. "Merci."

He held out the rabbit hides, and a raindrop landed on his arm. "I have the hides. Shall I put them in your moccasins to show you?"

"I think I know how." Her blush was demure and caused his throat to tighten. A rumble rolled across a sky that had turned grayer, and more fat raindrops hit the dirt around the campfire.

"I should take you back now, before the storm."

A shower hit the treetops, some of the rain making its way to the ground. "It would appear it's already too late." She stepped closer and stroked the hides clutched in his hand. The gentle pressure of her touch, as though she petted a live creature, stirred him. "They are very nice."

The fire hissed. "Come inside if you wish. If you trust me," he added.

Her eyelids flew up. "I trust you."

He stepped aside so she could duck beneath the opening of his rough shelter, poles tied together and overlaid by sheets of birch bark and the green boughs of many branches. He took a short stick from the fire that glowed on one end and carried it inside. As the rain's patter grew into a rushing sound through the forest, the inside of his lodge was dry though dim. He owned a single candle, which he lit and stood it up by digging a small hole in the dirt in which to anchor it. Ashwiyaa had already seated herself on the hides where he slept. He folded his legs beneath him and took a position facing her on the ground.

"It is cozy." Despite saying she trusted him, her voice held a nervous waver. Suddenly, with a crack of thunder, the clouds burst. She jerked, and a gray veil of water fell outside the open doorway.

Did she remember the day of her husband's death? "Have no fear. You are safe."

"I am not afraid. Only startled, that's all."

Water dripped off the shelter, pooling in a trickle by the door. Bemidii scraped a small trench with a stick so it would move away rather than flow inside. An occasional misty droplet broke through their covering, but for the most part, they remained secure inside.

Ashwiyaa eyed the ceiling. "I am amazed at how well we are sheltered. I can assure you, I was often much less comfortable on my journey here with the voyageurs."

"You will be more comfortable on your return to Montreal with the warmth of your lined moccasins and a good capote."

"Oui. Let me see them." She held out her hand, and he gave her the rabbit skins. He watched her continued stroking of the fur. She even raised the hides to her cheek and ran them over her face, closing her eyes. "They are very fine, Benjamin." She looked around. "You must give me a tour."

"I … do not understand."

"Show me your home, your things. What kind of trap is this?" She laid her hand on a pair of matching traps to her left.

"They are for beaver, muskrat, skunks. They are too small for some of the larger animals."

"I see." She turned her head to her right. "And this?" She indicated a thin hide rolled up like a tube. "Something to hunt with?"

His stomach tightened, but she waited expectantly. "I will show you." He reached for it and unlaced the leather ties holding the wrap around it. As he unrolled it, a glimpse at Ashwiyaa showed her mouth opening in surprise. He held the gleaming wooden instrument before her. "It is my flute."

Her eyes shone. "Play it for me."

Now the tightening in his stomach moved into his chest. He

shook his head and laid the flute down again.

"*S'il vous plait*, Benjamin. You must. I am sure you know how—since you own such a beautiful instrument, I mean."

"I know how."

She crossed her arms over her slightly rounded belly. "I won't let you take me back until I hear you play."

He stroked a hand over the dark wood. "I cannot."

"Why?"

Another thunderclap rolled, a little farther away this time.

"I must not play for you."

"It is my turn to not understand."

He stared at the instrument for a long time before raising his eyes, and it seemed by the downward turn of her lips he had hurt her. "It is not that I do not wish to play for you, but I cannot play my flute for a woman until I intend to woo her."

Her mouth opened again and closed, and her eyelashes fluttered. "I see."

Did he dare explain? His heart thrummed. "I wish to woo you, Ashwiyaa, but I cannot."

"Because I am French." Her tone sounded airy.

"Na."

She lowered her gaze and shifted her legs beneath her. He had embarrassed her, made her feel unwanted.

"Misawenim." He spoke in Ojibwe, for he could not keep his feelings in, but neither could he tell her. *I desire you in my heart.*

She raised her eyes slowly. "What are you saying?" she whispered.

He pinched his lips, but they would not stay closed. "There is too much between us. Our worlds too different. You must go back to your father, this great Clarboux, and live in his fine house. I must go into the woods and hunt. You cannot live like this"—he pointed at the branches covering their heads—"but must dwell in a better place."

She laid a hand on her stomach, shielding the baby. "Do you, too, tell me what I must do, Benjamin?"

He allowed her question to reach into him as they stared at one another. "We are different rivers, Ashwiyaa. Rivers must follow their courses, and the outcome cannot be changed."

Her lips parted and closed, and he could see her fighting his explanation in the sparkling green of her eyes. "So you will play for a woman on your flute someday." She had lightened her voice. "And I am not to hear one note from my friend?"

Outside, the rumbling grew more and more distant, even while the beat of Bemidii's heart pounded louder. His eyes remained steadily upon her as he picked up the flute and put it to his lips. A note spilled out, long and solemn, dramatic and lovely, and then another and still another. Finally, he closed his eyes and let the melody take him over. For almost a minute, he filled the lodge with sounds both haunting and passionate as he thought of her there, listening intently, and of how he wanted her.

He stopped abruptly and opened his eyes.

"I wish you had not stopped."

"You have heard it." He laid the instrument on its leather wrapper.

Her hand touched his, stopping him. "Play for me. Will you play for me?"

He stared at their hands. She did not move at first, then she slowly let her palm rest completely, and she wrapped her fingers over his. His chest rose and fell in a hot rhythm. His whole being longed to take her in his arms and tell her of his desire—that he would be a father to her child, too, and then their own. Yet … he could not fight the demon that whispered in his ear. *You murdered her brother. You will hang.*

Soul crushed, he slid his hand free and rolled the instrument into the leather. He could not look at her. He could not bear the hurt in her expression, so he did not. "The rain has stopped. I will take you back now."

CHAPTER 15

I saw a man pilloried and whipped today. He appeared near death itself. I shudder to think what his crime might have been.

—Journal of Camilla Bonnet

Camilla lay on her back, staring at the ceiling of her shared bedroom. She had claimed to be feeling a bit tired and ill in order to avoid going downstairs today. Madeleine had brought up some broth, telling her to rest as long as she needed, but Camilla suspected that Madeleine knew there was more than her pregnancy at work to bring her low. She'd hidden her tears when she left Benjamin and his canoe at the beach and come into the house yesterday. Yet Madeleine had sharp eyes. Nothing much remained secreted from her.

Camilla made out the shapes of trees and hills in the swirls of plaster above her—an entire world of rivers and rocks. A year ago, she would have seen nothing, only the dismal gray and white of the walls. Now she saw places and things she'd never dreamed of. People too. When had she learned to love both this place and this man of whom she knew so little? And did she really love him, or was Benjamin actually only a means to an end? A way to avoid her father's interference in her life?

Benjamin had never so much as touched her other than to assist her when she needed help. Yet the warmth in his eyes when he looked at her and the tenderness in his speech stirred her more than Ambroise ever had. Surely, he felt it too.

She clenched her eyelids tight and batted them open again. How could she help but love him?

Camilla's stomach burned anew with the humiliation she'd felt when he rejected her plea to play his flute for her. Did he not understand what she meant? *Non, that is not it. He understood. He did not want me.* In that moment, she had been willing to stay with him as his wife in this faraway land, except he had no intention of asking her. She would have remained with him if he only had put the flute to his lips again and played. She would have given him all of her.

The baby turned inside her, reminding her how much less desirable she was now. She was only meant for a man like old MacDaw or even the voyageur Monsieur Pilon. Not for a man like Benjamin.

And what of this family he spoke of—this sister and her husband who was a company partner? With such a family, could Benjamin not reasonably consider taking her as his wife?

Unless he waited for someone else. Perhaps a woman of his own people suited him more.

Perhaps she should have gone on with the brigade and trusted her safety to the Scotsman. Perhaps she should have considered Monsieur Pilon's suit. Perhaps she never should have gone with Benjamin to retrieve the hides for her moccasins. It would have been better to pine for him not knowing what might have been than to find out and face such rejection. Perhaps—

Marguerite tapped and poked her head in the bedroom door. "I am sorry to disturb you, but Maman wished me to see if anything was needed."

Camilla sat up and brought her feet to the floor. "Non. I am well. I am only heartsick."

Marguerite slid farther into the room and closed the door. "You went to see him yesterday." There was no need to mention Benjamin's name.

Camilla nodded. "He gave me rabbit skins for my moccasins. To warm me on my journey home."

"Then you will go when your père sends for you."

"Oui. Or sooner. I will go with the next boats leaving for Michilimackinac."

"I am sorry it did not work out for you with Benjamin."

"Merci, Marguerite. I am humiliated. Tell me, you once

mentioned that the right man had not yet played his flute for you. What happens when the right man does so?"

"At first, I will act shyly, pretending little interest. Then he will bring gifts to my parents, and with them, I will come to give my answer."

"Je vois." She had been too forward, then, perhaps. "How does this playing of the flute usually proceed?"

"He comes to my home in the night and plays outside to woo me." She sat on the edge of the bed, and her cheeks flushed. "I speak as though such a thing has happened, but it has not. If no one comes, then I will be content here with my family."

"You are a fine woman. I am sure someone shall."

"I hope so." With a sigh, she rose and walked to the small window. "Look, there are men coming up the shore. Hunters, I think."

Camilla rose and stood next to her. "Someone from the village?"

Marguerite shook her head. "I do not recognize them." A furrow bent her brow. "Unless … I think …" A tiny puff of air left her mouth, and she moved away from the window. "I must see. I will let you rest. If you do have need of anything, please tell me."

"I will come down. I am silly for feeling as I do."

Marguerite let herself out as Camilla pulled in a deep breath. The time had come to wash her face and brush her hair. Lying here abed would not solve her problems any more than waiting for a man of her choosing to rescue her. Never mind Benjamin. She could not understand his ways, and more than likely, she should not try. They were from different worlds. Two rivers running their courses, just as he'd said. Soon she'd be a mother with more important cares than her own comforts to think of. One day at a time. She must look no farther ahead than that.

When she went downstairs a short time later, Madeleine smiled up from her stitching on a new pair of moccasins. Several children sat around the table reading, and Marguerite mixed a bowl of cornbread. "You are feeling better?" Madeleine asked.

"I am well enough. I fear I overdid it yesterday."

"I am glad to see you rested. Augustin,"—she turned her attention from the leatherwork in her lap to one of the boys who was usually in his father's store—"tend the fire for your sister. I must start our evening meal before long."

"Oui, Maman." The boy pushed his chair back and brushed past Camilla, his expression surly.

"He is upset because I made him stay home and attend to his schooling. He saw the hunters coming to the store, and he wanted to hurry out and join his père. You know children. They do not like missing out." She chuckled.

"Marguerite saw them come." She glanced at her friend. "Was it someone you knew?"

Marguerite shrugged. "I am not certain. They were already at the store when I came down."

"Marguerite," Madeleine said, "I think I will send you to the village tomorrow with the basket I have prepared for Odahingum. Her child will be born soon."

"Oui, I will be happy to take it to her." Marguerite ladled the cornmeal mixture into a pan. "Perhaps Camilla will come along."

Madeleine pushed a lace through the punched leather as she spoke again to Camilla. "You have not spent time in the village."

"Non. I should have. I have wasted some of my time here, only thinking about when I would go. As much as I have enjoyed my time with you and the children in the gardens and … and even picking berries …" Her words stumbled to a halt, for she didn't wish to mention what was truly on her heart. "I should have learned more about the people of this lovely island."

"You might still go. I have cousins, aunts, and uncles who live there. They would be quite pleased to meet you. Odahingum will be happy to meet another expecting mother."

Camilla rested her hand on the back of Marie's chair. A pair of chocolate brown eyes smiled up at her. "I would be happy to meet her also. Then, I expect I should be packing my bags. I am sure your husband plans to send his canots to Michilimackinac soon. I must not delay him."

Madeleine rested her work in her lap. "I promise. There is time." She turned slowly back to her next lacing. "I am surprised Benjamin has not taken you to visit the village."

"He is a stranger to the island. He hasn't many acquaintances in the village."

Madeleine's brow bent. "Oh? I did not realize."

"Oui. He is from the western end of the lake. A village there."

"Does he expect to return?"

"He is waiting for his family—his sister and her husband. Then they will go away to hunt for the winter." She brushed her hand along the chair back and strolled toward the chair facing Madeleine. She lowered herself to sit and reached for a ball of yarn and needles in a basket beside it. Almost mindlessly, she picked up a recently begun stocking and began to knit. "I understand his sister's husband is a company partner."

Madeleine's head came up again, and she blinked in surprise. "You have not mentioned this before. Have you spoken to Michel? Perhaps he knows this man. This company partner might be your answer to returning to Montreal."

Camilla shook her head. "I fear not. Benjamin seemed very certain that they would be traveling into the interior. I cannot ask them to change their plans."

"I suppose not."

The door came open, and Michel strode in with a young man much like him. Madeleine cried out and rose up with the agility of a much younger woman. "Michel!" She rushed to the younger man and threw her arms around his neck.

"Ogiin!"

The children also leapt from their chairs. Even Marguerite let out a cry of delight and joined the throng gathering around their father and the younger man.

Madeleine leaned back and braced the young man's shoulders.

"We have a guest. You must speak French." She stepped aside.

He removed his hat and bowed his head.

"This is Madame Bonnet. Madame Bonnet, our eldest son, Michel."

He was a strapping lad of at least twenty. He wore the backcountry dress of a trader or hunter. "Booz—I mean, bonjour, Madame Bonnet."

"Bonjour, Michel."

The rest of the children rushed close to their eldest brother, and he handed out hugs and greetings along with maple sugar treats. He lifted little Charlotte in his arms and smiled at the baby playing on the rag rug in the center of the room.

After the initial hullabaloo, the children settled down, and the Great Michel slapped his son's shoulder. "He is only back for a short visit. He will leave for Lac Courte Oreille tomorrow and from there back to the Chippewa River post."

"So soon? I wish you did not have to go," Madeleine said, directing him to a bench to sit.

"I am sorry, Maman, but it is the way of things. The cold season comes soon, and the hunters will begin bringing in their pelts."

Great Michel explained to Camilla. "The place my son travels to is a long journey south of here."

They proceeded to talk about the trade and the coming season, about the difficult recovery since the raid on the Lac Courte Oreilles post last year, about their allegiances being forced to change from the North West Company to the Michilimackinac and the likeliness of the Americans taking over more posts in the west. Finally, they discussed rumors of native unrest.

Camilla's thoughts went elsewhere during much of their talk. To that mystery called *Ouiseconsaint,* the dark horizon south of the island, where her mind naturally settled again on Benjamin. How far would he travel into the deep green country where rivers made veins to unknown lands? Where villages waited, filled with life and laughter of people she would never see? Where he might find a bride for whom to play his flute?

Her ears pricked again at Michel's word, *murder*. "Word has spread everywhere. He will be forced to trade illegally."

"Plenty of *courier-du-bois* already roam the woods," his father said.

"No one is to trade with him."

Cadotte grunted. "How are we to know who such a man might be? Hunters … trappers … they come singly all throughout the winter to trade. Are we to judge a man's character on looks alone? Are we to ask him, 'did you kill a man at the great rendezvous?'" Great Michel gave an apologetic tilt of his head to Camilla. "I am sorry for speaking so callously about your relative."

"You are referring to my brother, Tristan?"

Great Michel gave a curt nod. "Oui. Your brother. There is a price on the head of the man who killed him, and some say he may have come this direction. *Pfft*!" He waved his hand. "He could have gone anywhere. If he left with other travelers south along the shore, there are a hundred places he could have gone. Back to his own village, most likely. Why should he come so far as these Apostles? More likely still, he has traveled up rivers to the west."

"We are a long reach from Fort William," the younger Michel said. "It is exactly your question that makes such a move plausible. I say we should keep our eyes open."

"Except, of course, for our guest"—he inclined his head again toward Camilla— "I am unconcerned. I do not believe the murderer would come here. He has no cause."

Camilla shifted her feet, uncomfortable with this talk of Tristan's murderer. Yet it was good that he was not forgotten and that there were those who sought justice on his behalf.

Great Michel heaved his shoulders with a sigh. "I will let the men of La Pointe know. Someone may have heard something. You never can tell," he conceded.

Madeleine tidied up the area where she worked on the moccasins. "I am sure the man who did such a thing will be found out. If not now, then by the time of next year's rendezvous. For now, let us speak no more about it. I will start your dinner."

Marguerite cleared her siblings' books from the table. Camilla stood to help with the meal, too, but her mind stayed on Madame Cadotte's words. *"If not now, then by the time of next year's rendezvous."* Would Tristan's death ever really be solved? Camilla had been set adrift in a land teeming with violence, both from nature and from man. And yet, a more beautiful land she had never imagined. If only Benjamin wished her to stay.

CHAPTER 16

"You are old enough to take on the tasks of a man. Learn well to provide for those around you now, and your family will not suffer when you are older."

—Etienne Marchal, to his son, Benjamin

Bemidii's breath rode upon crisp air as he and Coyote took Bemidii's canoe across the tranquil lake. Only the sounds of their paddles stirred the world. He would be back at his camp in a matter of days, for Coyote had reminded him more than once that they must return in time for the gathering of the annual fall celebration.

Coyote had begun urging Bemidii to join him on a hunt for venison on the mainland some days ago. The women had dried the rice harvest in the sun and parched it in a kettle to loosen the hulls. Then several of them, in clean moccasins, had danced over the rice, treading on it to remove the hulls. They'd thrown it into the air to winnow the chaff. All this was familiar to Bemidii, for the women in his village had done the same thing. But here at La Pointe, clans from around the region would take part in celebrating the end of the rice harvest and the beginning of the long season's hunting to come. Many men would soon be away from their families for weeks and months, while the women kept the fires burning at home. Therefore, for the celebration, a medicine man would bless their harvest and the hunters. The people would store most of the rice in birch baskets, but some would be boiled and sweetened with maple sugar or flavored with venison or duck broth. Coyote hoped to have venison to contribute for the event.

Tired of fish and the few squirrels he'd snared, Bemidii was ready for such a hunt as well, and it would be good to take part in the celebration, for it might help him to keep from thinking only of Ashwiyaa.

The month of the ricing moon was at an end, and days turned

swiftly toward the falling leaves moon. Frost had cast its ghostly coverlet over the ground on two occasions.

"My wife is preparing for the feast." Coyote's grating voice broke the quiet of the dawn. "She wants enough meat to feed all our relatives."

Bemidii grinned. "Then you had better shoot straight." Coyote loved to tell stories of his hunting exploits, but Bemidii had heard several of his stories more than once, convincing him those exploits had been few. "I will bring some of my meat to trade—should *Gitchie Manitou* guide my arrow." He would also dry some, if time permitted, and he would bring a haunch to the Cadottes along with the hide for trade.

His sister, Brigitte, always prayed for them before the hunt, and René prayed too. Would she be thinking of him now, with the season's change, and whispering her Christian prayers?

Coyote nodded. "I would not mind trading a haunch for some rum."

"Do your children fill their bellies on rum?" Bemidii had seen what it did to the men in his own village, how it harmed their families.

"There will be other meat."

"Let us hope so. Winter always brings surprises."

"Your father was a good hunter?"

Etienne Marchal had been a very good hunter. Bemidii would never forget the things his father taught him, even though their time together was cut short, first when his father left his mother, Keeheezkoni, for another wife, and then by his tragic death. "He had many deer, bear, beaver pelts, and more to trade. His family did not hunger."

Coyote fell silent.

Bemidii took a long, deep breath, filling his lungs with the freshness of the lake air. The sun crept higher into the sky as the hills of Ouisconsin loomed closer.

Fifty rods distant, another canoe glided over the glassy water away from St. Michel's too. Probably other hunters from La Pointe.

Coyote looked their way. "Little Michel leaves today."

"Who is Little Michel?"

"Son of Gichi-miishen. He arrived yesterday with some others. Now he goes to the Chippewa post."

Michel Cadotte's life was certainly full with his many children and his importance as trader, interpreter, and negotiator between the Indians, Frenchmen, and British in the region. What's more, he was fully committed to each of those things, unlike another trader Bemidii knew, René's own brother who ran the St. Louis post. That man had been ready to cast aside his native wife and family for a higher position. Perhaps he was changed. Claude Dufour seemed to regret that poor decision and had settled down since the days he sought to deceive Brigitte. He had grown wiser like his brother, René.

"You did not hear the news he brought?" Coyote caught Bemidii's attention again.

"What news?"

"Little Michel says that the murder of that Frenchman at the great rendezvous—the one who was brother of the woman at Gichi-miishen's home—he says, it is thought he might have come as far as the islands and that no one is to trade with him."

Bemidii's muscles tightened, and he stroked the paddle deeper. "How is anyone to know who this man is, that he is not to be traded with?"

Coyote shrugged. "Someone knows. It is only a matter of time before his identity is found out. There were many people at the rendezvous. Surely, someone saw."

Shadows of that night danced around the edges of Bemidii's mind, of the people at the celebration who saw Clarboux leave. People who knew that Brigitte had been accosted. People who saw Bemidii there as well. Even the maiden Anang must have wondered what had become of Bemidii after their dance and his flirtation. Surely, she and her family suspected him. Yes, someone would remember his name. Coyote spoke truth. It was only a matter of time.

He would need to deflect attention. "Some *coureur-du-bois* of a suspicious nature will turn up, or maybe some renegade bragging of his crime."

In the front of the canoe, Coyote wagged his head and let his paddle rest. "If tongues are to loosen, the company must offer a reward. As soon as this merchant in Montreal gets word of his son's death, there will be coin to gain."

Bemidii thought so too. Even Camilla's few words about the type of man her father was assured him the elder Clarboux would not forget. He would hunt down Tristan's killer at any cost. His pride would demand it. Bemidii pursed his lips in thought. There were many men like Coyote looking for easy gain.

"Hunting is a sure reward." He spoke evenly, suppressing his rising concern. "This other is like seeking for treasure that may not exist. I will fill my canoe with meat and furs for trade. That will be provision enough for me."

Coyote chuckled and pulled with his paddle.

When they reached the far shore, they carried the canoe over a sandy spit and hid it in the brush. Then they set out in search of deer sign. They soon found a trail with fresh sign and moved inland upon it. Bemidii's blood raced with anticipation as he threw his body and mind into the hunt. He would forget the words of Coyote. Worrying would do no good, but taking a deer today would. If only he were free to court Ashwiyaa, he would bring the meat to her family as a gift along with the hide.

By afternoon, they had seen several deer, but none close enough to shoot. The men agreed that since sign was plentiful, they would part ways for the evening and each find a place to wait.

He met Coyote in the darkness beside a creek they had agreed upon.

"Anything?" Coyote asked as he laid twigs for a campfire.

Bemidii took his quiver and bow off his back. "Not today. In the morning, I will go back. There are rubs and ruts. Plenty of sign. A deer will come eventually."

They finished building their campfire and unrolled their bedding in silence. Then they ate parched corn from their own packs. As they settled into their beds, Coyote resumed the conversation.

"I would not mind going to the Kaministiquia rendezvous next year. Perhaps I will sign with Gichi-miishen's brigade."

"You have never gone to the great rendezvous?" Bemidii couldn't cover his surprise. He figured a man like Coyote would not have missed out on such an adventure. Their fire burned low, so he could not see Coyote, yet Bemidii felt the man's gaze shift to him in the darkness.

"I have not, and this surprises you. You have been to Fort William yourself?"

Bemidii wanted to roll over, but he remained still and forced a casualness he did not feel in his reply. "I have gone many times. My father took me there when I was a boy, and I have gone with the others from my village. Members of my family are held in regard by the company." He didn't like bragging, yet this was the sort of thing that would awe Coyote and throw him off the scent of suspicion.

"Oh? How is that?"

Now Bemidii did roll onto his side away from Coyote. He let a yawn fill his voice. "Hunters … voyageurs … and my father was a trapper, a Frenchman. He came into this country many years ago and died in service to the company."

"I am sorry to hear it."

"He was a good man, my father." Bemidii let his voice drift off, certain now that Coyote would not speak further after treading upon his memories.

Rising well before dawn, they crept in different directions into the deeper woods. Bemidii took a six-point buck with his bow from the perch on an uprooted tree. The deer was heavy in body, and he would be a prize to bring back to the post. Perhaps he would give some meat to the Cadottes as a gift, anyway, because he could not help wanting to please Ashwiyaa.

Coyote took a young fork buck as well. With a lifted chin and much flamboyance, he told the story of his hunt, explaining how he came upon the deer in its bed but was able to bring it down before it escaped. Bemidii congratulated him, honoring Coyote with the approval he sought.

It was late in the afternoon before they arrived back at La Pointe. Coyote's children were among the throng rushing to the beach to meet them, their eyes bright at the sight of the two deer.

"A good hunt!" a voice called, and Coyote waved to a group of men gathered around a pair of hunters by another laden canoe.

Bemidii took a second glance as he tucked his paddle in the boat. One of the new arrivals looked familiar. Where had he seen those sharp shoulders and that wide brow before?

Rising, he stepped on shore and steadied the craft while Coyote disembarked. Together, they hoisted the canoe onto the beach, then grabbed the legs of Coyote's kill and hauled the deer carcass ashore.

Coyote's son ran to him and jabbered questions in quick succession. Coyote tussled the boy's hair and promised him a long story later, after they had the deer hung and skinned. He, too, glanced at the men. Did he feel slighted that they didn't rush over to hear his hunting tale?

"There will be time for talk later, when we are gathered around the fire with some rum to warm our bellies as well."

Bemidii acknowledged the invitation with a lift of his head. He returned to the canoe along with Coyote and the gaggle of children at their heels.

"Who are those men?" Coyote asked his son in a hushed tone.

"They come from Bad River. They share news and will join the celebration of the rice harvest."

Coyote glanced at them again and then at Bemidii. "Already,

the people come to begin celebrating. We will go over and see what news they have, eh?"

Bemidii shouldered Coyote's pack and laid it beside the deer. "I have my own venison to skin and cut. Perhaps later you can tell me what you hear. I will go back to my camp now."

"But it is early. Surely, you would like to have something to eat before you go. Many will want to hear about the hunt. Even them." He jerked his head at the strangers.

Bemidii gentled the canoe back into the water. "You go ahead. I will feel more at ease if I take care of the kill now." He threw Coyote a grin as he seated himself. "I have no woman to help me."

Coyote tossed back his head with a laugh. "You must remedy that before long."

Bemidii forced a chuckle and picked up his paddle. Coyote turned toward the crowd on the shore, and Bemidii glanced their way again. Had he seen that man before, or was his mind playing tricks? He had hunted and traded with hundreds in his twenty-seven summers. He could have crossed the stranger's path anywhere, even at the St. Louis fort.

Or had it been at Fort William?

In an effort to calm his disquiet, he focused on the rhythm of paddling. In another day or two, La Pointe would be teeming with such men and their families from the mainland villages surrounding the bay. He would probably recognize others as well. Perhaps even René and Brigitte might arrive in time for the celebration. It would be good to be with them again.

With each purposeful stroke, he pulled in a deep breath and eased it out.

Even if someone here should recognize him, only a few had been on the riverbank the night he fought Tristan. The odds were slim that any man or woman here would know his face from that dark eve. Weeks and miles lay between him and that time and place. He worried for nothing. Surely.

CHAPTER 17

The colors of spring have never seemed so bright, the sky so blue, the buds of the trees such brilliant green. Even the rocks that flash in the rivers beneath our canoes glisten with amber and silver. I have never been so happy or content. By the time we must return to Montreal, the colors will turn to autumn.

—Journal of Camilla Bonnet

Camilla dressed in her warmest frock and donned a wool shawl. The sunlight danced brilliant threads of light among treetops of scarlet, umber, and gold. The root cellar overflowed with squash, pumpkins, colorful cobs of corn, and now rice too. Camilla and the Cadotte women had gone to the village to help with the cleaning of the rice. Though none of them danced on it, they did their share of winnowing and collecting the long, dark kernels. Today they prepared food for the community celebration.

Canoes carrying cheerful Ojibwe and Métis had been arriving in droves. Women visited the post along with their men, and Michel traded away plenty of beads, kettles, and cloth.

Finally, the food preparations were complete. Camilla walked along with the rest of the Cadotte family to the village, where the singing, drumming, and dancing was already underway. The children ran off as quickly as they could get away to find their friends.

Camilla found a quiet place beneath a shady tree to tuck her skirts beneath her and rest while she watched the women's jingle dance. Never had she seen anything like it in the drawing rooms of Montreal. Exquisite beading and quill-work decorated the women's brightly colored skirts, and on the hem of each were rows of tiny bells that jingled with the rhythm of their dance. Camilla felt plain in her yellow dress and simple wool shawl. Then the baby tumbled inside her, filling her with the warmth of motherhood like the sun on her shoulders, and contentment soothed her. She would write about the colors and joy of this day later tonight, if she wasn't too tired.

The smell of cooking food drifted past her, savory and rich. She'd nibbled while—along with Marguerite and her mother—they'd boiled and baked their contribution, but the busyness of the day left her hungry. Once the dancing stopped, she rose and went in search of something to eat. She found Marguerite, who led her to a relative's home, where she was given a bowl filled with stew. How good it was to be over the early pregnancy sickness. To be able to enjoy every bite.

"You are smiling a lot today," Marguerite said, joining her on a blanket on the ground outside the wiigiwaam.

"It's a wonderful day. I wish it would last."

"Tomorrow we will gather again. Then many will leave. It is a good celebration."

"Oui. It is. I find that I am not nearly so homesick as I expected to be these past months. By now, my parents will have gotten word …" She caressed her budding abdomen. "Of Ambroise and the baby. My mother will worry. If I had a way, I would write to her again and tell her not to fear, for my friends have taken great care of me." She laid her hand on Marguerite's shoulder. "Merci."

"I have been happy to know you as well. I wish you were not going, but I suppose you must."

Camilla gave a small nod and took another bite of her stew. Quietly then, they ate while observing the dozens of faces moving about them through the throng in the village—elders, children, women chattering, and men laughing and smoking.

"I am going to join the dancing now. Do you want to?" Marguerite stood up.

Camilla chuckled. "It is very different than the kind of dancing I am familiar with. I believe I will remain here in comfort." She patted a hand on the babe again, and Marguerite grinned.

"Ah, oui, and so it is probably best. I hate to leave you alone."

"I am fine. I will sit a while longer, and then I will go to find your mother."

"All right. *Au revoir*."

"Au revoir."

Marguerite was soon swallowed up in the crowd, down the winding lane between wiigiwaams and cook fires. Camilla turned her head the other way, only to see the shape of a familiar back and shoulders some rods off. Her heart tripped over itself, and she carefully pushed herself to her feet. With the empty bowl in one hand, she used the other to brush off her gown and straighten it. Never had the sight of a man set her so off-kilter. That this man did, with his long hair hanging down the white shirt covering his back and the set of his elegant yet strong hands on his buckskin-clad hips, both mystified and thrilled her. She nearly felt faint and had to focus on deepening her breath. Might he turn soon and see her there? Would he come to her, or would he walk away, choosing instead to sever their friendship further? She nibbled her lip, her patience stretched taut until she finally noticed it was a man and a woman with whom he spoke.

Now her breath hitched again, for the man was dark and bearded. Clearly French. Was this …?

The diminutive woman beside him, she was native, or at least she dressed so. Her braid hung long down her back. Her arm wrapped around the bearded man. Was she Ojibwe or Métis? She looked so familiar somehow, but Camille knew no Métis or native women other than the Cadottes and a few others she'd met here on the island. She'd seen many in passing on her journey, but none that she recalled looking like this woman who stood beside the Frenchman speaking with Benjamin. A far-off memory plucked away inside her for release, but—

"Madame Bonnet!" Michel's voice called, startling her. She whirled sideways to face him. He reached for her hand and clasped it in both of his own. "I hope you are enjoying the celebration. There is much to do, non?"

She nodded and tried to steal a glimpse back at Benjamin and his friends.

"Here, let me take that empty bowl for you. May I get you something more to eat?"

She shook her head. "Non, merci, monsieur. I am filled to bursting." She laid a hand on her stomach. The baby wiggled. "Even my little one has had plenty, I think."

He chuckled. "Your little one will soon be well provisioned."

"Oh?" What did he mean by that?

"I have spoken to some of my men today. They are in good spirits. Well-fed and ready for the season to begin. I will send them by brigade to the Sault two days hence. From there, they will proceed to Fort Michilimackinac. You will go with them and be safely there in only a couple of weeks, well before winter. Come springtime, you can return to your family in Montreal. How does that sound?" He beamed, clearly expecting her to be pleased. And she was. Somewhat.

She took another glance at Benjamin, then back to Michel. "It is very sudden, just as you forewarned, but of course, I will be ready in time. I promise. I …" Her eyes burned without warning. "I thank you again for your kindness to me."

He clasped her hands again. "It is the very least we could do. You have been more than welcome. Perhaps, somehow, we will one day meet again."

She knew they would not, but it was a kindness to say so. She nodded.

"Now, if you will excuse me, I must go back to the store. Business is good today." He grinned and nodded farewell.

She blew out a breath and turned her head, cleansing away the unexpected emotion. Her eyes lifted to find Benjamin again, and this time, the small woman hugged him. Then she backed into the Frenchman's arm around her shoulders again.

Why, of course! It must be his family. The sister. The brother-in-law. Which meant he would go away with them. Perhaps even today.

So we both leave to return to the places we belong. We will never meet again.

She took one step. Was it better this way, to watch from a distance? Or should she go and say farewell once more? The woman's face flashed in her direction for a moment, and the puzzlement returned. Surely, Camilla had met her before, but when? How? At the Sault? Yet Benjamin spoke as though they'd never been so far east. And the handsome Frenchman was a complete stranger to her.

The woman stepped free from her man, and her face lifted toward the crowd. At that moment, her eyes met Camilla's.

And widened into stillness.

It couldn't be … It couldn't!

Camilla trembled. She clutched the fabric of her gown at her sides, and her legs shook. Those wide, brown eyes stared at her, just as they had done before, more than a year ago—almost two. She hadn't worn the colorful Indian dress then, but a simple gown of powder blue. She'd not worn a long braid then but had piled her hair atop her head. The girl had complimented Camilla's green gown and eyes while she sat crushed beside Tristan in their carriage. She'd come to the party at their home, and Camilla had warned her to be careful of her brother. Then, later, she learned that Tristan had taken her home unchaperoned. He was angry when he returned, and shortly afterward, the girl's mother—no, her aunt—had died. Tristan had spoken several times of his quarry, and the way in which he spoke tightened Camilla's throat with worry for the girl. But then she had vanished. Tristan thought she'd gone to the nuns, but the nuns claimed to know nothing. Then he supposed she'd run away to Quebec, but all leads that direction met with dead ends. Finally, he thought she'd died.

Tristan had turned his attention elsewhere then, or so Camilla thought. There was the servant who went away carrying a fatherless child. There was some other poor girl. Camilla couldn't recall her name, but if her memory served, she had taken over residence in a house belonging to this very young woman who stood before her now. There were others, certainly, but none that ever again struck the fancy that this woman did for Tristan. Could he have discovered she'd gone to the Upper Country? Surely not. Yet perhaps he'd suspected. When their father had demanded that both Tristan and Ambroise make their adventure, was Tristan's eagerness to comply less from boredom than from his ambition to track down this woman?

Camilla took a step forward. Would the girl shun her now? Camilla must speak to her. She was compelled to try.

Benjamin turned around, following his sister's gaze, and when he saw Camilla, a cloud passed over his features. Her step faltered. Did he wish not to see her? He must realize she would be at the celebration, mustn't he?

Maybe not. Maybe he'd hoped she'd be gone by now. Camilla raised her chin. It didn't matter what Benjamin thought now. Only that before him stood Brigitte Marchal, and Camilla must speak to her. She let a group of young women pass, then walked on, bracing her shoulders. At last, she stood only feet in front of her. The dark-haired trader faced Camilla on one side of Brigitte, and Benjamin stood on the other.

"Bonjour. You are … Brigitte Marchal, if I am not mistaken?"

The planes of her face smoothed. "Oui. I am Brigitte. Brigitte Dufour. This is my husband, René Dufour, one of the North West Company wintering partners."

Camilla dipped her head at Monsieur Dufour. "I see." She glanced at Benjamin.

"And my brother, Benjamin. I believe you are already acquainted."

"Oui." He had spoken of her to his sister? "Bonjour, Benjamin."

His expression was unfathomable, yet he didn't seem angry at her approach.

"I had to come and see if it was truly you, the girl I remembered from Montreal."

"And I am equally surprised." Brigitte chuckled, but it was a nervous sound. "To meet such a well-bred lady here in this part of the country … on this island!" She let a gasp of astonishment slip out and shook her head. "It is amazing, is it not?"

"I, too, married and came here with my husband, Ambroise Bonnet. Unfortunately, he met with an accident on the lake."

Brigitte nodded solemnly as though she already knew. Had Benjamin spoken of it? She seemed so well-informed. Perhaps Benjamin was not as immune to Camilla's feelings as she thought.

Camilla forced a smile. "In two days, I will leave here, however. Monsieur Cadotte has arranged for my transportation to Michilimackinac. In the spring, I will return home to Montreal, to my family." She could not resist another glance at Benjamin. His thoughts remained shadowed behind his dark eyes.

Brigitte's gaze dropped only briefly to Camilla's stomach, though she had the presence of mind not to let it linger. Camilla felt compelled to reject Brigitte's pity. "I am terribly sorry that Ambroise will not meet his child. However, that is the reason I must go soon to Michilimackinac."

"My congratulations to you, despite your terrible loss. I am sure your father will see to it that you are well cared for."

What was that sound Camilla heard from Benjamin? Was it a rumble? A growl?

"I am expecting as well," Brigitte went on. "When do you anticipate the birth of your child?"

Camilla fought against the urge to look again at Benjamin. "In *Janvier,* the heart of winter, I'm afraid."

Brigitte drew herself taller, moving nearer her husband. "I, as well." She drew her hand down over the round place beneath her bright blue skirt. They would have their children very close together, even though they themselves would be physically many leagues apart.

"I wish you well, then," Camilla muttered. Her nerves began to fray, and she could not keep going with this conversation. Awkwardness overcame her. Perhaps she should not have approached them at all. "I will not keep you. I am certain you and your brother have much to discuss." She turned partway and paused. "One thing. My brother … Tristan. I am not sure how far word has spread or if you have heard, but he has also died … unfortunately."

Brigitte's gaze dropped to the ground. "I did hear of someone by the name of Clarboux having been …" Did she wish to say *killed* but could not? It was an ugly word. Her husband's arm went around her again.

To Camilla's surprise, Benjamin raised his chin. "Will you walk with me?"

She nodded. Oui, she would walk with him. To turn away now, to say goodbye again like this, with such strain between them, would plague her future memories forever.

Brigitte appeared shaken when she lifted her eyes to Camilla again. "I am sorry for your great loss, madame."

"Merci." She looked to Benjamin, and then the two of them turned away together.

Benjamin was silent as he escorted her through the crowd. They passed the circle of drummers and singers, saying nothing, but only listening to the rhythmic beat and chanting melody.

Finally, as they exited the end of the village and left the gathering behind, he spoke. "My sister left Montreal to search for our father. She found me instead."

That was why? So perhaps she did not only wish to avoid Tristan? In some strange way, Camilla felt relief. "You never told me."

"I saw no reason."

No, of course not. What reason could there be? That their worlds had crossed so closely was the strangest thing, but it raised a question. "She knew my brother. Did she never tell you?"

He nodded. "When I told her of you, she told me about him. I knew there was someone who courted her before she loved René, but she was not to be wooed by him."

"Non. She was not. I still find it so amazing …" Camilla couldn't quite grasp hold of the fact that Brigitte Marchal was Benjamin's sister. "You told me your sister's name was Amoo."

"Eya'. It is a term of affection. My father also gave her her French name, Brigitte."

"I see." Did she? It was all confusing and shocking still. They strolled down the trail toward the trading post. Sunshine splayed from the west and cast the path in breezy shadows. "I am glad I got to meet her before I leave—before you go as well. It feels right to know what became of her. I did not know your sister well, but I liked her. She never seemed suited for her life in Montreal."

He halted and turned to face her. "How does someone seem suited? Is not home a place people make for themselves?"

Camilla pulled her shawl tighter around her shoulders, despite the heat that rose up her neck. How she longed to tell him how she felt—that she would willingly trade the fine homes and society of Montreal to stay here with him. Hadn't she tried after listening to him play his flute? Yet it was he who said their worlds were too different.

She leveled her look at him while trying to control the tight breathing high in her chest. "Oui, Benjamin. It is. Home is with the ones you love."

His brow flinched, then he turned his gaze elsewhere. "And in Montreal, you have people who love you and whom you love."

Dare she breathe the truth? She stared and waited. Then, as if he, too, had to know what she was thinking, he brought his gaze back. Camilla shook her head. "There is no one there I love, Benjamin. But here—"

Before she could speak further, he reached out and took her wrist, closing the space between them. He trailed his fingers up her arms, setting her nerves on fire. His gaze swallowed her as he leaned nearer … as his touch found the curve of her neck, shortening her breath and singeing the fine hairs along her skin. At the slight pressure of his fingertips, she tilted her head, and her lips met with his. Benjamin's kiss stopped her, stole away her concerns, diminished both their resolve. She curled her hands into fists at her sides, then loosened and raised them to his chest until she clutched at his shirt front, spreading her fingers wide and clenching them again.

Time hung immeasurable between them, and then it was but a moment. When they drew apart, Benjamin pressed his forehead to hers, almost painfully. "It is not possible."

"Oui, Benjamin. It is possible."

He lifted his gaze and studied her while she explored every angle of his face. What if she asked him again to play his flute for her? Would he answer differently now? Instead of her leaving for Michilimackinac and him to places west, would he stay with her, or would they travel on together?

He shook his head, almost imperceptibly, and her heart crashed to the floor of her chest. The baby rolled about within. "Is it because of Ambroise's child?" She had to ask. The question begged. Would a virile man like Benjamin Marchal be unable to accept another man's child? Was she destined only for a man who could pay her father to own her, then quietly put the child where he would never be bothered by it?

Benjamin's eyes found hers again. "Gaawiin." He spoke almost vehemently. "It is not for that. It is just … there are things you do not know, things you could never understand."

"What things?" She reached for his hand, and he let her grasp it. Despite his argument, he tangled his fingers with hers.

"Things that would cause you to feel differently. You would regret your choice."

"That's not true, Benjamin."

"Besides, as I have told you before, you know nothing of life in the wilderness. You think life on this island is difficult? This is a dream. How can a woman like you …" He searched her face, and his expression was nearly worshipful. "How can Camilla Bonnet live in a wiigiwaam and till the soil or work the leather? It is a harsh life." With his free hand, he tenderly pushed back a strand of her hair. "I cannot ask it of you. It would be wrong."

"It was not wrong for your sister. Brigitte grew up in Montreal."

He cupped her cheek. "She was born to this place, this country. She lived among her mother's people. You were not born to this."

He dropped his hands from her, and she felt cold despite the sunshine. Cold and empty. "It does not matter. I want to stay with you, Benjamin."

His gaze turned sad. What could he be thinking, that he should be so certain she could not live in the Upper Country with him? "You must go back to the party and then home with Madeleine and Gichi-miishen. You must go with the brigade as they say. It is the only way for you."

"It is not the only way. Surely." She grabbed his arms and held him. She wouldn't let him go away like this, not when he clearly loved her, and she loved him. What could he think was so bad that she would change her mind? Perhaps she could still change his. She leaned closed and turned her face upward. She could feel his heart beating beneath her palms. He blinked slowly, exposing the battle within him, but he did not pull away. He tilted his head toward hers.

Feet pummeled on the path, drawing their attention so that they each stepped back. Camilla lowered her hands.

"You are the one they call Benjamin?" Two strangers drew near, panting.

He turned to face them.

"What is it?" Camilla whispered.

Beyond them, she saw the man named Coyote. She recognized him because he was familiar around the post. Farther away, but striding purposely down the lane, came Michel Cadotte.

Benjamin's stance stiffened. "I am."

"You must come with us."

His gaze narrowed, and a glint sparked in his eyes. "Why? Am I needed for something?" He, too, glanced past them at Coyote.

Coyote hung back and gave a nod to Michel as he passed him on the road.

"Go," Benjamin said to her.

"No." She touched his arm, but he stepped away from her.

The two men approached almost cautiously, their steps purposeful yet without ease. They moved to either side of Benjamin.

"What is wrong?" Camilla held her hands out.

Instead of answering her, one of them addressed Benjamin. "You are under arrest for the murder of a North West Company agent some ten weeks past."

She gasped. They must be confused, but they were moving closer, and one man held a rope. Benjamin braced his stance but did not fight them.

"You're wrong," she cried out as they pulled Benjamin's arms behind him and tied the rope around his wrists. "You must let him go." She tore her gaze away to Michel, who drew close.

"I am deeply sorry," he said, not looking at her but at Benjamin. "I have no choice."

Benjamin said nothing, and he would not look at either of them. She followed his gaze to Coyote, still standing up the lane along with some other fellow. Coyote, who then turned and slunk away.

CHAPTER 18

"It is good you remember the wisdom of your Anishinaabe family, but you should learn the teachings of Jesus too. He was God come to earth as a man. Not a white man but a Jew, who brought new wisdom to teachings of old. He was much like us. He roamed about the earth, told good stories, and slept beneath the stars. He was not afraid of death but gave up His life for those He loved."

—Etienne Marchal, to his son, Benjamin

Bemidii peered through the crack where the chinking had fallen out between the walls of his log prison. The building was nothing more than a storage shed that had been emptied of its tools and padlocked to hold him inside. Wood was stored beneath a lean-to off one side. He was given some sacks filled with husks to sleep upon, and someone had brought him his own blanket from his camp. Likely Brigitte.

Who was responsible for his arrest? Coyote? Did the man's guilt eat at him? Doubtfully.

Coyote had watched the arrest, but he had not come forward to speak, and in that moment, Bemidii had known his friend was involved somehow. Still, he could not imagine what had happened to make Coyote point him out as Clarboux's killer. Was he merely guessing based upon Bemidii's acknowledgment of having been to rendezvous at Fort William? Was Coyote truly so desperate to gain a reward that he would spin a tale based upon lucky judgment? Or was Coyote guiltless in the matter? Did Bemidii's own guilt only seek to use him as a scapegoat?

His shame chewed away enough for both of them. For a while, the thing that he'd done at Fort William had not mattered. The life of Tristan Clarboux was worth less to him than the life of the duck he ate in his stew this afternoon. Yet, for her, for Ashwiyaa, it had begun to matter. Tristan was Ashwiyaa's own flesh and blood, and Bemidii had spilled it. He had not tried merely to stop the man from harming his own sister, but he had taken pleasure in watching him die, in making certain he could never hurt Brigitte again. What was worse, he had deceived Ashwiyaa. He had held her in his arms and tasted her lips. He had allowed hope and expectation to gain hold, all while secreting the lie between them. Now it was out.

And now she despised him.

The horror on her face when the accusation sunk in was not lost on Bemidii. He'd seen the revulsion as she realized the full extent of what it meant when he'd been captured. At first, she had disbelieved the charge and had cried out for mercy. Slowly, however, understanding dawned. It was not just a random man but her own brother of whom her Benjamin was charged with killing. Her eyes had widened, and her face paled. Her silken lips curled downward when he chanced a glance at her. Then she turned her face in disgust and fled, her arm wrapped around her dead husband's child in her womb.

Bemidii slung a fist against the wall, crushing open the skin on his knuckles. Today his side ached where Tristian had wounded him. Yet even the sight of his own blood or the ache of his wound offered no redemption for what he'd done. What would it take? A full confession? His life?

René has promised to speak, to tell the truth of that night. His good name will be recognized here, where there are fewer to fear reprisal from the merchant Clarboux. She will hate me forever, but I will be a free man before long.

The thought left little real comfort. Now that he had held her, he only felt emptier knowing he would never do so again.

Someone knocked on the door, and Bemidii faced it as he listened to the key turning in the padlock. Light spilled into the dimness, and he squinted at the shadow of Michel Cadotte filling the doorway.

"You are not too uncomfortable?" Michel took a step inside and handed Bemidii a bowl of corn mush and cooked meat. "There is no reason you have to go hungry. Later, I will see to it that you have an extra hide to cover yourself with. The nights are getting too cold for a single blanket."

Bemidii gave a nod of thanks as he accepted the food. "I am grateful for your kindness." He ate a few bites while Michel watched.

The man rubbed his chin. "There is someone here to see you."

Immediately, Bemidii both hoped and dreaded that Ashwiyaa had come, but when Michel waved a hand to someone waiting outside, another Métis stepped up. At first, Bemidii didn't think he knew who it was, but in only another moment, he recognized the stranger he and Coyote had seen on the shore after their hunt.

The man's expression was flat as he studied Bemidii. His eyes swept over him from head to foot, and then he gave a sharp nod. "It is him."

Michel frowned. "You must be certain."

"He is the one who killed the bourgeois."

Bemidii's stomach twisted. Michel Cadotte stood aside. "Wait for me outside the store."

The man swung away, and in that moment, Bemidii knew him. The knot in his gut unfurled, and a tingle chased up his spine. He was not a personal acquaintance. He was simply one of the people who had been standing among the others on the bank that night. One who had been watching as Bemidii staggered out of the river, his fingers bloody against the wound in his side, his other hand gripping the knife smeared red. Did this man not tell Michel of Tristan's own attempt to kill?

Michel faced Bemidii again, his face sagging. "I do not know what the circumstances of this incident were, other than what that man and Monsieur Dufour have told me. Dufour seems an honest man, though I do not know him well, and he is surely thinking of his wife. He tells me she was accosted by that man Clarboux and that you intervened."

"He stole my sister away, intending to harm her."

"Oui, that is what I am told. That he supposed to hurt her, but …"

Bemidii set the bowl of half-eaten food on a crate and pressed his hands together. Did Michel not believe René? "Not *supposed*. He came in search of her, intent to steal her for himself. It did not matter that she rejected him. That man who came just now, I do not know, but René Dufour does not lie. My sister does not lie."

Michel gave a slow nod. "I am apt to believe Monsieur Dufour. I am apt to believe you acted in defense of your sister. Still, Dufour is your relation, and such ties can be colored. I must not take the law into my own hands. Not where important company men are concerned."

"You are like the others who are afraid of the merchant." Bemidii's lip curled on the accusation.

Michel shook his head. "Not afraid, but cautious. I have my own family to think of. I cannot afford to run pell-mell into such a decision. There are higher authorities who must be consulted."

"Soon enough, it will be the Americans who rule this island. Then what will Montreal matter?"

"True." Michel put his hands on his hips and stared out the door. "But if I expect to earn their trust and their business, I must not have them believe that murder goes unnoticed."

"*Pah*. If I were more French and less Anishinaabe, I would be believed."

Michel speared him with a look. "I do not believe that is true. And I did not say that I didn't believe you. Yet justice must be served."

Bemidii bit his tongue on an acerbic reply. They did not seek justice but rather appeasement for Clarboux.

"Tomorrow I will send message of your capture. We must await word from the authorities. You will, unfortunately, remain incarcerated until we receive a reply. I thought about sending you with tomorrow's brigade. They might deliver you directly to Montreal, or at the least, to Michilimackinac. However,"—he gave Bemidii another accusatory glance—"they are not equipped to assure your safe arrival. And with Madame Bonnet going with them …" Michel stuck out his lip in thought.

"I am no danger to Madame Bonnet." He did not add that Michel was correct in reasoning that he would try to escape on such a journey.

"Tell me one thing, Benjamin. Did you know she was the dead man's sister?"

Bemidii ground his jaw. Why did Michel wish to know? Did he think Bemidii had intended to harm her, too, at some point? Michel must know he didn't. Bemidii didn't even expect to see her at the celebration today. He nodded. "Eya', I knew." He dropped onto his sleeping sacks.

Michel looked at him again for a long moment, then rubbed his chin again and turned away. Bemidii stretched his arm beneath his head as he listened to the heavy padlock latching on the door.

He saw no one else the rest of the day. When the next morning came, he woke with no sense of the time. Peering again through the cracks in the chinking, he searched for the sun to gauge its height in the sky. Since no one had brought him his breakfast, it must still be early. Finally, after what seemed an interminable amount of time passing, a voice called his name. René.

"Are you awake?"

"Eya'. Have you come to get me out?"

He sensed rather than heard René's sigh in the pause that followed. "Non, Bemidii." His brother-in-law sounded discouraged. "I came to tell you that we will do whatever it takes to make sure the truth is known. Unfortunately, there will be a long delay. The brigade is leaving even now. You must not worry."

"I do not."

"Are you certain?"

"What is the sense of worry? It cannot open this door. It cannot return me to my village or send me on a hunt."

"This is true." A smile entered René's speech. "'Who by worry can add a single day to their life?' That is what God says in His word."

"Does He?" René had often spoken of the words of God in His book, and most of the time, Bemidii listened patiently, though he wondered why man needed a book of God's teachings when He spoke so clearly to them all in the world around them. Yet this time, the words reached down inside him. Eya', who could add a day by fear, by worry, by regret? No one. He stood at the mercy—or lack of it—of men who viewed themselves above him or any other Métis or Anishinaabe. Worry would not save him.

"He also says we should not worry for our life and that tomorrow will take care of itself. The evil of today is sufficient."

"This I can understand, for evil has swallowed today." He looked around the dank, dark room.

"Brigitte and I have not ceased praying. Trust in God, my friend."

Bemidii's brother-in-law was a man of great faith, and now his sister had grasped hold of the Gitchie Manitou's teachings from the book too. Bemidii had learned from the teachings of his village elders, and he had taken part in many ceremonies over his life. Still, his father, Etienne Marchal, had also prayed to the Christian Gitchie Manitou and spoke occasionally of things that were different than the Anishinaabe believed. Bemidii had been caught between both worlds, with his feet more often set in the religion of the Midewiwin, yet Brigitte and René's faith was compelling.

"I will trust, as you say, my brother. But my trust will be in you and my sister, that you will prevail upon the authorities who hold me here."

"You must be prepared to tell all the truth, Bemidii."

"If I say that I killed this man who took my sister, they will kill me."

René remained silent for a spell. "Brigitte and I will trust in God that they will not."

Bemidii paced across the small space. Even now, a canoe set out to carry Ashwiyaa across the great water to her father, and she would tell him she'd seen the man who killed his son. She would confirm the worst. Yet Bemidii only wished her safety and wellness on her journey. After a time, he was unsure if René still waited outside. "Brother, I would know about the woman who went with the brigade …" His voice faltered.

"Oui?"

Bemidii sucked in a quick breath. "Did you see her? Did she look well?"

"She did, as far as I could tell. Why do you ask about her?" René's voice was closer, as though he leaned in toward the crack in the wall.

Bemidii tightened the blanket around his shoulders. "No reason."

"Brother?"

"She is the man's sister."

"I know this."

"Her husband died recently as well."

"Did he?"

Bemidii paced.

"Do you recall, Bemidii, those months last year when I hid my heart from your sister? When you wished me to accept and admit my feelings for her? I wonder … do you do the same?"

"My heart is not hidden."

There was silence and then a chuckle from outside. Bemidii leaned in toward the wall. "Do you laugh?"

"You care for her, then, this woman. You've spoken to her of your feelings."

"I care, and I spoke when I should not have done so. But it matters not, now that she has gone away knowing my knife took her brother's life."

"Is love given up so easily?"

Bemidii let out a ragged breath. "I do not give it up."

"You think she does?"

"Has she any choice? How can she reconcile the two men she has found in me? The black dog and the white. It is too late, anyway. She has gone to her home in Montreal. She will return to that other life she left behind and forget her weeks here on the island."

"I do not believe a woman forgets lightly." René paused, and Bemidii considered his remark. "If there was anything you could do to change her mind or seek her forgiveness—"

"I have often wished I could go back to that night on the river. That I could save my sister without bloodshed. Yet I do not know if I could have done so."

"Seek God's forgiveness, Bemidii. If there is doubt in your heart, begin there."

"I have nothing to offer Him."

"He wants only your heart."

Bemidii turned away from the wall and dropped onto his bedding. He was silent for a long while. Perhaps he would do as René suggested, yet he wished for more. It was one thing to talk to the Great Spirit who could hear him, but his voice could not carry to the heart of Ashwiyaa and plead for absolution.

CHAPTER 19

It would be ridiculous to believe that my father might be proud that I have at last settled and married Ambroise, but at least his scorn will cease to matter.

—Journal of Camilla Bonnet

She had refused to believe it.

All week long, she'd wrestled with the devastating discovery as the voyageurs drove their paddles deep around her. Camilla looked at the words she'd penned in their camp last night as she sat on her woven mat.

Benjamin was identified by a stranger as someone called *Bemidii*, the man who killed Tristan. Stabbed to death in a struggle in the waters of some far-off river during a festival.

Non, at first, she could not accept this, but then the evidence mounted. Benjamin had spoken nothing in his defense. What was worse, he would not look at her steadily, though her spirit pleaded for him to justify himself. She'd finally written about that day in her journal. She described the utter bleakness she felt at having to come face to face with the truth—Coyote had not invented the story to gain a reward. The Anishinaabe with him had been a witness, and all the man needed was someone to report it to. That man had been Michel Cadotte. Monsieur Cadotte had then done the only thing he could do, arrest Benja—*Bemidii*.

Her lips moved around this name for him, his true name. He had lied to her. Her heart splintered with the pain of it yet again.

"Le Sault!"

Camilla closed the book on her lap and raised her head to peer over the rippling expanse. In the hazy distance, an indent in the land appeared where a broad bay fed into the *Rivière Sainte-Marie*. The village there had grown, and a trading post stood on the south side. Camilla was familiar with it from their stop on their way into the region only a few months ago. Métis and Anishinaabe filled the place, and lately, more French had settled there too.

A week of traveling in the company of Michel's men had seemed longer than she even imagined it would, while carrying both the concerns for her unborn child and the questions that surrounded Benjamin's possible transport to stand trial. Would he be forced to do so in the presence of her father? Was there even the remotest of possibilities his life would be spared? Non. Not if James Clarboux's voice rang loudest.

Though the weather had been fair, she'd been uncomfortable, and in her condition, discomfort would only grow worse the farther she traveled. She was halfway through her pregnancy now. There was no more hiding it from anyone.

At least the voyageurs had been kinder than she expected. Each of them took great care to see that she was not unduly burdened, though their priority was to care for their own needs.

As the distant shore grew closer, Camilla dipped her hand over the gunwale and sipped a drink of cold water from her palm.

The smell of sweat and tobacco filled her senses as they finally arrived at the wharf above the falls more than half an hour later. Her relief to once again set foot on land was tempered by the fact that tomorrow she would embark again. At least the next leg of the journey to Michilimackinac would pass more quickly. Camilla pressed a hand to her back and paused for the welcome flow of blood into her legs. She tucked strands of windblown hair beneath her bonnet and moved along with the others down the trail toward the lower end of the falls and the village. Michel had assigned a man to carry her trunk, and he walked ahead of her.

Camilla trudged along the portage road that ran between the wharves on either end of the falls with her thoughts still on the past. Even though those days were filled with pain and perhaps self-delusion, it was better than thinking about what lay ahead. Could even God redeem her situation?

The baby flipped over inside her as if in answer. She cradled her stomach. *Oui, little one. You are redemption enough. I must not forget.*

Before long, they arrived at the well-established post of John Johnston, complete with storehouses and sawmill. Monsieur Johnston had played host to some of the notable settlers of the area and even to some of the passing merchants and company men such as her husband and brother when they traveled through previously. Perhaps she might prevail upon his family once again for a warm bed and meal before she was forced to embark tomorrow. Her stomach stirred with longing for something besides porridge and pemmican.

The man who carried her trunk deposited it outside the door of the main store, and she followed him inside.

"Bonjour."

The clerk raised his head at her companion's greeting. "Bonjour, monsieur, madame." He gave them a cursory study and spread his hands atop the counter, separating them. "How may I be of assistance?"

"I have need of some tobacco, but Madame Bonnet would be pleased if you can direct her to a warm meal and lodging only for tonight."

The man's brow furrowed as he touched a finger to his lips. "Your name is familiar, but I cannot quite place it."

"My husband and I passed this way in springtime. His name was Ambroise."

"I see."

"I am not the lady's husband," the voyageur said, and she felt her cheeks heat.

"My husband was, unfortunately, killed in a terrible storm."

"Ah! I am very sorry to hear it."

"*Merci beaucoup*, monsieur."

"If you will come with me, I will take you to Monsieur Johnston's home."

"Oui, merci," she said again.

The clerk spoke to his assistant, who filled small sacks of flour from a barrel, then came around the counter and directed both his visitors outside. "Have you met Monsieur Johnston and his wife, Susan?"

She nodded. She had met them with Ambroise. Johnston was a Scot who'd risen successfully in the fur trade and established his post more than ten years ago. He'd married Ozhaguscodaywayquay—or, Woman of the Green Glade—who was the daughter of a prominent war chief who—if Camilla remembered correctly—had come from the Bad River area not far from St. Michel's Island on the south shore of Chequamegon Bay. She'd taken the name of Susan after marrying Johnston and settling at the Sault. Like Cadotte and so many other fur traders, Johnston's kinship with the natives assured his success.

Passing through a lovely garden where faded roses still clung to their stems and evidence of other summer beauties still bore passing remnants, they approached Johnston's long, cedar log house, built in the French colonial style with its two dormers. By far the finest home in the village. Camilla breathed an inward sigh of relief, knowing that in a few more moments, she might be able to rest and sip a cup of tea.

Once again, her voyageur deposited her trunk. He knocked on the door and stepped back. "I will return for you before dawn tomorrow."

"You are leaving already?"

He shrugged. "You will be all right, madame." He tipped his head in farewell as the door swung open, and the prominent Mr. Johnston himself appeared, well-dressed as though he expected company.

"Who have we here? It is Madame Bonnet, is it not?"

"You remembered."

"How could I forget such beauty here in our lowly country?" He stepped aside and swept an inviting hand inward. "While I am quite surprised to see you, I believe I have a surprise which will delight you."

"I could ask for nothing more than a cup of tea." She smiled her thanks and untied the bow of her bonnet beneath her chin as she followed him inside. With a glance around the parlor, she recalled the many fine things she'd noticed in here last time she visited. She'd not expected to see such finery so far from Montreal, but the Johnstons' home displayed massively framed portraits upon the walls and many foreign pieces about the rooms. She particularly recalled the great sideboard in the dining room, which held many pieces of solid silver brought from Mr. Johnston's ancestral home.

"You shall have your tea, indeed, madame. Please, make yourself comfortable."

A man stood up on the other side of the room. That he was a company man was immediately apparent in the fine cut of his clothes and bearing. He was also a younger man than Johnston. Closer to her own age, perhaps, with a handsome jaw and blond hair swept back and tied in a queue. He bowed his head. "Bonjour, Madame Bonnet. It is a pleasure to meet you."

"Do you know one another?" Monsieur Johnston asked.

She shook her head, but the tall stranger smiled. "I know of Madame Bonnet quite well, but I am afraid we have never met. Now that is remedied." His blue eyes sparkled, and he smiled. "Allow me to introduce myself." He held out his hand. "I am Gabriel Thomas."

She lifted her hand, and he touched her fingers, bowing over them in a most debonair fashion. How did he know her, and what was he doing here in this country? Yet there was some familiarity to the name. Gabriel Thomas … It could be nothing. It was a common enough name. Perhaps he was some acquaintance of her brother's. If that was the case, had he heard of her brother's tragic passing?

She was getting ahead of herself. "*Pardon moi,* monsieur. May I ask how you know me?"

"There is no need to ask." The firm voice from behind her

caused her to spin around. She knew it instantly. It plunged through her like an anchor striking the depths of the lake bed.

Shock rippled through her as she faced him and forced herself to a calm she did not possess. "Papa."

"Camilla. I must say, I am surprised to find you here."

He was surprised? Why so? Had he not sent her and Ambroise to this country, while he, on the other hand, never left Montreal unless it was to go on business farther east. For the spark of a moment, she thought perhaps he'd come to rescue her. She took one small step toward him. "You are here."

"Of course, I am here. My son has been murdered. The heir to my company."

His words stung rather than consoled. "I am so glad to see you," she murmured.

"You've buried your husband." In his matter-of-fact tone, he continued to state the obvious. "How very unfortunate." His glance raked over her as if to take a measure of what was left to him. "I shall see you cared for, of course."

"Merci, Papa."

"How is it you've come here? I expected to find you on the island where they've captured your brother's killer."

Her throat burned. "I could not stay. I wanted to come home, and Monsieur Cadotte set me on my course." She lied. She had not wanted to come home, but she had not wanted to stay in the face of Benjamin—or *Bemidii's*—shocking arrest either.

"I see you've met my man." He gave a nod toward the other gentleman.

"Oui, I have met Monsieur Thomas."

"I am training him to take over the duties my son and your husband have left. There has been quite a vacancy."

"I hope to do my best to fill the gap in any way I can, sir," Gabriel spoke up. "Though I know there are ways it will be impossible to do so."

She regarded the man again for a moment, and he gave her a

sympathetic smile.

Now her father settled another look on the bulge beneath her dress. "I see your husband left you with something, didn't he?" His question harbored no note of warmth or anticipation, only disdain, as though she'd done something wrong by becoming pregnant with her dead husband's child. "It will make things more difficult."

"Difficult?" She forced herself to swallow.

He made a careless gesture with his hand. "Finding you a husband now that you are no longer a virgin, and with another man's whelp to care for—"

She cringed at her father's thoughtlessness and lack of emotion for his own grandchild, not to mention that he would speak so crassly in front of a virtual stranger.

That man now came to her aid. "I see no reason why Madame Bonnet should not have her choice of suitors asking for her hand. She is young and very beautiful. A little child should present no impediment." He gave her a generous smile that made her tumbling emotions stumble further.

"Oui … you may be right, Gabriel." Her father eyed his man, and Camilla could see the mechanisms of his brain working.

She cleared her throat. "I am very happy to see you, Papa. Greatly relieved, in fact. It has been a trying journey—a trying time such as I'd not imagined." She stepped closer and kissed his cheek. "Whatever your reason, I'm glad you've come. I had planned to go on to Michilimackinac, but if you wish it, I can remain here until you return from St. Michel's."

"You'll go with me back to La Pointe."

She blinked. "Back?" She stepped away, her head spinning. She couldn't go back there. Couldn't be near while he passed judgment on Benjamin. What if she was forced to see him hang? Her stiff and aching body had barely gotten used to being on land again, but of course, her père would not consider her discomforts. "Winter is coming. I have a letter to a family at Michilimackinac. Monsieur and Madame Cadotte assure me I will be welcome there to wait out my time with them."

"I am your father!" His shout made her lurch back. He quickly lowered his voice, but his eyes bulged. "You will attend with me, and then you will return with me. I will not have you traveling on alone without a husband or myself to guide you. I have a reputation to uphold and will not risk any more … *trouble* happening."

He had a reputation? What of hers? She lowered her eyes and gave the slightest nod, suddenly overpoweringly weak. "Of course, Papa."

Gabriel's voice, calm and even, came from behind her. "Perhaps you will allow me to assist your father in seeing to your comfort and aid during our journey."

She gave a nod, her throat tight. "Oui," she said at last, her voice small. "Merci." She swallowed back her embarrassment and faced him, turning away from her father's irritated countenance. "I would appreciate that very much, monsieur."

"You must call me Gabriel." His smile widened. Whatever his motives, she felt a moment's relief that at least he seemed a gentleman.

"Of course. Your thoughtfulness is greatly appreciated, Gabriel."

She moved closer to the hearth, hungering for the warmth of the fire, hoping that it might take the chill from her—a chill produced by more than the briskness of autumn.

CHAPTER 20

"If a she-bear charges you in the woods, you will want to run. But you must steady your bow and hold your ground. You must stand fast if you wish to take her. Fear is not cowardice. Bravery stands in the face of fear."

—Etienne Marchal, to his son, Benjamin

Rain beat down on the shed roof, carrying with it the weight of cold that seeped deep into Bemidii's aching side, even though the building was relatively dry inside.

How many days had passed? He squinted at the marks he'd made on the wall. Seventeen times the sun had set since they placed him in this room, with Michel Cadotte telling him little during that time. René confirmed that the message had been sent east and that it should not be long now until someone with higher authority arrived to judge Bemidii's fate. Not someone from as far away as Montreal, but perhaps an emissary from one of the bigger forts or villages.

It was hard for Bemidii to think of someone coming from across the lake. He thought more of the one who'd departed. Where was she now? Safe at the home of the Cadottes' acquaintances in the place called Michilimackinac? He hoped she'd arrived without mishap and that, even now, she was finding comfort in preparing for her child. Or would she decide to go on all the way to Montreal before the waters froze? It would be a cold and perilous journey, more so in her condition.

He huddled tighter in the extra blanket he'd received from Brigitte and René. Michel had given him a hide to spread over his cornhusk sacks, and Brigitte promised to bring him a capote as well. They'd also sent candles and food. His biggest struggle was boredom—boredom and the prodding of René's voice in his conscience, telling him to plead God's forgiveness of whatever sin lurked in his heart. If he did so, what would change? Would it be enough to remove Bemidii's guilt and the despair he felt for hurting Ashwiyaa? Would it be enough to proclaim him innocent in the sight of those coming to judge him? Would it keep him from further imprisonment or even the noose? Did confession do any good other than to ease his brother-in-law's and sister's minds? Would not better good be done if he were to dig his way free from his cell and leave this place?

Not for the first time, he considered the idea. In the corner where he'd moved away some empty barrels, he found that a bottom log had taken on rot. The soil beneath could be easily churned away too. With some effort, he could dig his way free in a few hours. He could return to his canoe if it hadn't been stolen, and he could escape the island. The only thing keeping him from doing so was the fact that René had vowed to speak for him, and Bemidii had no wish to damage René's reputation. Nevertheless, the temptation to run was strong.

Bemidii squatted at the corner and plucked some wood from the rotting log. He would be doing Cadotte a favor by revealing the problem with his shed's foundation. If he were to make a hole large enough to squeeze through, Cadotte would be able to replace the rotted section. Bemidii reached for a sharp, palm-sized stone he'd unearthed and used it to dig into the packed dirt. The rain pounded harder. No one would come by here in this weather.

Two hours later, his stomach roiled in hunger, but the hole had grown in circumference, and it burrowed over a foot deep beneath the sill log. The rain had stopped, and when he heard the rattle of the chain on the door, Bemidii quickly slid the barrel into place, hiding both the hole and the small pile of dirt he'd created. He brushed his hands on his leggings and wrapped his blanket over him as he stood.

The door swung open. "My wife sends food to warm you." Michel Cadotte carried in a covered dish. He set it on another overturned barrel along with a steaming mug.

Bemidii dipped his head in thanks.

Cadotte glanced over him. "You are comfortable enough? Not too cold?"

Bemidii spread the blanket open. "The trade wool is warm enough. It is the sunlight that is lacking."

Cadotte peered around the room, taking in the dark enclosure as a whole. "It will not be much longer, I am certain. Likely, someone from the Sault will be here soon."

Again, Bemidii nodded. He stepped toward the food and uncovered a bowl of hot fish soup. His stomach rumbled.

"At least the blasted rain has stopped."

Bemidii lifted the bowl and sipped while Cadotte went on.

"René Dufour has talked to me at length of your plight. I tend to believe what he has told me, yet it is not I who must judge."

Bemidii lowered the bowl enough to eye him over the rim. "Are you not the Gichi-miishen? Is not your wife the daughter of the Great Buffalo? Who has more authority over this country than you?"

"But I am under the jurisdiction of the North West Company. If I wish to keep my business, so it will remain—at least until the Americans arrive. Then my allegiance will go to the company and country which best allows me my freedom to provide for my family."

"Eya'. As men, we must protect those who Gitche Manitou has given to our care, just as I protected my sister." His gaze held for a moment before he took another sip of soup.

"If your brother can convince your judges as well as he has convinced me—and as you have as well—then there is no reason you will not soon be a free man."

"But if the bourgeoisie is not convinced?"

"Let us not borrow trouble."

Bemidii smiled and reached for his hot mug, but his smile was not from his heart, and it was not a smile of trust.

"I will take your slops." Michel retrieved the pail of filth on the side of the room and hauled it out. Bemidii had gotten used to the stink, but Michel's nose curled. Bemidii's body must smell nearly as bad. He would ask for water for washing, except he had made the decision to leave. He intended to be gone by morning. He would clean himself in the frigid lake soon enough.

The food and hot coffee filled and energized him. Rainwater soon trickled in where he dug, softening the ground so he could easily scoop the dirt away. When he broke through the sod, he used the stone again to cut the opening wider and to chip away at the rotted bottom of the log. Finally, he stopped to rest. He slept for part of the night but woke sometime in the middle and cleared out the edges of the hole a little more. Then, shoving his coat and blanket through, he laid on his back and pushed his head into the hole, tightening his eyes closed as he wriggled his shoulders and pushed with his feet. Two long minutes later, his upper body emerged on the other side. He withdrew his arms and hoisted himself free. After he'd stood and shaken and brushed most of the soil from his body and head, he picked up his bundles and ran into the night toward his camp and canoe.

Bemidii pulled fresh, chilly air into his lungs, expanding them and huffing out again. Run, huff, run, huff, run, huff … His legs churned over the uneven ground, but the clouds of the day had dispersed beneath a brilliant moon. The lake glistened through the trees, beckoning him like a dream.

The scent of campfire reached him before he saw the roughly built wiigiwaam he'd dwelt in. René and Brigitte now slept inside with the coals of the evening's fire keeping them warm, as well as the heat they shared together. For a heartbeat, Bemidii's spirit clutched hold of his heart. In the morning, René would find the canoe gone. Then he would come to the post and discover Bemidii had left them. He would be torn between gladness and shame … just as Bemidii was this moment.

Brushing aside his second-thoughts, he scurried down the rocks to the landing, but the canoe was not there. He turned in a circle on the flat rock, looking all about, in case it had only been moved. It was gone. He ground his teeth and fisted his hands. Would Coyote or someone else from La Pointe have taken it?

"It is safe."

Bemidii's shoulders dropped at René's voice above him. He turned around as René climbed down.

"I thought you might come for it."

His gut pinched. "I did not wish to leave this way, but I saw no other choice."

"You don't trust me to speak well for you?"

"That I trust. It is the bourgeois I do not know or trust, or the words of these witnesses. Men like Coyote." He shook his head.

"You must leave them to God and leave the speaking to me, brother." René clapped a hand on his shoulder. "You should not have run. It will not look good."

"Perhaps I would not have. Perhaps I would have waited for you to awaken. Then I would have let my sister cook my breakfast. Tomorrow—"

"Tomorrow is full of unanswered questions. Tonight, you should not have run."

"If I do as you say, I may still hang. The killing of a company agent will not go unpunished, no matter what you say."

"It is a risk."

They studied one another in the moonlight. Why was René not shaken? Did he trust so much in God's mercy that he would leave his wife's brother to a trial that might be anything but just in its proceedings? God had not spared Jesus, just as Bemidii would not have been spared at Fort William. The merchant traders did not take René's testimony into account there, and they had not given ear to his sister's accusations against the dead man. Why should it be any different here, where there were even fewer acquainted with the circumstances of Tristan Clarboux's death—not to mention the man's vile character? Yet René stood there looking at him as though the weight of life or death did not swing between them.

"I do not know why I am listening to you." Bemidii shook his head and looked again over the moon's shine on the water.

"You are listening because you know in your heart that Brigitte believes in you, and she believes that our voices will be heard."

"Does she?"

"It is not to say she is not afraid."

Now Bemidii clasped René's shoulder. "Then it is for me to be brave for both of us."

"Will you go back?"

"To that hole?" He shook his head. "Gaawiin. I will stay here. When the sun rises, you may tell Gichi-miishen where I am and that I will not flee. He will soon see that I could leave his jail in a moment if I want to. I will clean myself of the filth of that place, and I will stand before my judges like a man, not a *zhigaag*."

René smiled at his reference to the furry black-and-white-striped burrowers with their offensive scent weaponry. "You do need a bath."

"Go back to your warm bed beside my sister. When she wakes, she will find me a man clean enough to greet."

René chuckled and turned toward the rocks. "I will trust your word, brother."

Even Bemidii smiled at that. René's trust meant more to him than he would have imagined only a year ago. He would make certain it was not displaced.

René disappeared above him, and Bemidii faced the water. He disrobed, shivering in November's frosty, pre-dawn light. As he lowered himself off the rock, the water wrapped his thighs, almost instantly making his bones ache with numbing cold. Pushing discomfort from him, he moved into the deeper water and plunged beneath. He scrubbed his hair and sluiced icy water over his body, then exited quickly. He shook off the water and wrung his hair, shuddering against a violent rising of gooseflesh. Then he wrapped the blanket around him and sat upon the cold rock again. Once he was dry and warmed enough, he would dress again.

By the time he'd dressed, sunlight spread like melted copper along the edge of the horizon. Perhaps God would be with him, for in this moment of calm as the sun's rays edged nearer, Bemidii sensed His presence, as though Gitche Manitou sat beside him on the rock, watching the moving of creation together with him, telling him he had done right to stay, even if the cost to remain was high. As his spirit settled easier within him, Bemidii climbed up to the camp and built a fire.

Brigitte poked a sleepy head out of the shelter. "René told me you had come. I will come out and prepare some food."

"*Daga.*" Thanking her, he turned back to his task, searching for some small, dead branches that hadn't rested on the soggy ground. They would smoke but hopefully burn if tended patiently.

René emerged a moment later and tossed him a clean shirt, then cuffed his own sleeves. He looked well-rested despite the interruption of his sleep. "You look refreshed. You may as well look like a new man, too, eh? There are clean leggings inside."

Bemidii took off his old shirt and slipped on the new. "Now I am prepared to face my accusers."

"After we've eaten, I will go to Michel and tell him you are with me. I hope you will consider coming along. He will see that you do not mean to run away."

The fire flamed, and Bemidii added more sticks. Brigitte came out with a kettle to hang on her hook. If he went with René now, Michel might insist that he remain there, and yet if he did not go, Michel might become suspicious of René. He might think his brother was covering for his escape. If he was to follow through with his promise to face the trial, then he should prove himself and go with René this morning. Michel seemed an honorable man. Perhaps he would agree to let Bemidii remain free until the authorities arrived to judge him.

He stood and folded his arms. "I will go to speak to Gichi-miishen. Perhaps he will agree. If he does not …" Bemidii raised his chin. "If he says no, then I will go willingly back to the jail and wait."

René looked solemn.

Brigitte came to him. "I am not afraid to tell them what Tristan did. I will not hold my tongue."

Bemidii warmed at the expression of love and ferocity in his sister's eyes. He caressed her shoulder. "Amoo, you are a bee that stings, but I am afraid the bourgeois would swat at you with little care, just as they did at Fort William. My heart is glad that you feel this way, but once the bee stings, she is lost. You must remain calm, taking care of my niece or nephew. Whatever becomes of me, I will have joy knowing that you and this little one are safe." He gently touched her rounded belly, then withdrew his hand.

Tears sprang like mist in her eyes. "You will hold this child, Bemidii. I promise, you will."

She should not make promises, but he would not say so. Such a warning would only increase her fears. "My stomach growls. How long until we eat?" He smiled, turning her thoughts to her task instead.

They ate in a leisurely manner, for neither he nor René were in a hurry to face the inevitable. By now, though, someone had likely discovered he was missing from the shed. Michel would have brought him his breakfast on the way to his store. He would have found the hole in the back corner. Would he be angry … or possibly relieved?

The three of them strode the trail back to the post in silence. Bemidii ceased lingering over what was to come. He turned his mind instead to Ashwiyaa. She had called herself Camilla. The sound of it was like a song he might play, but even she might now think of herself as Ashwiyaa, one who would arm herself against him for what he had done to her brother. She could not know the kind of man Tristan Clarboux was, that he was a lewd man, evil, intent on harming an innocent woman. She would never believe it. She would be glad by now that she had gone back. She would forget her sorrows when her child was born. Soon she would marry again, no doubt. Bemidii would humble himself before the great God and repent of his crime if for no other reason than that he might be free to ask Him to grant joy to Ashwiyaa.

Even now, as they drew closer to the post, he turned to do so, letting no sound pass his lips as they moved in prayer.

There were voices ahead. Hunters, probably, or villagers setting out to fish. Unless it was Michel Cadotte and his sons searching for their captive.

"*Attendre.*" René halted them at the edge of the woods. Beyond, near the shore, people milled about, disembarking from canoes. Flashes of bright garments and tall beaver hats announced just who was arriving.

Those who will judge me guilty of murder. He shared a look with René and felt Brigitte's gentle touch on his back. They walked forward. Then another flash appeared, that of a long skirt and a bonnet, of a pale hand. Bemidii caged his breath in his chest. *Ashwiyaa has returned. To see me hung.*

Gaawiin. She would never do so. Yet here she was.

Bemidii and his family strode closer, halting near the path to the store. The shed stood dark and waiting.

Among those now making their way up the shore were several well-dressed men. They wore fine suits and towering beaver hats. One was tall with a generous girth, an older man with mutton-chop whiskers and a red face. He dictated orders to the others who carried trunks. Ashwiyaa walked behind him, followed by a man about Bemidii's own age. He supposed the second man to be handsome by French standards, with his queued blond hair and trim, squarely set shoulders. Michel halted when he saw Bemidii and his relatives standing there. His mouth gaped momentarily, then he clapped it shut.

Bemidii came forward. Ashwiyaa's head came up, her eyes wide with some expression he could not fathom, nor did he linger upon it. He forced his gaze ahead, only on Gichi-miishen. "I am here, as you wished it. I did not wish to meet the agents of the company in an unkempt way. You see, I am a man of honor and have not fled."

Michel took a step away from the others. "So it is true. I believe you, and I am glad you have not sought to leave. It will bode well that you have done so."

Bemidii's eyes drifted briefly toward Ashwiyaa. She covered her mouth and turned aside. In an instant, the handsome Frenchman was beside her, taking her arm in his and speaking some soft word.

The big man pushed past Michel with a scowl. *"Qu'est-ce que c'est?"*

Michel faced him. "This is your partner, René Dufour, and his wife. And with them ..." He let out a deep breath. "With them is the accused."

The man bolted forward, his face turning an even deeper shade. "Why is he standing free? Put him in chains." His bushy brows pulled together like a basket weaving, and he stuck out a fat finger. "Confine him immediately."

"He is going nowhere," René said. "He has given his word."

The man's glare shot to René. "You are a partner? How do you fit into this?"

"I am here to defend this man. His name is Bemidii, and some know him by Benjamin Marchal. His father was a Frenchman, a trader for the company."

The man's glare flicked toward Brigitte, and he squinted. Bemidii's guts tightened as they had the night he first observed Tristan Clarboux at Boucher's store. Understanding punched him in the stomach. This must be Tristan's father. Who else could it be? With whom else would Ashwiyaa return to St. Michel's? Any slight hope that he might yet benefit from impartiality was dashed.

The man pulled his perusal from Brigitte. "I don't care who you say he is. This man, Dufour, can speak for him all he wants. I want him confined. Now." He dashed his hand out in command to some men behind him. Three rushed forward.

Bemidii stiffened as they swarmed around him and yanked his arms behind his back. Someone had a rope, and soon his hands were bound, the circulation pinching off in his wrists.

René moved in front of Clarboux. "There is no cause for this. Bemidii has come forward willingly to face his accusers. He could have fled at any time." He glanced toward Cadotte for affirmation, and that man nodded.

The men spun Bemidii about, and while he could hear the continued argument behind him as they escorted him toward the shed, he no longer listened. All that mattered now was that he should behave honorably. Then, at least, *she* would know he was not a coward.

CHAPTER 21

Mon père has accepted Ambroise, promising my hand as quickly as a wedding may be arranged. While Ambroise's wealth is modest, Papa is not opposed to the marriage, believing that Ambroise's enthusiasm for trade will eventually land him well in years to come. He is young, so I should not have to worry about his health in the meantime or have him dying and leaving my right to dower less than a pauper's.

—Journal of Camilla Bonnet

Marguerite poured Camilla a cup of tea and sat down at the table across from her and her mother. Her brow bent with concern. "I am sorry you had to come back when your heart was set on getting settled at Michilimackinac."

Camilla looked into her cup and shook her head. "Please do not feel badly. *Mon père* has come, and it is much more than I expected him to do." She didn't bother explaining that it wasn't for her he'd come, but only for vengeance. He would have his vengeance soon enough. Then he would go about unsaddling himself of his pregnant, widowed daughter. She drew her head up with a smile. "I am quite happy to see you both again so soon and more than thankful for your generous hospitality once again."

"You must rest easy." Madame Cadotte touched Camilla's sleeve. "Your father will see to your every need, I am certain."

"Oui." Camilla took a sip, hiding her thoughts behind her teacup, despising the sting of how little her father thought of her. Had it not been for his need to avenge Tristan, whom he'd repeatedly referred to as his only heir during their return journey, he could have as easily waited until spring to hire someone to return her to Montreal. Yet Bemidii could not go unpunished.

She was still getting used to the name he was most known by—and in a way, it eased her not to think of him as Benjamin, for

Benjamin could not have murdered her brother, but Bemidii might have. Oui. Once again, she tried convincing herself he had to face the consequences. Camilla had held little regard for Tristan, but he was her flesh and blood, after all.

Thankfully, Gabriel had been there to fill in the lack of graciousness shown by her father. He sought out her company each day when they stopped to eat their evening meal before setting up their encampment. He visited with ease, telling her stories of his experiences that made her smile, though her heart was not in it. He'd been a soldier, but after his release from the military, he'd decided to embark in the business of trade. He'd been hired by her father only this year, and already his future looked bright in the business. Her father had taken him under his wing with special attention when word arrived back in Montreal of Tristan's death. Gabriel expressed his deepest condolences. She could almost think of him as a friend. As close a friend as she dared have on such a journey, at least.

Now, however, being safely ensconced again in the Cadottes' warm home, she cherished her opportunity to speak again with women.

"I fear my father and I will be wintering together at Michilimackinac. He will be very anxious to get back to his business."

Madeleine inclined her head. "It may be a good thing. He will have ample opportunity to know his grandson or granddaughter."

That thought had not occurred to Camilla. Would her father pay any true attention to the child while being cooped up together for the winter? He had never paid much attention to his own daughter. That thought made her hope the child was a girl. Her father would then ignore her rather than obsess over molding the babe to his own desired outcome, should it be a boy. He would turn her little one into a man like her brother, something Camilla could not abide.

The front door opened, and young Jean-Baptiste entered along with Gabriel Thomas. Jean-Baptiste had grown over the weeks she'd known him. He was old enough to be considered a man himself and stood only two or three inches below Gabriel in height. He carried a dead bird by its long neck, its gray-and-black-winged plumage draping the floor.

"Maman, Père would like you to cook the goose I shot for our dinner."

Madeleine rose from her chair. "Take it outside and pluck it. Make sure you put the feathers in the sack hanging in the kitchen."

"Oui, Maman." Jean-Baptiste grinned at Gabriel. "I can hardly wait to taste it."

Madeleine smiled. "My mouth already waters for such a fine meal."

Jean-Baptiste carried the goose back outside, and Gabriel faced the women. "An industrious young man." He inclined his head toward the women. "You ladies look quite at ease. I was hoping to speak with Madame Bonnet, but I will not disturb you now."

"It is all right." Marguerite stood. "I have finished my tea and must help Maman prepare our dinner."

Madeleine nodded in agreement. "We will get some of the potatoes we've stored to complement our meal. Go ahead with Monsieur Thomas," she said to Camilla. "We will visit again later."

Camilla set her cup on its saucer.

"I am sorry for the intrusion," Gabriel bent his head.

Camilla stood. "Is it some message from my father you have to tell me?"

"We will speak of it outside."

At his insistence that she wait, Camilla picked her shawl from the chair where it had slid from her shoulders and put it on. She lifted her bonnet off a hook on the wall and tied it under her chin.

"It is a fine day. One can hardly believe that winter is just around the bend." He opened the door and led her out.

"Oui, that is true."

Compulsively, her glance swept toward the jail shed. What

was Bemidii thinking even now? Was he awake, considering what might be his final days—his final hours? A tingling in her chest squeezed into a thick ball, paining her. She fought the sensation with a pulled-in breath. It was his own fault. Whatever led him to kill her brother, be it an argument over a woman, a drunken brawl, a bet gone wrong—Bemidii had succumbed to his most savage instincts. She took another shuddering breath. She should not—*could* not—love such a man.

"Is everything all right, madam?" Gabriel's blond brows tented as he studied her.

"I am fine." She gave a slight shake of her head. "It's just … so much has happened. I would have thought I would be home in Montreal by now with my husband."

"Oui. Such a state of affairs is more than you could ever have imagined when you departed Montreal in springtime. I was very sorry about your loss. You have my deepest sympathies."

"Merci. You have told me so before, and I appreciate your kindness."

"Shall we?" He indicated the village road.

She dipped her chin and walked beside him. They would have to pass very near Bemidii's prison.

"Please, take my arm. I do not want you to stumble."

She might have declined, but slipping her hand beneath Gabriel's elbow, she felt safe from the shadow of Bemidii's presence. It was as though he were looking at her, though certainly, he couldn't see her. The shed was a dark box without windows. Still, her breath quickened as they passed, and she struggled against the feeling that he could see her, and if he should speak her name, he might draw her to a standstill with a whisper.

"What is it you wished to speak to me about?" She raised her chin and looked straight ahead as they meandered down the lane where trees wore robes of russet, umber, and gold.

"Your père and I have often spoken in great detail during our travels to reach you."

He had her attention now. “Oh? Of his business, no doubt.”

“Oui, of the business and many other things. He is concerned for your situation.”

“He talked of me?”

“You are his daughter, so, certainly.”

“I wonder what my father could have had to say about me.” She didn’t truly wonder. She could imagine. He probably told Gabriel of the burden she would be now that she was pregnant and widowed. He probably explained his plans for her to marry with expediency, and in the process, to procure the wealth of someone like old MacDaw.

“He worries for your future.”

Camilla barely held back a snort. “Worries? About my future? I am afraid my father isn’t worried for my welfare nearly as much as he fears I will forever be a chain around his neck.”

“Why should you be? You are an intelligent, beautiful woman.”

A warm wind stirred a pool of fallen leaves at her feet and swept a flush up her throat. “You are kind to say so.”

“You might have your pick of any husband in Montreal—when you finish mourning Monsieur Bonnet, that is. Surely, there are many gentlemen in good standing who would seek your hand.”

“When I finish—” She cast him a sharp glance. Was he leading to something … something between them? The leaves swished beneath their steps. “You would be surprised how few opportunities there might be. My father would never let me marry the man of my own choosing if it did not benefit him in some way.”

“Your father holds so much sway? You are a grown woman.”

A grown woman, oui. A free woman? Never. She sighed. “Who are these gentlemen you speak of? If you know of one, please tell me.”

“I, for instance, would be more than charmed to attend to you. In fact, if you will consider me, I would, indeed, wed you.”

“Wed me,” she gasped, though softly. Did he not hear the absurdity in her tone? Instinctively, she caressed her child. “I am carrying Ambroise's child, in case you failed to notice."

He stopped and turned to her. "I noticed." His blue eyes lit with teasing, and he took her hand gently and raised her fingers to his lips.

She gently pulled them free, unsure whether to be amazed or flattered. "Has my father given his consent for you to speak to me this way?"

"He has more than consented. He wishes it."

Camilla looked away, her hands clasped over the baby. How was she to answer him? Why could he have not waited until they were far from this place to express his intentions? Shouldn't she be relieved that her father approved of a man like Gabriel rather than sell her off to old Monsieur MacDaw? And why did he?

"I am unclear as to how you gained my father's approval. What have you offered him?"

He made a noise with his throat. "I'm surprised that you would think I came to him with anything other than myself to offer. After all, I am in his employ. I am not an independently wealthy man, though I did serve in His Majesty's military and have been awarded my own bit of land … a small, undeveloped *seignory*."

"He saw some possibility in you." *Or likely, the possibility that old MacDaw would pass on before I could get back to Montreal in time to become a well-endowed widow.*

He raised his brow in acknowledgment. "Perhaps."

"I wonder …"

He threw back his head and laughed. She had not intended to speak aloud. "Wonder all you wish, madame." He took her hand and kissed it again. "But tell me you will consider my offer."

"Have you then made it?"

"Only in part, but I shall fall to one knee at the appropriate time, so you had best prepare yourself. Dine with me tonight alone, will you?"

She pushed out a humorless chortle. "Alone? At which tavern?" She looked around the woods, waiting for him to point out the nonexistent establishment.

"Allow me to figure that out. Just promise me you will."

There was every reason she should not agree. Mostly because she did not wish to marry Gabriel Thomas, no matter how charming he was. She could think of nothing else but that on the morrow, Bemidii would face his accusers for the first and perhaps only time. Would they condemn him immediately? Would they then transport him somewhere else to jail? Or would they simply pronounce his fate and put a rope over the limb of the nearest tree? Her gaze drew to a tall oak with a fat limb stretching over the road. She sobered.

It did not truly matter whether she answered Gabriel tonight or when they returned to larger civilization. Of course, she would agree to marry him. It was better than some other fate sure to await her if she hesitated. Her father was consumed with the fact that Tristan, his heir, was dead. He would, no doubt, have been happier if it had been Camilla who'd been struck by lightning instead of losing a man like Ambroise who could serve him in some capacity. Now her father had taken Gabriel Thomas under his wing. He must have shown considerable talents and possibility for advancement for her father to willingly wed her to a penniless man. Unless money really didn't matter, and it was just that he no longer wanted to bear the burden of her. It might be as simple as that.

She nodded. "I will dine with you if you insist, but you need not worry yourself as to what my answer will be, should you still be fool enough to ask. I will marry you if and when you wish." Resigned, she put her hand through his arm once again and turned her face toward La Pointe.

Gabriel caressed a hand over hers where it lay on his forearm. He led her farther down the road. "I know we are nearly strangers, though I must admit I have sought to learn what I could about you since our meeting only a week ago." He bent his head nearer to hers, and his voice held a contented smile. "What I can tell you about myself is that I am not a cruel man, Camilla. I will never raise a hand against you. In fact, you will find I can be most agreeable.

Perhaps you will come to care for me."

"I learned to care for Ambroise, so I know of no reason why I should not care for you." She crushed down the truth that her feelings for Ambroise were never so strong as what she longed for them to be. "You feel the need to assure me of your benevolence. I should not be incredulous. I should thank you. Perhaps you are aware of my father's … impatience."

He chuckled. "Once we are married, you will not be beholden to your father. If he is disagreeable toward you at any time, he will pay the price."

She was taken aback, slightly stunned at his audacity. "As he is your employer, what price might that be?"

His glance held a secret smile but did not reveal his thoughts. "That is nothing of which you need to concern yourself. Trust me, Camilla. I have your future well in hand."

CHAPTER 22

"Look into a man's eyes, and you will get a glimpse of his soul. Listen when he speaks, for his words will tell on him."

—Etienne Marchal, to his son, Benjamin

Bemidii's chest rose and fell in deep, painful breaths as he peered through the crack between the logs. Part of him wanted to frantically dig a new hole in the corner, run to the man, and tear his touch free from Ashwiyaa. But the look on her face stopped him. So peaceful, so resigned. Did her voice not sound so? Her words refused to carry to his ears, but a small laugh did. Did she forget him so easily? Did the blood on Bemidii's hands now stain her heart with hatred for him?

He pushed away from the wall, air huffing from his nostrils, but there was nothing he could do—no way to make her understand. Tristan Clarboux was her brother, and she shared his blood. Nothing was thicker, no tie stronger. Dropping to his bedding, Bemidii pressed his forehead in his hands, then clenched his hands together and rested his elbows on his knees.

"Gitchee Manitou, it is a good thing I am no longer in her heart, if ever I was. I saw the way the man spoke to her. Perhaps You give her someone who will care for her and her child—a man who is not like the one she feared. I am not worthy to look into her face again, even though I wish to tell her I am sorry. You must take care of her now, as You took care of my sister in the past. You must provide a way for her.

"I have no fear of death, though I do not wish it. I wish to be free again. If I am free again, I will not speak to her unless You will it, for she does not want my voice in her ear. I will let her live her life in peace—a peace I pray You will give her."

His breathing eased. He dropped his hands onto the dirt floor at his side. Only God's will could be done.

The loud jangle of a key in the lock outside startled him, and he rose to his feet. The chain rattled free, and the door was jerked open. Two men filled the doorway, and with a command from beyond, they stepped inside and reached for him. He let them lead him out without resistance. Outside, the sunlight blinded him while they secured his hands behind him once again.

His eyes focused in the brightness, and he took in those who'd gathered. The merchant Clarboux and the two guards who were probably mere voyageurs set to the task of escorting him, another man in European dress, Gichi-miishen, René, and ... He glanced casually toward the La Pointe road. In the distance, the man squired Ashwiyaa away. Neither of them seemed to have heard the commotion nor looked back.

The men jerked him forward, leading him to the trading post. Michel went ahead and opened the door. He showed neither accusation nor understanding in his gaze as Bemidii passed, but he did meet his eyes. René came in and nodded at Bemidii.

Several others filed inside. They spread about the room while Michel strode around to the back side of his counter. He opened a book and filled his quill pen, ready to write down all that transpired. Bemidii studied each of the men in turn. One was the stranger who'd identified Bemidii as the killer, and behind him followed Coyote. Bemidii leveled a long, hard look at him before glimpsing the well-dressed man who'd strolled out with Ashwiyaa entering the door. She was no longer with him. Bemidii lingered on him, studying him further, from his upright posture and broad shoulders to the long fingers that held his hat.

Gichi-miishen cleared his throat. "We shall begin with Monsieur Taylor taking charge of the proceedings." He gave a nod to the other man in European dress. He was older than Bemidii by perhaps a decade. He had brown hair and mutton-chop whiskers—a style Bemidii always found curious with the men of European nations.

Taylor took off his tall beaver hat and laid it aside on the counter as he stepped to the front. "We all know why we are here. We have in our midst a man accused of the murder of Tristan Clarboux, merchant son of our own esteemed Beaver Man, James Clarboux. A man of rising importance in his own right, young Clarboux was killed by the strike of a blade during a fight at Fort William during the annual rendezvous of July last. We have in our presence eyewitnesses of that occurrence."

"I demand justice for my son." James Clarboux shouldered forward, his eyes boring into Bemidii with nothing short of pure hatred. "I expect this man to be dealt with in the same haste with which he stole Tristan's life."

Bemidii felt every muscle in his body stiffen into stone, though he betrayed as little as possible, despite the sense that even the pupils of his eyes hardened at the man.

Clarboux strode close and jutted a finger in front of his face, his breath putrifying the air Bemidii breathed. "May your flesh be rotting by tomorrow morning."

"Please, Monsieur Clarboux," Gichi-miishen said. "If we can continue with the proceedings."

Bemidii stared the merchant down as he backed away.

The man called Taylor cleared his throat. "Oui, monsieurs. Let us continue." He glanced beyond Clarboux. "Will the witnesses come forward."

The Métis stepped to the fore, with Coyote remaining behind.

"Please state your name."

"I am Alfred Cormier. Some also call me Bluefoot."

"Monsieur Cormier, were you at the Great Fort William Rendezvous in July?"

He nodded. "Oui. I was there."

"Please tell us when exactly."

"I was there when this man was there." He pointed at Bemidii.

"The dates?"

Cormier rubbed his chin. "Let me see. I arrived with my fellows on the day of the heavy rain. The thirteenth. Oui. That's when it was." He snapped his fingers. "I did not leave until several days after the young man was murdered. My fellows and I paddled south to the St. Louis, but one of them first had something important to do, which led us here to this place. I can tell you what that was—"

"It is unnecessary at this point. Please tell us what you saw on the night in question."

"On the night this man murdered the fellow—"

René raised a hand. "I object to Cormier's assumptions, monsieur."

The man in charge frowned. "And you are …"

"I am René Dufour, North West Company partner and brother-in-law to the accused."

For the first time, Cormier addressed Bemidii. "Is this true? He is your brother-in-law?"

Bemidii gave a deep nod.

"Do you wish him to speak for you?"

"It is well that he speaks if I am not allowed to speak for myself."

Heads bent in whispers.

"Go ahead and let him speak," Clarboux said, his voice heavy with disdain. "It will not change the fact that he plunged a knife into my son and will pay the penalty for murder."

The blond man with the fine brow touched Clarboux's arm and leaned close to his ear. Clarboux narrowed his eyes but fell silent as though rebuked.

René stepped in front of the counter and addressed them all. "I do not doubt that this man, Cormier, was present the night of the unfortunate events in question. In fact, I can attest to having seen him there, among others present. *Many* others were also present. If we were able to locate all of them individually, we might have an entirely different testimony to tell of those events." René lifted a quizzical brow. "Providing, of course, that they did not know a reward would be given to anyone willing to condemn Monsieur Marchal." René nodded toward Bemidii. "Since those individuals cannot now be found, we are reliant upon the testimony of someone who only has something to gain by making the accusation of murder. An unreliable witness, if you will, Monsieur Taylor."

Clarboux fumed. How had such a man sired a woman of such grace and loveliness as Ashwiyaa? The man's heavy body quivered. "*This* man is the unreliable witness. He himself admits that the prisoner is his own relation. How is his word to be trusted?"

"Gentlemen, *s'il vous plait*." Taylor drew himself straighter. "We shall sort through all the testimony. First, let us consider the record. We have it on the authority of those who wrote letters from Fort William that a woman was involved. Is this true?" He looked to the witness.

Cormier nodded. "She was there with them in the water."

"In what way was she involved?"

Cormier frowned and splayed his hands with a shrug. "That I do not know, though I supposed they fought over her. Some said she was with the man who was killed, and then this man came along." He glanced toward Bemidii but quickly averted his eyes.

Bemidii huffed through his nose. One of the guards prodded him in the arm.

"Did your letters also say who the woman was?" René asked. "Did they not say that she was Madame Dufour, wife of René Dufour?"

Clarboux's eyes bulged first, then squinted.

"So it was your own wife, monsieur," Taylor said to René. "If that is the case, then we should interrogate her."

"A *woman's* word!" Clarboux nearly spat his remark. "Are we to subject ourselves to the opinion of the fickle sex? Heaven knows what her husband and brother have convinced her to say."

Bemidii glared at him, and his forearms tightened against their restraints.

René narrowed a look as well, his dark eyes smoldering. "This woman is my wife, Monsieur Clarboux, and I expect that as a member of the Beaver Club, you will speak of her with respect."

Clarboux seemed to simmer down. His jowls relaxed. "My apologies, Dufour. You must understand my passion over my son's death. Of course, as a partner, you may have chosen a wife of a more level mind than most. By all means, if Monsieur Taylor sees fit, allow her to speak."

Bemidii shifted his feet. He didn't like the idea of Brigitte being submitted to this farce of a trial. She had been through enough at the hands of her attacker and need not subject herself to that same man's father.

René glanced at Bemidii, his expression grim. With a sharp nod, he turned to the door. Gaawiin! He should not! Bemidii took a step but was hauled back by the two men holding him. He eyed Clarboux, then turned his face to Taylor. "My sister will speak the truth, only this man will not like it." He curled his lip at Clarboux. Clarboux breathed an oath, and Bemidii raised his chin, sneering with a satisfaction he'd not felt in some days.

While they awaited René and Brigitte's return, Michel pulled out a bottle of spirits and poured a dram for himself. "A glass for all when this business is concluded, eh?"

Coyote elbowed Cormier with a grin, but the man had the sense to ignore it. Bemidii exchanged a look with Michel, who then gave the slightest shrug.

The blond man who stood behind Clarboux moved forward. "I have no testimony to bear. Perhaps I'll take that glass now."

The store's door opened again, and Brigitte accompanied René inside. Her gaze lowered to the floor, but Bemidii took in the determined set of her shoulders, the tidiness of her hair braided and wound at the nape of her neck, a pretty dress in russet and yellow René had purchased for her in trade. She held her hands at her sides, but the dress flowed gracefully over her protruding belly to her ankles. She was the image of modesty and grace as she gave Taylor a short curtsy.

He smiled. "You must be Madame Dufour."

"Oui, monsieur."

"Be at ease, *s'il vous plait*. We only wish to ask you a question or two."

She nodded.

Taylor's glance slid to Clarboux and back to Brigitte. "We understand you were with the deceased, Tristan Clarboux, on the night of his death. Is that true?"

"I—"

"Only answer oui or non."

"Oui, but—"

"And this man to your right. He is your brother, is it not so?"

Her deep brown eyes, shining with hope, lifted enough to catch Bemidii's. "Oui."

"And while you were in the company of Monsieur Clarboux, your brother came to the place where you were and stabbed Monsieur Clarboux."

"It is not so simple—"

"Did he, or did he not, stab Tristan Clarboux?"

"He saved me," she blurted.

Taylor's nostrils flared, and Clarboux let out a frustrated gasp. "What nonsense."

The others murmured, and even the guards exchanged looks.

"Will we not hear my wife's story?" René's voice rose above the rest.

"All right." Taylor peered at Brigitte again, and Bemidii willed her to speak calmly. *Spirit above, enable her.*

Brigitte pushed her shoulders back and turned to the men in the room. Rather than lower her eyes, this time she raised them and peered directly at Clarboux. "You do not remember me, do you, monsieur?" She leveled her gaze with an intent Bemidii recognized as determination that would not be put down.

Clarboux squinted, but his own unease became apparent. "Should I?"

"I have been a guest in your home, though I would not say it was a pleasant experience."

Now even the blond man with Clarboux narrowed his eyes, giving Brigitte curious study.

"A guest in my home?" He let out a humorless laugh. "A servant, more likely. I don't …" Suddenly, his eyes widened. "*You*."

Her left brow tweaked as her chin rose even higher. "Oui, Monsieur Clarboux. I was a guest with your son Tristan well over a year past. It was in the springtime, on the eve before my aunt's death. Tristan insisted I come, and he would not be put off. I had no interest in your son then, and to his dying day, I shunned his cruel advances. I came to this country to escape him. Unfortunately, even after I traveled so far and married a much better man"—she glanced at René—"Tristan would not let me go when he found me at Fort William. Your son, monsieur, dragged me away against my will. He forced me into his canoe, and I do not know what would have become of me had my brother, Bemidii, not intercepted him to rescue me." Her voice had begun to waver, and she fought tears shining in her eyes, but she bravely went on, pushing out her words. "My brother is innocent of murder. But your son is not innocent of treachery. Of kidnapping. Of intent to harm. Of threatening my brother. He shot at my brother, monsieur. He supposed he would kill him and escape with me. He likely would have killed me as well."

"Enough!" Clarboux's shout consumed the room. "I will not listen to any more of this wanton's accusations. What kind of woman attends to a man if she has no intent of capturing him for her own? I remember her at my home, dancing and partaking of my food, her coquetry obvious to all. What kind of woman joins a brigade of men to travel with them for months in the wilderness without a husband or chaperon? I will tell you what kind. The kind who sells herself." He smirked at Brigitte. "A common whore, who duped this company partner into some common law *marriage à la façon du pays*."

Bemidii strained against his captors even as René grabbed Clarboux by the collar.

Immediately the blond, Cadotte, and Bemidii's accusers swept in, pulling him back. Brigitte rushed to René's side.

Taylor pounded a heavy object against the counter and shouted for quiet. The room stilled, but the air was stifling. "We have heard enough. I will give the matter the utmost consideration, but it seems clear that Madame Dufour's testimony is tainted. We will meet together in the morning for my judgment." His glance at Clarboux, though brief, was clearly reassuring. The older man straightened his back and sniffed. Bemidii's gut twisted even as the guards pushed him toward the door.

They marched him back to his jail, only this time, they left his hands tied, and they proceeded to bind his feet as well. Bemidii sank down to his bed, now ridden with fleas. "We'll be right outside, so do not suppose you are going anywhere," one of the guards said.

He turned his face away as they backed out and padlocked the door. Their voices continued to carry, chortling as they discussed the excitement of the trial and the execution to come.

CHAPTER 23

The Métis girl came with Tristan to the party. He was like a rooster, crowing over his victory. Non, more appropriately, he was like an owl swooping down from the sky and pinning his prey to the earth to toy with her as he wished. Now she has disappeared, and I find myself quite happy over the fact. His frustration is felt by all, but I remain quietly pleased.

—Journal of Camilla Bonnet

Camilla left her room in the Cadots' home and held carefully to the rail as she descended the steep, narrow stairs to the main room below. Her father raised his head upon her entrance.

"Ah …" He smiled. "You look quite lovely, Camilla."

She stepped toward him and allowed him to kiss her cheek. She was familiar with his flattery. It presented itself whenever she pleased him by heeding his expectations without complaint, and right now, he seemed to expect she would accept his new employee as her husband. Once again, she wondered at the agreement he had made with Gabriel. At least Ambroise had some family money to offer for her upkeep, but what did Gabriel have? Land, he'd told her. That was all. Ambroise's brothers would receive the bulk of the Bonnet inheritance now. She would only receive a minuscule allowance, a third of what might have been Ambroise's if he'd lived. Later, if their child was a boy, he might receive something better, but that was yet to be known. The Bonnets might claim that the child did not deserve a share.

"Thank you, Papa. It is kind of you to say so."

"I am sure Gabriel will agree."

She tilted her head to the side. "You are quite certain. Yet I wonder what Gabriel has to offer that can interest you so."

Her father chuckled and shrugged. "He has youth. Right now, I find that a commodity in itself."

Camilla frowned. Her father had often remarked upon old MacDaw's fortune for exactly the opposite reason. "I do not understand."

Her father's gaze went to the single window, but it didn't seem to settle on any particular thing beyond. "My son, my heir, is dead. Your husband, Ambroise, as well. Who will run my business when I am gone?"

She lowered her eyes and laid a hand on her babe. "You see Gabriel as capable, then."

"There is no one else," he said, turning to her again. Their eyes met, then he looked at the position of her hand. "If you bear a son—a legacy for which we can only hope—there will be another generation. But it will be years until he is grown. I might not survive so long. If I can call Gabriel my son … so be it."

A knot formed in her throat. As she suspected, her only worth to him was as a commodity, not unlike the furs he bought and sold, shipping them from one place to another. If only she could climb aboard one of his ships and go far away. To Europe, perhaps. To disappear. Just as she had once thought of doing here.

Such a silly idea.

"Gabriel will be ready to take the reins. He is intelligent. He is also more mature than Tristan was, I am afraid." He let out a breath. "He served in His Majesty's army over there, in France. I should think you would be pleased in this choice."

With a small and forced smile, she swallowed against the knot binding her throat and nodded. "Oui. I am pleased."

A knock on the door was answered by Madeleine Cadotte. Gabriel removed his cap as he stepped inside. His presence immediately caused Camilla to pull in a breath and exhale it slowly. She hadn't realized how tense she'd been until her shoulders relaxed.

"Bonjour, madam … monsieur," he said. "Are you ready for our evening, Camilla?"

"Oui." She raised her head and accepted his arm, only catching his nod to her father as they exited.

The heart she thought numbed shattered inside her as they passed the jail shed and strode toward the store. Today they had held Bemidii's trial, so Madeleine had said. None of the women were privy to the outcome, yet the fact that he was still locked inside and now two guards stood posted, one on each end of the tiny building, could only mean one thing. She blinked against the unnerving truth that Bemidii had been found a murderer and that whatever the decided punishment, she would never see him alive again. Her father would see to it.

"We are dining inside the store?" she asked, forcing her thoughts elsewhere with little success. The images of Bemidii playing his flute inside his lodge, of his face turned to the sunlight as it glistened off the lake, of his hands gently holding hers, of his lips molded to her mouth … they haunted her.

Gabriel's voice brought her back. "Monsieur Cadotte has been most accommodating. He has ordered our dinner prepared by his wife. One of them will bring it shortly." He opened the door and led her inside. A conjunction of smells assaulted her, and she touched the back of her hand to her nose. Tanned hides, kerosene, gunpowder, dried meat and fruits, aged wood, candle wax—a myriad of mixtures embedded into the building itself. Along the side of the room before the mud-daubed, glowing fireplace stood a small table set with pewter plates, copper cups, and candlelight. Gabriel drew out her chair and seated her.

She picked up her cup and sniffed the contents. It smelled like berries and herbs but unfermented.

"I remembered your condition," he said as he removed a flask from his coat and poured a splash into his own cup.

"That is good of you. Merci."

"I promised that I would present myself properly. I hope you will forgive our surroundings. They are not quite what I'd hoped them to be when I asked a woman to be my wife, but considering the lesser alternatives of children scattered around or the density of a cold woods"—he gave a sweeping glance about the room—

"firelight seemed better."

"It is not so bad," she admitted, now that she'd grown accustomed to the strong smells.

He swirled his cup and held it aloft. "To a pleasurable evening."

She raised her own but kept her reply inside. After she'd sipped, she glanced around. "They held the trial here today."

He drank back his beverage and set the cup down. "Oui." He ran his tongue over his lips. "Quite a trial it was."

She sharpened her look at him. "Oh? How so?"

"As you might imagine, your father was anxious for the man's guilt to be quickly proven."

Her heart stammered. "Was it not?"

"It was delayed only momentarily. Monsieur Taylor thought it appropriate to let the woman involved have her say, only to appease the partner Dufour, I suppose. Taylor would not have it get back to Montreal that the trial was less than fairly and justly administrated."

"And was it?" She twisted her brow along with her hands.

Gabriel served himself another drink, only this time, there was no juice in his cup with which to mix it. He poured the contents down his throat and cast her a deeper look. "He killed your brother. That is fact. The woman was someone who made claims against Tristan—and even claims against your father. She was viewed as untrustworthy and of low morals. Her testimony was not to be regarded."

Camilla's hands fell limply in her lap. "I see."

The door opened then, and Marguerite and Julie carried in their dinner. The aroma of roasted goose quickly overcame the less pleasant smells in the store. They set the food on the table before Camilla and her suitor. "Maman wishes you both will enjoy your meal," Marguerite said. "We will return for the dishes after perhaps an hour." The two curtsied and left as hastily as they'd arrived.

Gabriel didn't delay. He dished both their plates, then picked up his utensil and forked a piece of goose into his mouth. How often she had sat thus with Ambroise, who always enjoyed his meals to the fullest. Gabriel ate with less … exuberance. She lowered her eyes and picked at her food.

Does Bemidii eat tonight, or do they withhold even that small comfort?

Why did she care? He was a murderer, and Brigitte, something of an accomplice. Yet that did not seem fair—nor honest. She had only spoken in depth to the woman when she was at her parents' party in Montreal more than a year past. Even then, it was clear that Tristan intimidated her, that she hoped to find something redeeming in him but was hard-pressed to do so.

Gabriel leaned back as he finished and poured himself coffee from the pot the girls had set for them. He raised the rim to his lips and watched her above it. After he'd taken a drink, he moved his cup aside and stood. He came around the table and dropped to a knee before her. The firelight shone golden against his hair. He reached for her hand.

"As I promised to do this thing well … Camilla, will you do me the honor of becoming my wife?"

Camilla's breath stole from her chest. She had practically begged Bemidii to play his flute for her, and now she could see his dark eyes again before her. Tears burned her eyelids, and Gabriel smiled, surely thinking they were for him—or, at the least, her dead Ambroise. He turned her hand over and caressed her palm. "Are you hesitating, or does the pulse beating at your throat mean I have captured enough of your heart to say yes?"

She swallowed and drew her free hand to that place at her throat, wishing rather her heart might stop altogether, but it continued to beat. Finally, she nodded. "I have already told you I will marry you."

He bent and kissed her palm, pushing back the lace on her sleeve to press his lips to her wrist as well. She gently withdrew it from his touch and turned to hide her face.

He chuckled. "I will not press you, my dear. There is time for love-making."

Now her neck felt aflame.

He sat in his chair again. "We will marry as soon as we arrive at Michilimackinac. Since we cannot return to Montreal before the rivers freeze, we will spend the winter there with your father."

Her head jerked up. "My father."

"It would not be my perfect choice to spend my honeymoon sharing quarters with my father-in-law, but alas … there is little to be done about it. I suspect our marriage will be worth a winter's inconvenience."

But I am to birth a child well before springtime. To share quarters with her father and Gabriel—still more a stranger than lover—while she gave birth to Ambroise's child …

She leaned forward. "I hope we are able to find lodgings suitable, seeing as how I will give birth by mid-winter."

A tiny frown flicked across his brow. "Oui, there is that."

"And though I have agreed to marry you, I must have assurances about my child. That he or she will be safe and loved in our home."

He reached across the table for her hand again. "You mustn't worry, Camilla. I am a man capable of accepting the child as my own. In fact, by the time we return to Montreal, no one will think the babe as being anything but, although … I will want my own, of course." He squeezed her fingers. "As soon as possible."

The baby stirred inside her. Did the infant sense her mother's fears?

"We will raise a dozen if you like," he added with a grin. "Enough to fill the house and farm I plan to build."

"I have no dowry."

He leaned away again. "You have many assets. As I said this morning, you are a beautiful woman. However, I have already arranged a sort of dowry from your father in the form of a rise in my circumstances. I've made it very clear to him that I will return you to him if he fails me." At the horror flushing through her and no doubt showing on her face, he chuckled. "Do not concern yourself, my dear. I am in jest, though your père need not know it."

Ignoring his coffee, he reached again for the flask in his pocket.

Camilla could do nothing but stare as he finished the contents while intermittently telling her of his grand plans.

Half an hour later, Gabriel returned her to the Cadottes' home. "Let us say goodnight here," she said, stopping at the door.

"Your father will be waiting for our news." He rested an arm against the doorframe above her.

"I will tell him." She raised a hand to his chest as he bent closer. "*S'il vous plait.*"

His eyes roved over her face, deep, blue, searching. "On one condition." He leaned down to kiss her, his breath foul with the liquor he'd consumed before, during, and after their meal. His lips were gentle at least, but she withdrew from them as quickly as she could. He smiled, and she saw in his face he wanted more.

She stiffened, and with a sardonic smile, he drew back and put his cap on his head. "You may tell him when you wish. *Bonne nuit, ma chérie*."

"*Bonne nuit*, Gabriel." She turned as though to go inside and waited while he strode away.

He called to the guards at the jail. "I am to be a married man!" Then he whistled a tune, disappearing to his own lodgings among the natives at La Pointe.

The laughter of the guards reached her, and she stormed away from the door, seeking the solitude of the lakeshore. How much she longed to be away from them all. All except Bemidii.

Why, God? Why did You let him do it? My brother was an evil man, and yet … why let Tristan pay for his crimes at the hand of the one man I have ever cared for? Why did Bemidii's heart drive him to do it?

The air was crisp, and she shivered. There would be frost come morning. She counted long seconds between washes of surf, for the water moved little but for the ripples upon which the moonlight shone like a million points of light.

"Camilla."

She whirled at the sound of a soft voice calling from the shadows. A female voice, thankfully. "Marguerite? Is it you?"

A woman stepped from the darkness into the moonlight. "It is Brigitte Marchal."

Camilla clutched her skirt. "Brigitte Marchal? Whatever are you doing here?" Her voice shook with cold and nerves. Did Bemidii's sister mean to harm her? Quick breaths brought her back to her senses. The girl she'd met in Montreal would not harm a soul.

Brigitte hurried closer. Close enough for Camilla to see the sheen in her eyes. "I had hoped to speak to you, to find you alone. I had dared myself to knock on the door and ask for you, not believing you would listen, not dreaming I would find you outside, here." She cast a hand at their surroundings. "May I speak to you?"

Bemidii's sister … What strange world had brought them together? Surely, her heart must be as broken and torn as Camilla's own. She nodded. "Certainly, you may."

Brigitte glanced about and directed them farther away from the wharf where no one would stumble upon them or spy them. Brigitte faced her again. "You know what I say to those men is true. You yourself warned me about your brother."

Camilla blinked at the memories of their first meeting. "I asked you if you were charmed by him."

"And implied that I should not be."

"Did I?"

"In as many words. And you said—"

"I know what I said."

"They did not listen to my testimony. They did not believe me."

"What do you mean?" Camilla studied Brigitte. "What could you have possibly told them? Knew you something of my brother's death?" Anger tingled beneath her skin. "I have not been told yet what brought my brother and yours together. I know only that he was murdered. Stabbed by Ben—by Bemidii." Her heart pounded.

"Were you there?"

Tears dripped from Brigitte's eyes as she nodded through Camilla's questions. Camilla's heart skipped as the truth dashed against her like the cold water of the lake in her face. "Why? How?"

"My brother only tried to save me from Tristan." She shook her head, and her voice quavered. "He took me from the festival that night against my will and would not let me go. He attacked Bemidii."

Camilla remembered the wound in Bemidii's side that he'd made light of. "Continue."

"You know yourself what kind of man Tristan was."

She knew Tristan had indeed sought Brigitte for weeks after she disappeared. Camilla had secretly cheered for her escape, even if she thought Brigitte had only chosen to go to the bottom of the river just as their servant girl had done. Even with that other girl, there was no certainty that the liaison had been consensual with her brother.

Camilla turned to face the darkness. "Why do you tell me this? What do you want from me? If they would not listen to you, there is nothing I can do."

"Do you care for my brother? Despite what happened, is there something in your heart for him?"

Camilla bowed her head. Was there still? Even after … even after knowing that he'd killed her brother? Or rather, that he'd defended his own sister? Yes, Tristan was likely as accountable for his own death as Brigitte made it seem. And in such a case …

Shameful memories washed over her. She'd only been ten the first time her brother came into her room. How many times had she wished someone would step in and rescue her? But no one ever had. Eventually, he'd moved on to others. Serving girls, the daughters of rich men who thought they meant something to him. He then settled his mind on Brigitte. Shocking, for she was of no important family and had little to call her own. He'd brought her to meet his family. Camilla had felt sorry for her, for she could see what an innocent the young woman was. Perhaps even that was a game to Tristan. He'd been furious when she slipped his grasp, determined to find her. Surely, he must have decided there was a chance of finding her in the Upper Country. A trip to Quebec City had yielded him nothing. Camilla knew better than to think he really cared for Brigitte, but there was something about her that appealed to Tristan. A different sort of conquest, likely, and nothing more, for Brigitte had been reared by nuns and strict relatives. Oui, that was probably it. Tristan had always loved a challenge.

What a different kind of man Brigitte's brother was. Camilla's shoulders sagged, and she nodded. "Yes, I care."

"Then is there not something you can do? Beg your father's mercy. Surely, he will listen to you."

A harsh sound pushed from Camilla's throat. "If you think so, you are greatly mistaken."

Brigitte moved beside her and grasped her arm. "Please, madame. I believe God has led me to you tonight. You are my only hope to save Bemidii."

CHAPTER 24

"It is a beautiful day, Benjamin. Look at the earth. Smell the air. Can you feel it? It is a good day for hunting. If I were to go to the Father today, I would be at peace."

—Etienne Marchal, to his son, Benjamin

"Bemidii Marchal?"

Bemidii jerked to life at the feminine voice hailing him softly beyond the wall. "Ashwiyaa?" He scooted forward, inhibited by the ropes binding his hands behind him and cutting into his ankles.

"I am Camilla Bonnet, sister to the man you murdered."

Eya', it was Ashwiyaa's voice, but her tone was stiff, forbidding, unfamiliar. His chest caved with the pain of his sinking heart.

"I hear you."

She stood near the crack out of which he had so often peered into the yard. If he could get to his feet and somehow draw near … He shuffled backward and pushed himself up against the wall.

"I have come to speak."

"*Bekaa*. Wait." He hopped toward the crack in the wall, losing his balance and striking his shoulder against it. Fleshly pain did not matter. He could feel her there, inches beyond the logs separating them. "Camilla." He said the name he was not used to speaking, even though he'd whispered it in his thoughts a hundred times today alone. He played it in notes in his mind without the presence of his flute.

"I must know the truth." This time her voice was gentler. "*S'il vous plait*." Her words crumbled apart.

He pressed his forehead against the wall, the agony of their separation breaking him in two. "I am sorry. I care not what happens, only I beg you to forgive me."

"Why did you kill him?"

"Do you truly wish to hear?"

Her silence echoed in the dark. "I would," she said at last. "I must know precisely what happened."

Dare he tell her the truth? Was he willing to put the images of what really happened that night into her mind in order to vindicate himself? He clenched his jaw. He could not bring her to suffer so. "I cannot say it. I do not wish to hurt you further."

"You hurt me by keeping silent, Bemidii." How desperate she sounded, and she had called him by the name his family used.

He wrestled. Tomorrow he would be no longer among the living. She would have only her memories. Be they good or ill, did he have any right to keep truth from her? Could he not speak it without making himself out to be a better man than he was? She would hate him.

Gaawiin. She already did, but at least her hatred might be justified.

"We met in the river Kaministiquia, above the encampment outside the fort. I had been searching for my sister."

"Brigitte," she interjected.

"Eya'." He remembered the fires and music, the face of the young woman dancing with him, her eyes alight. Brigitte disappearing into the crowd. "I thought her resting in our lodge, but she was not."

"Where was she?"

"Tristan Clarboux—your brother—had found her there at the festival."

"She went to the river with him."

"Gaawiin. Non." His voice deepened. "She was taken by him against her will."

Ashwiyaa was silent. He waited a long moment for her response. Moonlight flowed through the crack where she had stood. Had she heard enough? Did she go back to the warm house where her father waited for her?

"And then?" Her voice released the tension in his body.

"He had her in his canoe and was taking her away." He had threatened to kill Brigitte. His ugly words still resounded in Bemidii's ears.

"What did you do?"

His arm pressed against his side where Clarboux's knife had pierced him. He put his mouth against the crack in the logs. "I went into the water, but your brother had a pistol. He fired it, so I dove into the river and swam to them." He could still feel the pressure of the water on his ears, hear the bullet hissing past, see the man trying to paddle, hear Brigitte calling out René's name. "He also had a knife, as did I."

"You reached them."

He nodded at the darkness. "I spilled their boat. We were all in the river. I fought your brother. His knife found me first, and mine found him as well." She needed to hear the worst. He steadied his voice. "I made certain he could never harm my sister or any woman again."

His eyes searched the crack for light, but there was none. He could hear Ashwiyaa's breath against it. It seemed to intake and quicken.

"If you cannot forgive this, I understand," he whispered.

A sniffling reached him, and when she next spoke, tears filled her voice. "I forgive, Bemidii. I forgive."

Then the moonlight shone through the crack again, and he knew she was gone.

Bemidii fell backward onto the hard-packed floor and pushed himself onto his pallet. He looked up into the darkness. "Tomorrow I meet you face to face, God of my brother and sister. I am ready, for I have known what it is to be forgiven. Now of You only do I ask it again." His breath eased out in a peace he had never known, and Bemidii closed his eyes in sleep.

The rattle of the lock woke him the next morning. Bemidii pushed back on one elbow to right himself and welcomed the blast of morning light through the door. His neck and shoulders ached from sleeping bound, but acceptance continued to leave him feeling rested. Today he would look to the sky and breathe deep of this unexpected serenity.

Gitchee Manitou, be blessed.

The gruff commands of the two tired guards and their rough grasp hauled him to his feet. One of them bent and slit the rope between them so he could walk, but each one took an arm, making certain he could not run. Bemidii would not have run if he could. He let his captors lead him without struggle. Today he would face the man whose son had meant to harm Brigitte, and despite the great loss of Ashwiyaa's love, he would not bow in humility before a man whose only thought was not justice but vengeance. Bemidii would face his accusers and accept the fate that God allowed.

Too soon, though, they reached the store, and again the sunlight was locked out, all except for the washed-out haze filtering through the small, dusty window. The other men were present, moving quickly today. Brigitte had not come, and René did not look at Bemidii as he was led to the front of the room. His judge, Taylor, already stood behind the counter along with Cadotte, who waited with his book spread open before him.

Bemidii had not bothered looking at Clarboux, but when everyone took their places, he pierced that man with a long gaze.

"Let us get this over with," Clarboux said, adjusting his shoulders in his greatcoat.

"I have gone over the evidence and the testimony of the eyewitness. I have also taken into account the word of Madame Dufour, who, as we all know, is kin to the accused." Taylor looked at a paper in front of him.

Evidence. Bemidii smirked inside.

"I have no choice but to find the accused guilty of the murder of Tristan Clarboux. I will hear arguments for his punishment. As it stands, I think it is most conducive to our situation and location to carry out punishment to its furthest degree today. Unless, of course, Monsieur James Clarboux would prefer we seek higher counsel. Then we can transport the prisoner to the military post at Michilimackinac."

"I say we put him before a firing squad now. I don't—"

"Wait!" René spoke as the door opened. Brigitte entered, and behind her …

Ashwiyaa. Bemidii's breath hitched in his chest. Would she, too, come to see him condemned? He fought against the threatening heartache. How much better was the peace filling him only moments ago.

The blond man straightened and seemed ready to hurry to her side, but René reached them in the front of the room first. "With utmost respect, Monsieur Taylor, your conclusion is premature. We have further testimony."

"This is ridiculous!" Clarboux eyed the women coming through the door and spun forward, his face reddening. "We've heard what this strumpet has had to say."

René extended his hand and guided Ashwiyaa to the front of the room, giving her father a rough shoulder as they passed. He positioned her only an arm's length from Bemidii. For all Bemidii wished to turn his head and gaze at her, he didn't. The blond man had no such compunction. Confusion knit the man's brow, mirroring Bemidii's feelings, as the Frenchman studied the woman they were both drawn to.

"What is this outrage?" Clarboux shouted to the room, but his eyes bored into his daughter, drawing Bemidii's glance.

Her head lifted, and she answered him. "Am I allowed no opportunity to speak? Was not Tristan my own flesh and blood?"

At this, her parent's feathers seemed to smooth, though his nostrils still flared. "Tell them why this savage must die." He settled his shoulders back and sniffed.

Taylor cleared his throat. "All right. Since we are not in Montreal and this is not a traditional court, I believe we can allow for a concession. What would you like to say, Madame Bonnet?"

She looked at them all, her eyes moving from one to the next, and Bemidii felt them settle upon him. He tilted his face toward her. What he saw was not the condemnation he expected, but she'd schooled her features well, and he could not be sure how she felt.

"I believe him."

Breaths escaped. Uncertain. Questioning.

She looked at him again, and this time her eyes shone with a mix of emotions—sorrow, fear, purpose. But what purpose? "I believe Bemidii Marchal. He is innocent of murder. Tristan is responsible for his own death."

A clamor erupted. Even the guards came to life, murmuring between themselves. The blond man took two strides toward her, but her father's thunderous voice overrode them all. "What right have you to speak so of your own brother?"

The blond man reached for her hand and leaned close, but he was within Bemidii's ear-shot. "Camilla. Think what you are saying."

"I am speaking the truth, Gabriel."

"There is no need for you to say anything at all."

"There is every need." The way she looked at him tore into Bemidii, telling him some understanding had passed between them. Gabriel nodded and loosed her hands.

"Please let us restore order." Taylor darted a glance at Clarboux.

The room slowly settled into quiet, though the agitation in Clarboux's demeanor remained evident in his clenched fists and grinding jaw.

"I believe Brigitte Marchal." Ashwiyaa's voice was even firmer. If anything, fear had fled from her face. Bemidii's spirit lurched. "My brother was not a man of character."

"How dare you." Spittle fell from her father's lips.

"How dare I what, *mon père*? How dare I reveal the kind of man my brother truly was? The kind of man who would abduct a woman with every intention to ravage her, to threaten her life and the lives of those she loves? How dare I tell the truth that Brigitte Marchal fled Montreal out of fear of him—and of you—because of your long reach?"

"You know nothing. You have been hoodwinked by that woman. You are mourning the loss of your husband and are not thinking clearly."

"My thinking is quite crystal."

Taylor raised his hands and patted at the air, speaking over them both. "Madame Bonnet and Monsieur Clarboux, calm yourselves, *s'il vous plait*."

Ashwiyaa pinched her lips closed, and Bemidii watched her eyes settle forward, a study of composure.

Taylor shrugged. "This testimony to your brother's character is enlightening. However, it provides no solid proof of what he was doing with Madame Dufour that night. Unless you or anyone else can prove he really did the things you say, I am afraid—"

She spun on him. "I have further testimony."

Taylor quirked a brow but held his tongue. She turned back to the others and blew out a slow breath. "My brother spent months seeking Brigitte Dufour, who was then Brigitte Marchal. He could not rest for want of conquest of her. I believe the only reason he agreed without argument to come to this country was on the chance he might find her, and he did."

Clarboux's face was ashen, his eyes bulging, but he listened.

"My brother's lusts first began overcoming his sense when he was still quite young." Her voice dropped a notch and slowed. She blinked rapidly. "When I was a girl, he came to my room, and though I tried to resist him, his strength was far greater than mine." Her chin began to quiver, and every desire in Bemidii was to reach out and gather her into his embrace. "My brother has always been ruled by his passions. If my father were to admit it, he would tell you this is true." She stole a steadying breath and stared at him. "How many times have you paid to have one of

Tristan's inconveniences resolved, Father? What became of the girl a fisherman pulled from the river, the one who used to tend the fires in our rooms?" Tears glistened on Ashwiyaa's cheeks. "Do you know? Do you care?" She pressed her hand to her rounded belly.

Her father blustered curses in undertones.

Bemidii stirred, hardly able to keep from jerking away from the guards. How he wished his hands were free so he might press them into her tense shoulders and comfort her.

She turned around and faced Taylor. "My brother meant only ill to Madame Dufour. I am certain of it. You surely cannot condemn a man for protecting his sister and himself against violence." Her head dropped forward, and tears dripped to the floor.

Bemidii looked at Taylor as well and was gratified to see the man's composure slip. His jaw slacked, and his eyes shifted away from the other men in the room. "Non," he said at last, sounding resigned. "I cannot."

"What is this?" Clarboux roared once again. "Women have no right to voice in a court of law. You!" He pointed a shaking finger at Ashwiyaa. "I am ashamed. You are unfit to be called my daughter." His eyes ablaze with madness, he reached into his belt and withdrew his pistol, swinging it toward Bemidii. "I will handle this myself."

Gabriel reached for Clarboux's arm but was unable to stop the blast. Pain exploded through Bemidii's shoulder and drove him back. He stumbled against the counter.

Then she was there, crying out, grasping him in her arms.

"Ashwiyaa," he whispered.

Cadotte appeared at Bemidii's side along with René. With two quick jerks of a knife, his bonds were cut free, and the pair urged him to the floor, but he refused rest, despite the blood soaking his shirt.

"We have you," René said.

Brigitte moved in beside them, asking for cloth, and soon Michel was pressing something firmly and painfully against his shoulder.

Ashwiyaa faced her father. "You call *me* unfit." She shook her head. "That is just as well, for I do not choose to call you my father."

The man's lip curled, and he drew his arm over his shoulder to strike her with the back of his hand, but Bemidii staggered free from those tending him and lurched forward, grabbing the knife off the counter that had been used to cut his bonds.

"*Arrêtez!*" Taylor shouted. He jerked his head at the guards, who rushed forward, weapons drawn. "There will be no more violence."

They stared at one another, he and Ashwiyaa at her father with the man Gabriel beside him. Her father slowly lowered his arm and shifted his shoulders. "You all see what a mistake you make."

Bemidii's legs shook as Brigitte moved beneath his good arm for support.

Gabriel stepped forward. "Do not be rash, Camilla. I will still marry you. We will leave this place and never speak of it again."

The man spoke pleadingly with Ashwiyaa, but weakness from blood loss blurred Bemidii's vision. He wanted to step between them, but his legs would not obey. He wavered. His weight crashed against his sister, and voices became an incohesive rumble as the floor rose up to meet him.

CHAPTER 25

Maman says I should not set much store on hope. Hoping, she says, is chasing a kite's tail. Ah, but how I would like to catch it.

—Journal of Camilla Bonnet

"Ashwiyaa ..." Bemidii slid heavily against his sister, and René hurried to ease him onto the floor.

Gabriel reached for Camilla's arm, but she shrugged him away. She lowered herself to the floor beside Bemidii and reached for his hand.

"You cannot be thinking of remaining here with these people." Gabriel's voice fell down over her, but she looked only at Bemidii, praying in her heart that he would not die. "You are a lady, Camilla. You are not one of them."

Her eyes met Brigitte's warm brown ones, filled with compassion and understanding. "I cannot go with you, Gabriel. Especially not with him." Camilla peered over her shoulder at her father. She felt freed rather than hurt by his declaration, and she could not fathom the thought of ever returning to a place where he could rule her again. "I have no wish to have my baby elsewhere, especially where my father might interfere."

Gabriel leaned down. "I told you, once we are wed, he will not interfere. He will not dare to—"

"Or you will return me to him?" She raised her chin and stared at him. "I see no reason to join myself to a man I do not love, Gabriel—now that I am no longer my father's daughter."

His eyes narrowed. "I have credited you too well, Camilla. Now I see you are not the woman I imagined you to be."

"And what woman was that? A woman whose own life and desires mean little compared to the position she can give her husband or the heir she can provide? A woman who can be easily led?" She sniffed. "No, I am not that woman. You would do well to find one who is." She turned her face away.

"Camilla!" His urgent voice demanded she change her mind.

"I will not marry you, Gabriel." She gazed upon the still face of Bemidii as other hands ministered to him. The door opened, and light steps approached. Madeleine and Marguerite set a basket of bandages and tinctures on the floor beside them. "Tell me how to help," Camilla said.

Slowly, heavier footsteps faded, and the door shut with a thud. When Camilla looked up again, Gabriel was gone.

The bullet had passed through Bemidii, damaging only muscle and tissue, but a significant amount of blood pooled beneath him, soddening his shirt. René cut if off, and Brigitte worked to clean the wound.

Camilla's baby somersaulted in her womb as she watched them work, handing Brigitte whatever she needed. Cadotte contributed whiskey to clean the wound.

At last, René stood and placed his hands on his hips. "The wound will bear watching, and he will need to rest for some days. My wife and I will take him to our lodge."

"I will come too." Camilla pushed herself up with effort. "I will help to care for him." She looked to Cadotte, who stared at her. "I can return to sleep at your home at night if you will still allow me, but I will sit with Bemidii during the day. *S'il vous plait,* Monsieur Dufour." She pled with René again. "I do not want to be in your way, but I owe him this much for what my family has cost him."

A hand touched her arm, and she jerked to see Brigitte. "You may come. We will make room."

The men lifted Bemidii and carried him out. Michel had his son fetch their travois, and both Madeleine and Marguerite saw to it that hides and bedding were swiftly placed upon it before the men lowered Bemidii again. He groaned but did not fully waken.

As René and John-Baptiste each took a pole to drag the travois, Camilla stepped closer to Michel. "I pray you will forgive me for the trouble my family has brought to you here. I cannot say what will happen to my child or me now, and I do not wish to burden you further. You have given me shelter for such a long time. Perhaps you can give me work to do. Something by which I may pay you."

Michel squeezed her shoulders. "You have been a help to us, *mon cher*. My wife and daughters have often remarked how your kindness and assistance have benefited our home. You must not worry for tomorrow. Winter is nearly here, and there will be no more brigades going east. You must make yourself comfortable now and wait out your time in peace."

Her heart sighed with relief, yet she regretted the crowding of their home for the duration of winter. However, it eased her mind to know that Madeleine would be present to tend the birth of her child. Madeleine's plentiful experience in birthing children would certainly be a blessing. She thanked Michel again and followed Brigitte and the men carrying Bemidii.

She had not been to their camp since that day when she had convinced Bemidii to play his flute and he had stopped abruptly to return her to the Cadottes'. Soon after, he had kissed her, and again she'd pleaded to stay with him. Did she dare force her feelings upon him again? Even now, the familiar scents of pine and leaf mold, of woodsmoke and damp earth reminded her of him and what it felt like to be in his arms. She wanted to be there again—if he would have her—if he healed. Would he send her away once more?

René and Brigitte had enlarged Bemidii's lodge and layered it with more bark. Brigitte held back the door flap, and the men carried Bemidii inside. "Please, come inside," she said, waiting for Camilla to enter.

Camilla ducked her head through the doorway. Light filtered in from the smoke hole above, and coals from the morning's fire burned in the center of the widened room. On one side, the men moved Bemidii off the travois, settling him gently on a thick bed of pine boughs and hides. He shivered, and Camilla clenched her skirt, holding herself back while the others covered him.

Brigitte faced her. "I will heat him something warm to drink and food for when he is ready. Sit by him." Her smile encouraged Camilla.

As René and John-Baptiste backed away, Camilla tucked her dress around her legs and kneeled down beside Bemidii on one of the mats covering the floor. In another moment, they were alone inside the shelter. To be able to freely study him filled her heart. Emotions swam over her, filling her eyes until they ran over silently onto her cheeks. "Oh, Bemidii," she whispered. She touched his forehead, smoothing strands of raven hair from his weathered brow. She traced a finger over the line of his jaw to his chin. Movement behind his eyelids told her his body had recognized a touch. "Please be well." She doubted he could hear her, yet her spirit urged her on. "I need you to be well. I need to tell you how sorry I am for doubting you, even for an instant. Bemidii … God …" She bowed her head. "I beg You to heal him. *S'il vous plait.*" She batted open wet lashes and glanced the length of him. Already the bandage showed blood soaking through. Camilla pressed a fist to her mouth.

Then she spotted the rolled-up leather wrapper holding Bemidii's flute. "I am praying to God, asking Him to make you whole. You must get better. I want to hear you play again on your flute." She shook her head. "It does not have to be for me, though I wish it so terribly. You are a good man. A wonderful man. You must play it again."

René had not said Bemidii's life was in danger, yet she knew how easily men died of such wounds. A poisoning in the blood was all it would take. How could her heart bear it if she lost him, after all?

He is not mine to lose.

She pulled in her quiet sobs and wiped her nose on her apron.

"Ashwiyaa …"

The name rode on a breath, jerking her head up. Camilla clutched his hand and felt the slightest pressure returned. "Bemidii."

His eyelids moved, batted, lifted with difficulty. Then he turned his head toward her, and his throat worked again to say the name.

She leaned over him and stroked his face with a shush. "It is me. Ashwiyaa. I am here with you for as long as you allow it."

His hand twitched at his side, then lifted to touch her face, lingering there, filling her with hope on wings of eagles. "Thirsty."

She nodded and lowered his hand. "Brigitte!" she called. "Bring water."

Bemidii's sister stooped into the door little more than an instant later, carrying a copper cup. "I was getting it as you called. Can you lift his head?"

Camilla slipped her arm beneath him and supported the solidness of his back and shoulders without reaching as far as his wound. She helped him gently raise his head to drink.

He laid back down again, exhausted, his eyes closing in sleep once more.

"His weakness is from the blood loss," Brigitte said. "By tomorrow, God willing, if there is not a fever, he will feel better."

Camilla pinched her lips, not daring to speak lest she break. She nodded. Brigitte stroked her arm with a gentle warmth.

He woke once more before darkness fell, and this time, his focus remained on her longer. Though he did not speak, his eyes seemed to recognize her and not want to let her out of sight. Perhaps he thought he mistook someone else for her or that she was a spirit. Softly, she reminded him that she was Ashwiyaa, and she would see him again in the morning.

René saw her safely back to the Cadottes' home as darkness fell. Exhausted, her feet nevertheless carried her to the room upstairs that she shared with the Cadotte girls, where she was drawn again to her journal. She had not written in it since agreeing to marry Gabriel. The words had been too painful to say, even in writing. Now the leather book called to her. She sat down with her candle at the tiny desk and picked up her quill.

I am to remain at La Pointe in the home of Michel Cadotte until my child is born. I dare not think what will happen after that. The man who once was my father has already gone away. Should I be saddened by his departure? By the fact he has rejected me? I am not. He left along with Gabriel Thomas while I was with Bemidii and his family, and I can only be relieved.

Sitting beside Bemidii, a man I know so little, I am at home. Yet I no longer belong to anyone except within my own heart. And I wonder and hope and pray … Am I in his? He spoke my name so gently.

She stopped writing and raised her head to the darkness outside the window. There was no moon tonight. Only the candlelight flickered against the pane. "*Cher Dieu,* I beg You, make him well," she whispered. Lowering her gaze, she dipped the pen into the inkpot again.

I pray to God above that he sleeps well tonight. Tomorrow I will go to him again.

Camilla laid aside her pen. She had no sand to sprinkle over the page, so she left the book open to dry. Then, rising, she removed her dress and blew out the candle. Camilla climbed beneath the blankets on her bed, never disturbing the girls who slumbered several feet away.

She woke at dawn and moved slowly as she rose. At nearly seven months pregnant, she had more difficulty beginning her day. Stepping quietly between the beds, she tugged her dress on.

"Are you going to them? To the Dufours?" Marguerite's whisper carried across the room.

Camilla nodded. "I will help your mother with breakfast first, and then I will go."

"You care for him very much."

Camilla paused as the feelings she held so deeply rose to the surface again. She nodded. "I should have spoken long before today. If I had been courageous enough to face my father, none of this would have happened. Tristan might never have done what he did. Brigitte would not have suffered at his hands. And Bemidii ... we might have never had cause to guard our hearts."

"You no longer call him Benjamin."

"He is both to me." A smile touched the corners of her lips.

"You love him."

Camilla sat on the edge of her bed and held a shoe. She longed to admit her feelings to someone but feared the impossibility of such a thing, for Bemidii had told her their lives were too different. But were they still? "Oui."

"This is a wonderful thing." Marguerite flashed her an encouraging smile as she sat up and pushed back her covers.

"I am so soon widowed. You do not think it wrong of me to feel this way?"

"Why should it be wrong if the great God has given you someone to care for and love, and perhaps a father for your child?"

Camilla laid the shoe beside her and cradled her unborn love. "I dare not hope so."

"Why not? Life is hope."

"Until yesterday, I would not have agreed."

"Today is not yesterday."

Marguerite rose and reached for her own dress. What did the young woman herself hope for? She was of an age and past to marry. Did any man ever catch her eye? If so, she never let on.

Camilla laced her moccasins and stood. Her eye fell to the journal lying open on the desk, and she looked at the words she'd written. But as she closed the book to put it away, she could only think of all the blank, unwritten pages. The future so hard to see.

More than an hour later, she followed the trail along the high shoreline to the camp of Bemidii and the Dufours. She carried a basket containing dried medicinal herbs and bandages from Madeleine to refresh the treatment of Bemidii's wound. She also brought bread.

Her pace quickened, and she grew more anxious as she approached the site. René chopped sticks outside the wiigiwaam. He lowered his hatchet at her approach. Brigitte's husband smiled behind his full beard, and even his eyes crinkled at the corners. Camilla could easily understand how the young woman had preferred this man to her brother.

"Bonjour."

"Bonjour, Monsieur Dufour."

"I am always René."

"Oui, and I am Camilla."

"It is good to see you looking rested this morning, Camilla."

"I feel I have slept a week."

"You have slept the deep sleep of peace."

"Which rather surprises me," she said, raising her brows, "given Bemidii's condition."

"I think you will be pleasantly surprised. Go inside. He is awake."

Her heart skipped a beat. Without further word, she obeyed René and raised the flap of the door.

"Welcome." Brigitte reached for her basket and bid her come inside.

"I've brought bread and new bandages." She spoke to Brigitte, but her eyes went to the bed where Bemidii had been propped up on layers of fresh cedar boughs and blankets.

He was watching her as well.

She pulled in a breath. "How is your pain?"

A slow lift of his lips, almost imperceptible, sent a wave of tenderness washing over her. "It is bearable."

She lowered herself beside him, and their hands found one another, clasping at the wrists. Rather than speak, for she could not think of the words to say when so many things jumbled inside her—the desire to apologize, the love she felt, the fears for his health, the needs to comfort, to hold, to know … A knot formed at the base of her throat.

The flap opened again, and René stepped in. He took a bowl of food from Brigitte's hands, and Camilla saw that a half-eaten bowl also sat beside Bemidii's bed.

"We're glad you've come, Camilla." René took a cross-legged seat on a hide on the ground. "We must talk about your future."

Air rushed out of her chest, and she swallowed against the tightness binding her vocal chords. Bemidii squeezed her hand gently, and hers replied instinctively.

"Bemidii will need more time to rest. A week or two. Then, if he is well enough, we must leave for the hunt. In the meantime, I will move this lodge to La Pointe for Brigitte. We had intended to be far south of here before winter set in, with a dwelling in place. Now, with all that has happened, that cannot be. She cannot travel so far and so quickly with our child on the way."

Brigitte's face was bathed in acceptance. Did they plan to winter here at La Pointe? Camilla's heart dared to hope.

"Brigitte and I have agreed that she will remain here at La Pointe near help. Bemidii and I will go to the mainland to hunt and trap for the season. We will also check in with the other posts, for that is my job with the company."

He would leave Brigitte? Camilla flashed another glance her way, and the subdued look on Brigitte's face told her this was so. Somehow, this was Camilla's fault.

"We will come back in December, one month's time, well before the babies are born."

Camilla's child kicked. Babies? He was speaking for the needs—the *wants*—of both women?

"You have a warm bed and a comfortable place with the Cadottes, but I hope that you might consider staying with my wife, if you feel capable."

Camilla's lips parted. René was asking her to live in a wiigiwaam with his wife during the harsh winter months when she was expecting a baby herself at about the same time? Bemidii's hand lay looser in her own as she hesitated in her reply. Did they test her?

Did Bemidii? She looked at him, her heart lurching to action, and she pressed her hand tightly to his. "Oui. I most certainly will stay with her. We will weather this time together."

A stirring lay behind Bemidii's dark eyes, but Brigitte's brightened. "I knew you would agree. Thank you, Camilla."

"Non. You do not understand. It is I who thank you for trusting me."

A slight pressure grew on her wrist, and Bemidii moved his fingers into hers. Now he smiled softly. He spoke words in his language she did not understand except for her name, Ashwiyaa. Nevertheless, his very tone sent heat into her body. Her answering smile made his grow.

And yet they would be separated for most of the winter.

Somehow, she was not dismayed. The Cadottes would still be near if help was required. René would see them well-prepared. She and Brigitte would learn to know one another better. And hope, like that which Marguerite spoke of, would find room to spread itself wide and grow.

CHAPTER 26

We have been married for six months, but I have yet to find myself with child. What if I am barren? What if I cannot provide my husband with an heir? I know it is what he wants more than anything. To speak the truth, I could wish for nothing more myself than to cradle my own enfant *within my arms.*

—Journal of Camilla Bonnet

Two months later

December came and went. January buried the island in cold so deep that no one left their firesides or their heavy robes. René had paid a man well to deliver firewood to the two women, and Camilla worked at adjusting to the kind of life she had never imagined in the wildest stories she'd heard growing up. Even though her daily thoughts lay in the tasks it took to stay alive—to cook, eat, sew, carry water cut from a hole in the lake ice, and prepare for the coming of her baby—she would not have gone back to Montreal for all the comforts of His Majesty's kingdom.

Except that Bemidii and René had not returned. Days ticked by, one after another beyond their promised return, and even Brigitte's eyes glimmered with worries she could not hide. What if something happened to them? She remembered how Bemidii told her of his own father dying when he fell through the lake ice one winter. But there were so many other perils as well. They might get lost and frozen. They might have been injured in the course of their work. They could have encountered dangerous opposition. Brigitte spoke of difficulties with the Sioux. She also mentioned that there were even Ojibwe who followed the Shawnee prophet and might be bent on stirring up trouble for the traders. Perhaps they'd returned to the village of Bemidii's other family and needed to remain there or at some other post for motives she could not fathom.

Some men went into the wilderness and never returned for reasons no one ever discovered. Injury and death could arrive in a myriad of forms.

"We must not allow fear to overtake us," Brigitte said, pausing in her lacing of a moccasin to cover Camilla's hand with her own, as if she could read every thought running through Camilla's mind.

"I am hard-pressed to avoid my fears."

"Then let us talk of our hopes instead. You first."

They had played this game of words a number of times over the frigid weeks. One of them would express a hope, and the other answer encouragement, then she would acknowledge her own hope, and the encouragement would be returned. In doing so, Camilla had found herself expressing her deepest feelings to Brigitte. Brigitte, too, had opened up her heart, and the two had become friends. Closer friends than either had ever had—as they both admitted during their "hope talks."

"I hope they are safe." Camilla ushered out her words on a sigh as her fingers braided a sash.

"They hope the same of us, I am sure. The snow is so deep, the rivers frozen. I am sure that is what delays them. I hope they arrive before the babies come."

"God knows best. He will birth them in his time, and it will be a perfect time, whether or not your husband or brother returns for the day. I hope—I hope Bemidii's wound is fully healed. He left too soon."

"René will not let him overwork it. He knows the risks. I hope they bring back so many pelts that they will not have to return to the wilderness."

"Will they have to?" Camilla broke off the game with her question.

Brigitte nodded, her eyes downcast on her work, but it seemed a sad nod. "René will stay as long as he can with us, but he is a partner …" She didn't need to explain all that his company obligations entailed.

"And Bemidii a hunter."

"What else?"

"What else what?"

Brigitte raised her brow. "What else do you hope?"

"I hope …" Camilla had confessed her love for him, yet at times she feared she loved him far too much and that saying so again would somehow jeopardize her hopes.

Brigitte waited expectantly. "Let it be a prayer."

"I hope—and pray—that he will love me as I love him."

Brigitte lifted a smile to her. "I think such prayers were answered long ago."

A shiver raced through Camilla and then a laugh. "I hope you are right, for I also hope we will be sisters."

Both women laughed aloud, and suddenly, a new warmth burst inside her. A warmth that trickled through her dress and into the blanket tucked beneath her. Shock silenced her laughter.

Brigitte's face fell. "What is it?"

Camilla stared at her and down and up again. "My waters … *Le bébé*."

Brigitte scrambled to put aside her work and rose, her movements remarkably speedy and agile in her own fully pregnant condition. "I will help you to get dry and comfortable. Then I will fetch Madeleine."

Camilla could only nod.

And hope the men did not arrive just now.

Madeleine arrived just over an hour later, bringing with her such things as she knew might assist in the birth. A local mother joined her, a woman who had attended almost all the births in the village. It had recently been announced that Madeleine herself was expecting again, a fact that made Camilla gladder still that she had yielded the space she'd taken in their home.

But where would she go come springtime?

Questions both dark and disconcerting pulled at her mind as she labored to bring Ambroise's child into the world—a world in which she longed to find a place for both of them. Would springtime find her with Bemidii as she hoped? Or would springtime prove him lost to her in that great, dark wilderness, and might she be forced to return east, anyway, at least as far as the Sault or Michilimackinac? Might she be compelled yet again to wed outside her heart's choosing so that her child would be provided for?

She cried out, both in physical pain and anguish over her fears. But at last, as the day went from afternoon to dusk, to nightfall, and to dawn again, her baby was born. When Camilla held her daughter for the first time, all other fears and dreads fled away in the face of a love she'd never imagined.

"Tell me how to say *little girl* in the language of your and Bemidii's mothers," she said to Brigitte, as she studied the tiny fingertips curling around her pinky and the soft lobes of her baby's ears.

"*Kwesewen*." Brigitte peered down on the child.

"Kwesewen. I love you, *mon chéri*."

"Will you name her after her father's mother?"

An unexpected tear edged from Camilla's eyes. "He would have been pleased, but somehow, I think he will not mind this name. He admired the people of this country. He was not a bad man."

"Non. Of course not." Brigitte squeezed her shoulders.

Camilla stroked the baby's crown of light brown, downy hair.

The Ojibwe midwife rattled off a string of words, as she had been prone to do throughout the course of the previous hours, and Madeleine came forward. "It is time for her to try and eat. I will help you learn."

Camilla laughed softly as the baby found her breast and suckled. All the women smiled, and for the moment, all was right with the world.

As the days went by and she healed quickly, only the care and tending of Little Girl helped Camilla endure the longing to know what kept Bemidii from returning. Brigitte helped to tend the child as well as taking care of many of their daily needs. The distraction seemed to help her fence in her worries, too, until the morning she awoke with pains, and it was clear that Brigitte's child would come, too—with or without the presence of its father.

Brigitte rose and set water above the fire to heat for washing. She paused with a glance and smile at Camilla. "Not to worry. My waters are intact. I think there will be many hours before the baby comes."

Did she seek to reassure Camilla or herself?

"You sound so certain. Go ahead and wash. I will take Little Girl with me to the fort and tell Madeleine."

"Tell the midwife too. She will know when to come."

"Oui." Camilla nodded and quickly swaddled the baby. She wrapped herself in a warm robe, though they had been enjoying several days of thaw. Winter in the north would not leave anytime soon. The months of February and March could bear down on them with more thick layers of snow, and even April could show two faces.

She warmed beneath her robes as she carried Kwesewen. The baby slept peacefully, nested against her. Camilla sang softly to her, a lullaby of sheep and flitting clouds, as she trekked through the trampled snow down the path. A deer stepped into the road, startling her, then moved on with a bound into the woods.

She smelled smoke from the chimneys even before she reached the post. Her warm breath spread into the air as she huffed along. She would need to hurry, or she'd have to take time at Madeleine's to feed the baby before she returned. Hopefully, Brigitte was right, and the child would not decide to come too quickly.

Camilla looked toward the trading post as she always did when she passed by. Michel must have visitors. A sled mounded with bundles stood outside. Hunters bringing in furs, no doubt.

She continued to hum as the lake broke into view. The sheet of white glistened across the bay. Tracks came up from the shore. *Oui, hunters to trade. Probably from—*

Her breath caught, and she whirled around to look again to the post. Could it possibly be Bemidii and René? She backtracked several steps and peered again at the sled from across the distance. Someone had brought plenty of furs, more than might be brought in by a single hunter. Possibly furs that had been collected from other posts. Her heart hammered. Yet what if it wasn't them? It could be any trader. Any hunter. Any number of people from around the country. Her hopes would plummet and dash to pieces as quickly as they sprang to life. Still, what if Bemidii and René had finally come back?

Her breath huffed out in deep gasps as she trudged through the snow. A trickle of sweat streamed down her back. She should be getting Madeleine, and she would. But she would see Michel first.

She barely glanced at the sled as she passed it by and shoved open the door. Warm air pushed against her. Air filled with all those wild scents she recognized, as well as the smell of smoked meat, making her stomach jump in anticipation. It took a moment for her eyes to adjust to the dimness of the interior after walking against the brilliant light of the sun glaring off the snow.

"Ashwiyaa."

"Camilla."

She heard their voices before their forms took the familiar shapes she loved so much.

She puffed for breath, joy creating a clamor inside her. "Bemidii!" Her outcry brought them rushing over. "René!" They took her arms, and she longed to lean into Bemidii's embrace, but so much—*too* much needed to be said.

Some things did not. His gaze swiftly fell to the baby tucked inside her robe, then rose to meet hers.

She blinked wordlessly for only a moment, then dragged her attention to René. "I was coming for Madeleine. Brigitte is in labor this very minute. She—"

He turned around and strode to the door before she could finish.

"She is fine!" she called after him as he left at nearly a run, jerking the door closed with a bang behind him.

She looked to Bemidii, and they both shared a glance with Michel. Then they all laughed.

"I suppose this concludes our trade for today." Michel spoke with a patient grin.

"I will unload the rest of the packs." Bemidii's smile remained fixed, and he seemed reluctant to leave her for even a moment.

Michel came around the counter. "I was about to feed them some meat. The packs will wait. I will take your message to Madeleine. The two of you should rest here and eat. I think you have much to talk about."

Rather than give them leave to answer, he lifted his coat from a peg near the door and left them, though not in such a hurry as René. The sound of a tune he whistled grew distant.

They turned to one another again. Bemidii stepped close, and Camilla drew in a breath as he edged away the blanket that covered Kwesewen and studied her.

"It is a girl," she said, her voice a whisper of hope that Bemidii would approve, though why should it matter to him? He was not the father.

"She is beautiful like her mother." He stroked the baby's fine hair. "I wished it to be a girl."

"You did?"

His gaze met hers, and he moved his fingers to stroke Camilla's hair along the side of her face. "But to be as beautiful will be a triumph."

Her chest filled more with every heartbeat, and when his fingers followed the curve of her chin and drew her face upward to touch his lips to hers, it nearly opened wide.

The baby wiggled against her, and Bemidii leaned back, the

moisture of their kiss pulling her to look at his lips, to feel a swelling of love.

"She is hungry."

He turned her to the stools sitting by the hearth. "Come, let us eat the food Michel has left, and you can feed your little girl."

"Kwesewen. That is what I call her."

Now his eyes filled with something that mirrored her longings.

He turned his back to get them a plate to share food from while Camilla opened up her robes and dress to feed the baby, covering herself modestly before Bemidii sat down again. She blushed at the suckling sounds that occasionally came from beneath the baby's blanket.

Bemidii did not seem to mind. "I was worried when we could not return as soon as we hoped. I feared something would happen to you during the birth. I am glad to see you so well."

She could hardly believe she'd given no thought at all to his wound in her excitement to see him and to be kissed by him. "What about your shoulder?" Now she noticed that he didn't move it as freely as the other.

"It improves. I have been impatient. My mother tells me it is a problem I have always had."

"Have you seen her?"

He offered her a bite of venison from his fingers, and there was something very sensual in the way he watched her lean and accept it from his hand. He nodded with another smile. "Briefly. My family is well. I hope to bring you to meet them when we go to rendezvous this year."

She stopped chewing. The succulence of the meat sat on her tongue. Finally, she swallowed enough to answer. "You will take me with you?"

The baby pulled away, full and satisfied. Camilla spent a minute adjusting the strings of her blouse in such a way as to preserve her modesty, though this time, Bemidii did not bother to turn away. He watched her movements as though fascinated while he swallowed and brushed off his hands. She blushed again as she lifted the baby, dribbles of white milk on her chin.

"You are most beautiful, Ashwiyaa. Most beautiful of all women I have ever seen. Your spirit, too, is the loveliest of all." He set aside their shared plate, and he rose. "May I take her?" He held out his hands.

She offered the baby up to him, and he placed her against his heart, murmuring to her in Ojibwe as he gently patted her back. Camilla had never seen a thing so perfect—a man so perfect. A tiny bubble of air came from Kwesewen's puckered lips, and she fell asleep again.

Bemidii looked down at Camilla. Behind him, a log rolled in the fireplace, and a flame burst higher, warming them, though, at the moment, the ardor in Bemidii's eyes sent sparks bursting inside her.

"Do you wish her father was here this day?"

His question confused her. "I wish he did not have to die without ever knowing his child. He would have been a better father than my own, perhaps. But this day?" She rose from the stool and faced him. "This day, I have no greater wish than to see you hold her in your arms as you are doing now."

He took a step nearer. "Do you wish for another man to be father to this child?"

She, too, took a step. "I wish it."

"I was wrong to say our worlds could not be the same."

"Were you?" His breathing was even, yet his heart beat at the side of his neck, giving him away. She moistened her lips.

"The child is not of my giving, and yet …" He broke his gaze to peer down and kiss Kwesewen's silken head. "I wish to call her mine."

"Do you?"

"Have I not said so?" A playfulness came into his features, belied by the lines around his mouth.

She returned it. "And what does this mean, Bemidii Marchal?

What do you intend?"

Holding the baby close against the wounded shoulder, he wrapped his stronger, free arm around Camilla and melded them together with a kiss that was long and claiming. With her arms around both him and Kwesewen, she leaned her head back as his lips moved down her jaw, beneath her ear, and along the side of her neck. When his mouth found hers again and the hand behind her back caressed her, every question or uncertainty she ever had fled.

CHAPTER 27

"To dwell alone is not in the making of man. Someday you will understand what I mean by this. There is more to hunting than the going. There is always the coming back."

—Etienne Marchal, to his son, Benjamin

April 1809

A year ago, his family had begun urging him to find a wife. Bemidii had not expected to ever find such a woman as Ashwiyaa, called Camilla by his family and others. Camilla was a good name. She told him it was the name of a flower. Bemidii would like to see such a flower.

He hummed a tune as he paddled in the bow of a canoe that was laden to the gunwales with bales of fur from the inland posts. They'd done well. These they could trade at La Pointe. Later they would head toward the *fond du lac* region and collect more for the rendezvous at Fort William in July. Bemidii kept a cache of his own furs near his family's home on the St. Louis. This year, they would not meet another Tristan Clarboux.

Neither would Bemidii search for another such as Anang if God willed that Ashwiyaa was safe and waiting for him still.

René steered silently from the stern, listening perhaps, enjoying the reflection of the springtime sun shining on the water. Most likely reflecting, as well, and dreaming of their upcoming arrival at St. Michel's. Leaving Brigitte had been hard for René so soon after the birth of his son, Etienne, named after Brigitte and Bemidii's father. Etienne's sweet complaints sounded less like cries and more like the chirping of spring birds to Bemidii, and Bemidii fondly nicknamed his new nephew Chibenashi—Big Little Bird. René was anxious to return to wife and child.

No less so did Bemidii's heart strike an anxious rhythm with every broad stroke of his paddle, each one bringing him closer to

Ashwiyaa. They had parted with soft-spoken hopes and words of love, along with kisses that lit him on fire. Yet there were things left undone before he could make her his wife.

He hummed again, repeating a melodic line. A wind lifted strands of hair that had freed from the braid he wore and whipped around his face. He squinted into the distance. "Ahead!" He threw the word over his shoulder at René, and they dug their paddles deeper.

Gradually, the line of islands grew up from the horizon. Bemidii ignored the burning in his muscles and the especially unique ache just below his shoulder where the wound had knit cleanly, though the muscle was slightly damaged. Perhaps Ashwiyaa would rub away the knot with her long, smooth fingers. *Soon enough, with hope.*

They paddled almost an hour longer. Sounds came from children casting hook and line along the shore as their canoe drew near. They waved, and the children waved back. Other canoes were turned over on the beach near the post, and two heavy bateaux were anchored at the wharf. They coasted near, and Bemidii reached out to stop them from hitting the boards. As soon as he and René had the canoe steadied, he climbed out. René tossed his bundle up along with a rope, and Bemidii tugged him farther in.

René's feet splashed into the shallow water, and together they gently brought the canoe ashore. Young Antoine Cadotte ran alongside them with a shout. "Boozhoo!"

"Bonjour!" René matched the lad's enthusiasm and tousled his hair.

"You come to see my père."

"I do, at that."

"He is at the store. *Ma mére* is digging in the garden."

"Preparing the soil, eh?"

Antoine nodded. "I carry for you." He reached for René's bag and hoisted it over his shoulders, where it hung to the ground. Without letting the weight and size deter him, he dragged it up the shore, grunting as he went.

"I see a voyageur in the making!"

"I am very strong!" the boy called back.

Bemidii chuckled. "Someday, that will be Etienne waiting for you when you return."

"In truth, it will be hard to be away when he is of such an age."

"All fathers must provide, and all sons must wait."

"And their wives," René added with a grin at Bemidii, which he returned with a nod.

"Eya'. With their wives."

René clapped him on the back. "Let us get this business over so I can keep mine waiting no longer."

An hour later, their transactions complete, Bemidii and René got into their empty canoe and launched it toward the village. Minutes later, they again disembarked. Again, children gathered and chattered. Men mended fishing nets, and among them was Coyote, who glanced Bemidii's way, then slunk behind the others. Did he fear reprisal from Bemidii? At one time, Coyote would have been right to fear, but Bemidii had given vengeance to the God in heaven who gave and took away. Bemidii lived, and Ashwiyaa waited for him. That was enough.

They strode up the road and spotted the women from a distance, sitting outside their lodge while they wove willow baskets. Their heads were bent over their work, and they talked and smiled a lot. The golden crown of Ashwiyaa's hair kindled yearning in Bemidii's breast. The day was bright and cool, but she had shed heavy robes for a shawl over a blue dress, one he remembered from last summer. The sound of a cry came from inside the lodge, loud enough to reach his ear, and she laid aside her work and rose.

"Ashwiyaa." He called her name, and she stopped. Her dress spun around her ankles as she turned and shaded her eyes. Then her hand fell to her side, and a smile broke out on her lips. Her eyes were bright like spring grass in the sunlight.

"René!" Brigitte, too, leapt up and rushed to meet her mate.

Ashwiyaa took only a step, and Bemidii met her slowly.

Now both babies cried inside the lodge. Big Little Bird's voice had grown.

They stopped face to face, and their fingertips touched. He searched her face, her eyes, her lips, her throat, and her gaze moved with his. Finally, they leaned close, and Bemidii kissed her forehead. His heart beat hard, wanting to make her his wife this very moment, to take her into the lodge and be one with her, but he must wait. Such a treasure must be discovered slowly.

The baby's wailing increased. "She cries for you."

Ashwiyaa nodded. Reluctantly, he released her hands, and she went inside to collect the unhappy infant.

Bemidii brightened again when she returned bearing Kwesewen in her arms. The baby was small, but her cheeks and fists showed she had filled out. Her hair had lightened also and seemed only a shade darker than her mother's. Ah … such a gift. He stretched out his arms for the babe and nestled her against his body, laughing when she curled her lips and bent her brow, then turned red as she belted out her disgruntlement that Bemidii had no food to offer.

When the baby would have no more of it, he handed her back to Ashwiyaa. He turned to speak to his sister, who was already nursing Etienne, while Ashwiyaa prepared to do the same.

"Welcome home, Bemidii." Brigitte offered him a warm smile but quickly went back to conversing with her husband. Bemidii lowered himself near Ashwiyaa.

"Oui, welcome." She looked at him again.

"It has been a long winter. Now that spring has come, life will be easier." He wanted to tell her that he would not go without her again, but that should wait.

"It is enough that you are here," she said. "You must tell me about your travels."

Bemidii gave her the briefest recount of parts of their journey. He told her he'd spent almost a week at his mother's village near the fort on the St. Louis helping to collect some of the sugar sap while René took care of business with his brother, who was chief clerk there. This interested her, as well as talk of Bemidii's younger sister and brother.

"You have a good family who loves one another." He heard the longing in her voice. Would he soon be able to share his family with her?

René, too, talked about the fur take of the season and the trouble they'd had procuring as many furs as other years because of the Americans' encroachment. Sooner rather than later, this part of the country would come under their control, just as Michel had said. How then would life change for them all?

Once the babies were content and the women had heard enough stories of the men's two months of travels, they went about preparing an evening meal of lake trout René and Bemidii had paused to catch yesterday. All the while, as they continued to visit, Bemidii shared looks with Ashwiyaa that made him want to switch places with his sister and brother-in-law. It had been decided that Bemidii would spend another night camped under the stars, and Ashwiyaa and Kwesewen would seek a place with the Cadottes to give René and Brigitte a night of privacy. At the appointed time, after their meal was complete, Ashwiyaa tucked Kwesewen in one arm and held a small bundle in the other. Carrying his own roll of bedding, he walked beside her down the road to the Cadottes'.

He wanted to linger with her, but he could not invite himself inside, and the temperature had fallen. Neither did he wish for Kwesewen to catch a chill. Marguerite stepped out to meet them, and too soon, Ashwiyaa whispered goodnight and went indoors.

Bemidii did not kiss her in the presence of Marguerite. When the door closed, he strode with his pack toward the woods, but he didn't go far. Just within the edge of the forest, he spread his robes and blankets. Tonight, he would not let himself be far from where she was.

As the hours stole by, he watched the house and the candlelight glowing inside. She'd pointed out the window of the room where she would be. The hour was growing late, and one by one, the candles were extinguished. Frogs croaked in the low-lying places, competing for a song in the night, but Bemidii's song would silence them.

Stars filled the heavens. Only now and then did a wispy cloud pass over them on a breeze as Bemidii withdrew his flute. Leaving his bedding behind, but with a blanket wrapped around his shoulders, he strode into the yard beside the house and gazed upward. Only one light remained. Did the baby keep her awake? Or did she sit by the light and write in her book? She had carried it with her in the things she took along to the trader's house.

He set the flute to his lips. In moments, a melody lifted into the night. It was the same melody he had begun months ago when she sat inside his shelter with him above the lake ledge. The same melody he'd hummed often during the long winter months. The melody he'd finished only today as he hummed and paddled to this place where she waited. It was his courtship song for Ashwiyaa.

He'd once told her that rivers must follow their courses and the outcome could not be changed, but he had been wrong. Even now, the rivers flooded from the melted snows and spring rains, and the courses found new channels and fresh ground to cut through. Then they joined again at the places in the big lake where they were meant to flow. Just so, he and Ashwiyaa no longer had to follow the courses on which they'd begun, for they had found another way. A better way. A way where their hearts might be joined together into something greater.

A shadow rose in the window, and he saw her there. Then she moved away.

Bemidii kept on playing until the door opened and she came out, an apparition at first, and then warmth and flesh before him. He lowered the flute as she drew near.

"Do you play for me, Bemidii?" Her words sounded breathless, even though she must know the answer.

"There is no other." He stepped closer. "I have told you of the tradition of my people. If I woo the woman I love, and she agrees to become my wife, she will join me in my blanket." He opened up his arms, spreading the material covering his shoulders. Ashwiyaa pulled in her breath, and she stepped inside. He drew the blanket around her. While they had kissed passionately before, never had her body been pressed so close to his. "When I burn my flute, it means I will never love another."

Her palms pressed against his chest, and she shook her head. "You must not burn your flute."

"I must not love another." He coasted his lips over her ear, and her body responded with a pleasing shudder.

"Will you make another?"

"Not for courtship, unless ..." He leaned away to look at her. "Unless, at last, you refuse me. Your heart is free to choose."

Her hand slipped up, and she stroked his face. "My heart knows you, Bemidii. It knows no one else." She cupped his jaw. "It wants no one else."

He tightened her in his embrace and lowered his head, anticipating the taste of her lips, then reveling in their touch. When her answer deepened the kiss, he knew she'd forgotten all others who had ever sought her. "Tomorrow ..." he whispered against her cheek. "We will honor our French blood. Tomorrow we will ask René to marry us. We will go to the store of Gichi-miishen and ask him to bear witness, he and his wife and my sister."

Once again, her eyes shone into his, like the aurora borealis that danced in the night skies. "Tomorrow?"

"It is too soon?"

She shook her head and gave him a smile that told of her desire. "Non. Not too soon."

Their bodies warmed beneath the blanket, and their kisses as well, until finally, Ashwiyaa lowered her head. "I must go back inside lest Kwesewen wakes and I am not there."

Bemidii groaned but reluctantly released her. "Go to our daughter. By this time tomorrow, you will not have to leave."

She stepped from the blanket, and their fingertips fell apart. "Au revoir, Bemidii, but only for a little while."

CHAPTER 28

"I am my beloved's, and he is mine."

—Song of Solomon

Morning came on eagle's wings. The cry of the great bird pierced the sky above the waving white pine, soaring over Bemidii and lifting him from a sleep that had been deep and sweet. He rolled up his bed and jogged down the path toward his old camp, then he bounded down the slippery rocks toward the frigid water, where ice crystals still formed along the edges each night. Disrobing completely, he let out a whoop wilder than any he'd shouted since his youth and plunged into the glassy lake. Even his bones ached when he emerged, gasping, moments later.

He sang as he untangled and combed his hair, sitting in the cold morning sunlight on the rock. Gooseflesh covered him, reminding him he was alive, and this was real. Today he would take as his wife a woman of whom he had only dreamed.

Half an hour later, clean and dressed in a fine new shirt made by his sister, he returned to La Pointe. He carefully watched the Cadottes' house as he walked by, but no one was about. He smiled to think of Ashwiyaa readying herself inside with the help of the Cadotte women who would flutter around her.

Bemidii met Brigitte and René outside, eating bowls of corn mush and leftover lake trout, and he joined them. René leaned back against the side of the lodge, his face as relaxed as Bemidii had ever seen him. Brigitte served Bemidii a bowl, and the softness in her expression made him wonder when he would have another nephew or niece.

"Tonight, you will have the lodge," René said.

Bemidii had been a bit uncertain as to where he would take Ashwiyaa for their first night together. He had thought he might easily re-construct a quick shelter at his old camp if necessary.

"Where will you sleep?"

"I will speak to Michel. I think he will let us spread our pallet inside the store. Perhaps we can keep such an arrangement until it is time to leave."

Bemidii nodded in relief that he would not need to build another shelter just yet and that he and Ashwiyaa could remain alone for a few days, at least.

René went on. "Depending on when she is ready, we can plan our trip back to the head of the lake without delay. There will be room at the fort there for Brigitte and me, and you will undoubtedly want your family to meet Camilla."

Bemidii swallowed down the remains of his mush and wiped his mouth. "I think she will not wish to delay."

"*Bien.*" René grinned. "If you're finished eating, what do you say we collect your bride and get on with the business of marrying you?"

Bemidii was more than finished. Even though he'd been hungry, eating seemed another thing to steal the time he wanted to spend only with Ashwiyaa and Kwesewen. He set aside his bowl with a happy sigh and got to his feet.

René chuckled and patted him on the back. "I hear your impatience. Soon, my friend."

Brigitte had gathered Chibenashi and now looked squarely at Bemidii. "I know you will be a good husband to her, as you have always been a good brother to me, even when I did not know you were my brother. I will be blessed to have another sister as well, though I would not ever have dreamed it to be Camilla, especially since I fled such a possibility at one time."

"Come, wife." René wrapped his arm around her. "Let us take him to her and rejoice that God has taken what was evil and turned it to good."

"Oui." She laid the back of her head against his shoulder.

Bemidii whispered his own amen.

Young Marie Cadotte opened the door to them when they

arrived. She bid them to come in, and they found themselves in the main room of the home, a fire in the hearth warding off the morning chill and the scent of roasting meat and herbs wafting throughout the house. Madame Cadotte had dressed the table in a lace cloth, and the whole family was clad in their finest. Bemidii had never been inside so fine a home, even though he was certain that it was a mere shadow of the homes in Montreal and other places to the east. Surely, his bride was used to more magnificence than this, and yet she desired the simplicity he offered. He might have felt shame, but the fact she trusted in him enough to leave all such things behind made his chest swell with a greater love for her.

Footsteps on the stairway drew his attention, and Marguerite emerged carrying Kwesewen, a smile on her face that made her appear lovely also. She stepped away from the staircase then, and Ashwiyaa entered the room.

She wore a pale gown covered in a print of pink and yellow flowers. Her hair fell in golden ringlets to her waist. She walked to him and looked into his face. Her green eyes glistened, and they both smiled.

Bemidii struggled to find the words against the tightness in his throat, but she must hear his heart. "On the day I first saw you, I could not take my eyes away."

Her lips bowed into a smile, and he wanted to bend his head to kiss her now, but René cleared his throat and captured their attention.

"Madame Cadotte, it seems, has been preparing a wedding feast, so if we get started, it will not be overcooked."

Everyone chuckled, and Bemidii and Ashwiyaa faced René with the families gathered around.

"I have never performed a marriage before. As we know, many in the Upper Country are not so formal."

The pair nodded and shared a smile.

"Today, not as a priest, but as company partner with some small authority, and with these Christian witnesses, and with belief in the God who brings us together, I will marry these two, Camilla Bonnet and Bemidii—sometimes called Benjamin—Marchal."

They faced one another as René went on. He read from the Holy Book, and afterward, Bemidii and Ashwiyaa promised their lives to one another until death separated them.

Even the children cheered when René pronounced them husband and wife.

Then Kwesewen cried, startled from her sleep, and Bemidii took her from Marguerite. He laid a kiss upon her cheek. The baby's eyes blinked open and crossed as she studied the face of the man holding her, but her crying ceased. "Boozhoo, Little Girl." He smiled at Ashwiyaa and again at the baby. "See? You are coming to know me, and that is well, for you are my daughter now."

The baby's lips puckered into a tiny *O*, and Bemidii's pulse thrummed with another kind of love. Then she turned her head, rooting to be fed. He handed her to his wife, whose eyes shone with tears she quickly blinked away.

At last, the hour came when the party ended. They had all eaten. The couple had thanked their hosts. Ashwiyaa's things had been carried to the lodge at La Pointe by the Cadotte boys. Bemidii clasped her hand in his and thanked the men who'd helped him win both his freedom and his love. Then they turned toward home.

The midday sun stayed higher longer now. Though it was still cool on the island in this northern body of water, the promise of warm days ahead satisfied. As they walked, he brought her hand to his lips and kissed it. He turned it over, looking at the flowers printed on the arm of her dress. "What are these flowers you wear? Could they be the ones for which you are named?"

She shrugged. "Perhaps. I've only seen them in a book. I think they might look so."

"I would like to see these flowers."

"There are others just as lovely."

He cast her another smile. "But not as lovely nor as sweet as the woman who wears the name."

She laid her head on his shoulder for a moment, then picked it up again. "Tonight, perhaps, I will not be Ashwiyaa."

Defends herself.

Bemidii chuckled at her implication and squeezed her hand before kissing it again.

They reached their lodge, and he opened the flap for her to step inside. While she nursed Kwesewen again, Bemidii built a small fire. Just enough to ward off chill and light the room so they might see each other. Then he sat beside her and unwrapped his flute.

Ashwiyaa moved the child to her other breast, and this time, she did not cover herself, nor did Bemidii look away, but he lifted the flute to his lips and played her song.

When she finished, she laid Kwesewen on a tiny, soft bed. Then she drew close to Bemidii and reached for his hand. "Last night, when you played outside my window, I realized there is something I have never done."

"You have done many things, so I wonder what that is." He kissed her brow.

She looked into his eyes. "I have never told a man I loved him. No man. Ever."

Thunder pounded in his chest at her words. "And now?"

"I have never longed to say such a thing—until now. I love you. I love you so much ..." Tears filled her eyes, and he kissed each eyelid.

"*Gi-zaagi'n*," he whispered, then leaned back and translated. "I love you, Camilla."

She laughed, a joyful sound that rippled through both of them as he laced his hand along her neck and stroked his fingers through her hair. Then they sobered as his gaze fell first to her mouth, then to the pulse beating at the opening of her dress at her throat where she had not closed the buttons after nursing their daughter. Slowly, he shifted his hand downward, toward the opening, and her breath caught. With a gentle caress, he kissed her again, and they leaned back onto the bed.

His side brushed against an object—his flute, and for one more moment, he pulled himself away.

It brought him no pain to put his flute into the fire. He would make another. A better instrument to play for her of their ever-growing love. To teach to their children of the way of love and the Great Manitou who directed their paths as easily as he steered the rivers. The flute was merely wood, but the song that remained in their hearts would never end.

THE END

AUTHOR'S NOTE

Thank you for entering the world of the Lake Superior fur trade with me. While the story of Bemidii and Camilla is completely fictitious, there are a number of people mentioned in my novel who did forge history, at least somewhat similarly to the way I showed them doing so in the story.

Michel and Madeleine (Equasayway) Cadotte, indeed, headed the most renowned fur trade family of the Apostle Islands and in northern Wisconsin, and their sons carried on in their stead. The largest of the Apostle Islands where their trading post was built is now called Madeline Island—named in her honor. The La Pointe post was built near the ruins of an old military fort that had been occupied at the southern end of the island during the French and Indian Wars. Today, visiting La Pointe by ferry, you are not only afforded the joy of basking in the windswept beauty of the island, still sitting like a gem in sparkling Lake Superior among the archipelago of the Apostle Islands National Lakeshore, but you can also take in the lovely setting of historic Bayfield, Wisconsin, on the distant hills of the mainland.

Michel's great-grandfather, Mathurin Cadot (changed later to Cadotte), was the first family member to arrive at Lake Superior in the 1600s. It was Michel's father, Jean-Baptiste Sr. who, most critically, established fur-trading posts along the southern shore of the lake, all the way to Chequamegon Bay where this story takes place. Three of Michel and Madeleine's sons continued the tradition, serving important roles in both the fur trade and the War of 1812. It was their son-in-law, Lyman Warren, who took over the post on Madeline Island after Michel retired. Under Lyman's direction, the post became the American Fur Company's primary trading post in the region.

Around the middle of the novel, Michel mentions that his stores at Lac Courte Oreille had been robbed the year before. That was an event that took place when the famed Indian called the Prophet, brother to the great Tecumseh, began preaching his religion that advocated banning the trade of whiskey. He also taught that the Indians should not furnish meat to the white traders unless it was boned. As his religion spread, some Indians took to harassing traders wherever they could, including breaking in and destroying stores, as happened to Cadotte at Lac Courte Oreilles, some seventy-five miles south of Chequamegon Bay. The Prophet was defeated in 1811 by Mad Anthony Wayne at Tippecanoe, and the death of Tecumseh followed in 1813.

The novel also mentions that the Americans would be coming soon to take over French trade in the area. As a matter of fact, there were plenty of American fur traders already in Wisconsin. In 1787, Congress passed the Northwest Ordinance, in which territories and states were formed around the Great Lakes. While Wisconsin was part of Indiana Territory, it was not much affected by United States laws until Jay's Treaty of 1795, which contained a provision for British withdrawal from the region. If you read Brigitte and René's story in my novel *Mist O'er the Voyageur*, you might recall how the French had withdrawn from Grand Portage, leaving it to the British, and now that, too, would fall under American jurisdiction.

Michel Cadotte, though a Frenchman, was an independent trader who plied his trade in whichever direction his interests were best served. He transitioned his work from Canada's North West Company to John Jacob Astor's American Fur Company shortly after the conclusion of this novel.

As to the presence of my heroine, Camilla Bonnet, history tells us that—but for the occasional company partner's wife taking a summer trip with her husband into the Upper Country—there were only two white women who permanently resided in Wisconsin at this time. They were Mrs. Charles de Langlade at La Saye and Mrs. Jean Marie Cardinal at Prairie du Chien. Nevertheless, I felt it plausible that someone like Camilla might have arrived with her bourgeois husband Ambroise, and … let's just say my imagination took over from there. Perhaps there actually was someone like Camilla living here in this vast Great Lakes country, and history simply lost track of her.

I hope you'll leave an online review for Bemidii and Camilla's story, and if you enjoy the rich history of America's past as much as I do, I would love it if you'd hang out with me on social media and sign up for my monthly newsletter. You can find me around the web at places like these:

My website and Northwoods Faith & Fiction newsletter: https://naomimusch.com/

Bookbub: https://www.bookbub.com/profile/naomi-musch

Goodreads: https://www.goodreads.com/author/show/4617551.Naomi_Dawn_Musch

Amazon Author Page: https://www.amazon.com/Naomi-Musch/e/B00727J758

Facebook: https://www.facebook.com/NaomiMuschAuthor/

MeWe: https://mewe.com/i/naomimusch

Instagram: https://www.instagram.com/naomimusch/

Pinterest: https://www.pinterest.com/nmusch/

"*Bent Tree Bride* offers a rare glimpse into the hidden history of the past where larger than life, unlikely heroes helped forge our nation in remarkable ways. Well done!"

~ Laura Frantz, Christy Award-winning author of *The Frontiersman's Daughter*

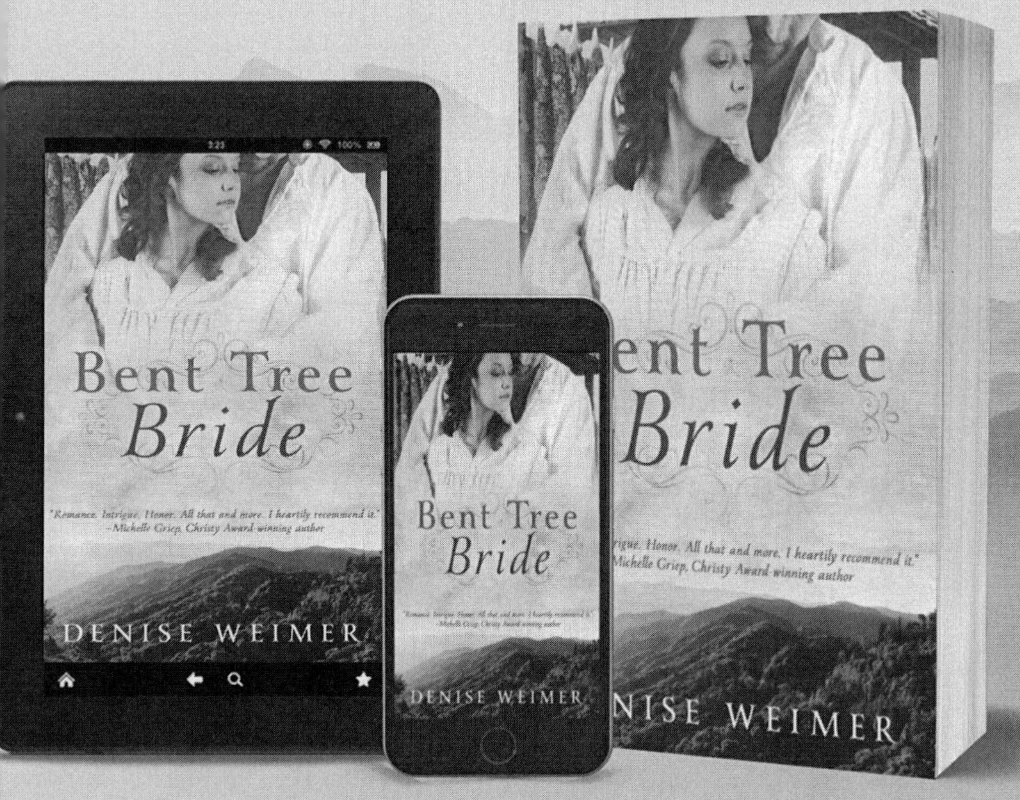

Available from ShopLPC.com and your favorite retailer.